# ADAPTATION

Pepper Pace

The last woman on earth...
meets the last alien on earth

ADAPTATION
BOOK I

PEPPER PACE

Now Available on Audio Book Exclusively
through AUDIBLES!
Exclusive bonus preview of Adaptation Book 2
included in this volume!

Adaptation


*Sign up for the Official Pepper Pace Newsletter for your free reads and exclusive giveaways!*
http://eepurl.com/bGV4tb

# Adaptation

**Editor:** JJ Murray
http://www.johnjeffreymurray.com/id63.html
**Cover Art:** Kim Chambers © July 2014
**Published by Pepper Pace Publications**

ISBN-13: 978-1500640743
ISBN-10: 1500640743

# Adaptation

# Reviews for Adaptation

Who makes a Blob sexy? Pepper Pace does, that's who. This was freakin awesome.
- **M. Hallahan "Grint Girl (verified Amazon purchaser)**

This is one of the coolest sci-fi books that I have read in a long time. It's funny, adventurous, dangerous and heart warming. There's even a touch of comedy.
- **Eleanor M. Walker "elgin" (verified Amazon purchaser)**

This is a really unique among the romance genre. Its truly something only an artist of Pepper Pace's quality could create.
- **BookDevour "M2M" (verified Amazon purchaser)**

I loved everything about this book!!! You know how you search for a book that has everything you're looking for, well I finally found it and I can't wait for the second book!
- **KDubLew (verified Amazon purchaser)**

Eagerly awaiting part 2. Loved this. Pepper Pace always delivers.
-**Hope McGill (Author of Pearls, Pearls II)**

# Author's Note

This story is dedicated to the memory of an amazing writer whose stories inspired me to write 'outside of the box'. In 1987-1988 I was just 21 years old and had read a book entitled Dawn written by Octavia E Butler. It became a three book series called 'Lilith's Brood' and then renamed Xenogenesis. Over the years I have re-read Xenogenesis countless times and it is the root of the book you now read.

Miss Butler explored themes that as a writer I now explore in my own stories. I like to think of Octavia Butler as the ultimate IR writer. Not only did she write about strong, independent black women involved in multiracial relationships—but her stories often crossed into inter-species relationships between humans and aliens, hybrids and even vampires.

Miss Butler's stories tackled racism, feminism, gender, self-preservation, love and desolation. In tribute to this amazing author I have written my own version of a post-apocalyptic world where aliens and humans intermingle. There are some common themes in our stories but Adaptation is not a work of fanfiction nor does it attempt to re-tell, re-construct, or mimic Dawn, Adulthood Rites or Imago. These amazing stories are merely my inspiration.

The writings of Octavia Butler has allowed me to dream of the world where my own characters thrive. I thank this wonderful writer for being a forerunner to a genre that still struggles for recognition. My hopes are to bring multicultural and interracial stories into the 'light'.

In memory of **Octavia Estelle Butler** (June 22, 1947 – February 24, 2006)

Adaptation

# TABLE OF CONTENTS

REVIEWS FOR ADAPTATION .............................................................VI

AUTHOR'S NOTE.........................................................................VII

OCTAVIA E. BUTLER .....................................................................XI

PROLOGUE................................................................................1

CHAPTER 1~MAGGIE~ ....................................................................2

CHAPTER 2~WOLF~ .....................................................................12

CHAPTER 3~THE BLOB~ .................................................................18

CHAPTER 4~MICAH~......................................................................25

CHAPTER 5~THE LONE TRAVELER~........................................................32

CHAPTER 6~THIS SO-CALLED LIFE~......................................................38

CHAPTER 7~WOLF AND THE ALIEN~.......................................................46

CHAPTER 8~RIGHTING A GREAT WRONG~...................................................51

CHAPTER 9~DECISIONS AND CONSEQUENCES~ ..............................................56

CHAPTER 10~MUTATION~.................................................................63

CHAPTER 11~BILAL RESURRECTED~ .......................................................71

CHAPTER 12~COMPROMISE~...............................................................78

CHAPTER 13~WOLF COMES HOME~ .........................................................84

CHAPTER 14~BILAL MEETS HIS SON~ .....................................................91

CHAPTER 15~I AM NOT ALONE~ ..........................................................99

CHAPTER 16~FIRST BATH~...............................................................103

CHAPTER 17~THESE STRANGE FEELINGS~..................................................113

# Adaptation

CHAPTER 18~ASKING FOR HELP~ .................................118

CHAPTER 19~BABY~ .................................................124

CHAPTER 20~BABY MAKES THREE~ ...........................133

CHAPTER 21~ABILITIES~ ...........................................138

CHAPTER 22~PLEASURE~...........................................144

CHAPTER 23~TURNING THE CORNER~ .......................150

CHAPTER 24~THE TRUTH~..........................................157

CHAPTER 25~SHOPPING~ ..........................................163

CHAPTER 26~LOSS~ ..................................................173

CHAPTER 27~SOMETHING NEW~ ...............................180

CHAPTER 28~BATTLES~ .............................................186

CHAPTER 29~ESCAPES~ .............................................195

CHAPTER 30~ENDINGS~ ............................................203

CHAPTER 31~HOME~..................................................212

EPILOGUE~THE FIRST DAY OF THE REST OF OUR LIVES~.................219

ADAPTATION BOOK 2 PREVIEW ...................................226

ABOUT THE AUTHOR ................................................238

AWARDS ...................................................................239

# Adaptation

# Adaptation

*Intelligence is ongoing, individual adaptability. Adaptations that an intelligent species may make in a single generation, other species make over many generations of selective breeding and selective dying. Yet intelligence is demanding. If it is misdirected by accident or by intent, it can foster its own orgies of breeding and dying.*

*-Parable of the Sower*
**Octavia E. Butler**

# Prologue

**A hint of the song** played somewhere deep in her mind, and with it came the memories that were both a blessing and a curse. They only came when she slept and always with a whisper of the song that Jody had played on the school's piano.

No one else was around, and she certainly should not have been roaming the school halls after hours. But the quiet peacefulness of school was comforting when there was no one else around. She preferred the quiet, which caused people to think she was shy when she was actually a loner.

In some ways it was good that she had never needed people around.

Carmella followed the faint tinkling of the piano keys, liking the melody.

Later, Jody would explain that it was a song called "*Arpeggi*" by a group called Radio Head. But that would be a future—one that she would have liked to keep frozen and permanent.

Carmella stared through the glass of the closed door and watched the teen's fingers as they moved across the keys. She recognized him but hadn't known that he'd had a talent for more than reading books and making good grades. In a word, he was a nerd—but it was still one step up from being a loner.

The dream-Carmella watched the pale skinny boy with the strikingly black hair through the glass of the door, and she longed to throw open that door and fling herself at him.

1

## Adaptation

But the dream-her didn't know him yet, and the real-her had lost him a long time ago.

# Chapter 1
## ~Maggie~

**Carmella blinked** her eyes but didn't otherwise move. For a moment the memory of Jody was so fresh it sent a sharp pain right to the center of her chest. She stared at the ceiling until she could breathe. It always took her a moment to push the memories back into a place where they did not drive her mad. And perhaps there would come a day when they would no longer retreat neatly back to that special place where she kept her memories, and then she truly would be mad.

Carmella leaped to her feet as she remembered what day it was. It was Sunday, and there was a lot to do. She used the slop bucket, and as she carried it outside she paused on the back porch and scanned the yard.

Yard?

Yes, she considered the acres upon acres of farmland to be her yard. Her "yard" didn't stop at the end of the farm. Carmella's land ran as far as the eye could see to the Ohio River and beyond.

She began the arduous task of pumping and hauling water back to the house and heating it on her wood cook stove for her bath.

Sunday she could luxuriate in the bath. Heating the water and filling the big tub was too much of a task to do every day, so for the rest of the week she used a washbasin to clean herself. But on Sundays she allowed herself this small luxury. She sang old songs but only the parts she could remember. And as the water heated she tended to the bread. Her kitchen always had a pleasant,

# Adaptation

fresh-baked smell because of the starter dough that sat on the counter. Every morning she fired up her cook stove, baked her bread, milked the cow, and collected eggs. Her breakfast was usually scrambled eggs, bread with fresh butter, and milk still warm from its source.

It took nearly two hours to fill the tub. She had timed it long ago. Carmella lit several candles and situated them in her large bathroom, and then she tested the water and found it was bearable. She kept one bucket of hot water in the corner to heat the bath as it cooled. Carmella stepped into the tub with a sigh of pleasure. The most expensive bath beads that she could find in Macy's in downtown Cincinnati colored the water sea foam green and exuded a fresh ocean aroma. She picked up a book, a paperback imprinted with the image of two white people on the cover, which promised an interesting romantic journey. She had several hundred paperbacks that neatly filled one room. Sometimes she picked them because the cover made her remember something she had long forgotten, like cell phones. How could she have forgotten cell phones?

But after so long a cell phone was the last thing worth remembering …

Carmella lost track of time in the bath. She had the book half-read and the water was tepid by the time she stepped out. She padded into the bedroom naked and dried off while standing in front of her mirror. She had no interest in the way she looked, but if she bothered to glance into the mirror she would see a thirty-eight-year-old woman with medium brown skin and long dreadlocks that ran down her back to her buttocks. She stood 5-9, and though more thickly built than thin, she was almost pure muscle. Her face was unpleasant, not because she was unattractive, but because her eyes fluctuated between a look of wild desperation and lost confusion. Her eyes rose momentarily and took in the sight of the wild thatch of black hair that nestled under her arms and between her thighs.

"When I was back at home I used to trim that," she said dispassionately before dressing in a pretty blue dress that still had

4

the price tag on it: "$1,799.99." She examined it before ripping off the tag with a cackle. "That one *fucking* penny! Always that one *fucking* penny!"

By the time she reached the bottom of the stairs, Carmella had tears in her eyes from laughing so hard. When she reached her neat kitchen, Carmella put the chicken in the oven. She'd slaughtered it yesterday and got it ready so she wouldn't have to spill blood on Sunday. Once a week she sacrificed a chicken to Sunday dinner, but there were enough chickens left that she would never have to worry about it. There were probably more chickens in the world than there were humans.

She knew this to be true, because she was the last person on Earth.

Not that she'd walked the entire Earth. But the last time she'd seen a person was eight years ago. Maggie. Maggie was mad, the crazy kind of mad — though she was angry too, which was why they couldn't continue to live together. So yeah ... two people on Earth.

Carmella and a crazy white woman named Maggie.

**In the beginning** Carmella had roamed. She felt that it was her job to find others. She had been raised in the Cleveland suburbs and had kept to them for several years. There were so many houses to live in. At first, living in the large, luxury homes made her feel good, but soon living in the homes of dead people and seeing the evidence of a life long gone began to haunt her. She began to seek out hotels, which were impersonal and without history. But the solitude began to eat at her even more, so she decided to put being a Midwestern girl to use and began searching for a farm where she could keep animals and plant fresh vegetables instead of living off the canned goods she found in abandoned stores.

That was when she found the old lady living in a rambling old farmhouse that had seen better days. The wolves drove her to

# Adaptation

the house. She'd forgotten about the wild animals when she had decided on this journey. Animals had taken over the manmade communities, but they were domesticated animals that used to be kept as pets or ones hunted as food and not ones Carmella would run from. It was Cleveland, after all, and she would never think of lions and tigers ... perhaps bears — even if all of the animals in the Cleveland Metroparks Zoo had been released during the end of days. And even if they were now roaming the streets, there surely wouldn't be enough of them to be concerned with.

But she'd forgotten about the wolves.

Carmella had adopted a motorcycle that allowed her easy access to regular and dirt roads alike. She knew how to unlock the pumps at gas stations, and when there was no working back-up generator, she knew how to siphon gas from underground tanks using a two-way rotary hand pump and two eight-foot fuel hoses. The gas found in abandoned cars was no longer good. She didn't know why. She thought gasoline lasted forever, but evidently it didn't. The only gasoline still somewhat usable was hidden away in tanks under gas stations.

She had been riding for hours when she decided to stop and pee. Driving down I-71 through Ohio was tedious, nothing but straight road and decaying, rotting corn and soybean fields as far as the eye could see. But she didn't want to live so near the highway. The image of the endless people in buses and trucks being carted away was still imprinted on her memory. That was a long time ago ...

She had ventured off the highway southeast of Columbus and had found overgrown roads to explore. The sun was hot and beat down on her relentlessly until Carmella spotted a clearing where she could stretch her legs and rest a while under an oak tree. After relieving herself, she pulled out beef jerky and a can of Coca-Cola for a quick snack. Maybe they had been tracking her for a while. There were four of them, and she smelled them before she had ever seen them. They had surrounded her before she even realized it.

6

# Adaptation

They knew the moment she realized their presence because her scent changed even to her own nose. She smelled the acrid funk of her own terror as the two wolves in front began a slow advance, head low and teeth bared. They were skinny, half-starved, and mangy. She had a rifle secured to the bike, but they would be on her tearing her flesh before she could reach it. There was a pistol in the satchel that sat next to her.

Carmella's throat went dry, and she nearly choked on the jerky. Sweat rolled down her scalp as she reached into the jerky bag and grabbed a handful. One of the wolves seemed to dislike her movement and growled as he advanced, his growl a signal for the others to move in. Carmella flung the jerky at them while leaping to her feet. The two wolves in front scrambled for the jerky, which gave her enough time to dig into the satchel for her gun. She gripped the cool steel in her right hand when something hit her hard in her left shoulder and a second wolf clamped down onto her left calf. Though the pain was horrible, she squeezed the trigger and shot wildly through the satchel.

The explosive sound caused the wolves to retreat a few feet. Carmella backed against the tree while her shoulder and leg exploded in pain as the wolves advanced again. She didn't have time to aim and pulled the trigger again, clipping the closest wolf in the neck, causing it to cry out before scurrying away.

Two others followed the hurt wolf, but a third had Carmella's blood on its mouth and wanted more. He jumped at her, and Carmella screamed and shot repeatedly, the animal landing on her in a death spasm. She pushed its emaciated body away and clamped her hand on her bleeding shoulder. It was bad, but it hadn't gotten her artery. Still too much blood …

Her heart pounded in her chest and she could barely catch enough breath to fuel her movements. She stumbled to her feet and saw her bike, but somehow it seemed to move further and further from her. She was going to black out … God no. And then she fell and panted while she lay on the grass. *I am dead. After all of this, I am dead.*

# Adaptation

When Carmella's eyes opened, she was met by a stench of such magnitude that it must have been like smelling salts to her system. Her eyes blinked and she tried to focus. There was the face of a woman hovering above her, and it took Carmella a long moment to understand why this was so strange.

Hers was the first face she had seen in about two years.

The woman seemed just as intrigued as they stared at each other, and then the woman's lips parted to expose the source of much of the funk. Her breath smelled of decay because she had a mouthful of rotten teeth.

She was old, her hair was completely gray, and it didn't appear to have been combed in months … or longer. She was too thin but had lively blue eyes set in a face that smiled easily.

"Wolves got you good," the woman said in a surprisingly strong voice. "Took a chunk out of your shoulder."

Carmella's stomach turned at the rankness of her breath. She reached up and touched her shoulder, surprised to feel that it was bandaged heavily.

"I stopped the bleeding. Had to take a hot knife to it. It'll be ugly, but you'll live." The woman moved away.

Carmella looked at the filthy, trash-strewn bed where she lay and then at house that was a hoarder's dream. There was so much stuff Carmella couldn't see the floor except for a narrow path that led out of the room.

The woman returned with a filthy mug, with food smeared along the lip. "Here." She offered the mug to Carmella.

Carmella struggled to sit up.

"It's soup, Campbell's chicken noodle. It's good for you."

Carmella was happy the soup helped to mask the other smells, and she tried to take it, but her shoulder screamed in pain and she gasped.

The woman held the mug up to her lips.

"Thank you, but I don't think I can drink any right now."

"No?" The woman prodded her lips with the dirty mug as if she was an insolent child.

"No. Thank you, no."

8

# Adaptation

The woman slurped the soup. "Good stuff." She eyed Carmella. "I heard your gunfire. I didn't know what it was at first. It's been so long ..." The woman's eyes hazed over before clearing and refocusing. "What's your name? I'm Maggie."

Carmella tried to look at her shoulder. The bandages appeared clean. She needed to remove them to see the damage, but she was tired and it hurt too bad to move much. She looked at the woman. "Carmella Washington. Thank you for rescuing me."

"You would have been wolf food if I hadn't. Get some rest, Carmella. We'll talk in the morning. I broke a pain capsule open into some water and spooned it into you. You'll be sleepy for a while, but maybe you'll sleep through some of the pain. I had to sew your leg up, but it only took six stitches, one on each puncture." The old woman smiled ruefully.

Carmella considered the likelihood of a staph infection. Maybe it was the mention of the painkillers or the trauma of her attack, but Carmella fell asleep.

When she awoke, Carmella's bladder felt as if it would explode. She slid off the bed gingerly, and as she stood, her leg nearly buckled when pain flared in her calf. She sat and pulled up her pants leg to examine the wound. Although covered in a clean bandage, it had begun to seep. She carefully pried the tape away exposing an angry wound, the uninjured flesh ringed with iodine. Relieved, she secured the bandage. Maggie might have been dirty, but she knew to keep a wound clean.

Carmella stood and stumbled out of the room on the narrow path through the trash, careful not to topple towers of junk rising to the ceiling on either side of her. "Maggie?"

She came to a landing with a stairwell leading down. Boxes stacked to the ceiling lined the corridor, and Carmella tried not to lean against them as she limped to the stairs. How had that skinny old woman managed to get her up these stairs?

Carmella eased down the stairs and looked around. What should have been a living room on her right was a mess of chaos. At least upstairs there was some semblance of order. It was as if someone had flung trash into the room. Another room to her left was in a similar state. Rotting food, opened cans, and human and animal waste littered the floor.

Grimacing, Carmella made her way outside. "Maggie?"

A cat came scurrying out the door and almost made Carmella fall.

"Carmella," Maggie called. "Come down around the side. I'm picking tomatoes. There's a patch of poison ivy so leave it be. Leaves of three, leave it be."

Carmella followed the voice and saw the woman tending to a small garden. Maggie had a basket filled with fresh lettuce, cucumbers, and tomatoes, and Carmella's stomach groaned in hunger.

"Good morning, sleepyhead." Maggie smiled.

"Good morning. Um, where can I ..."

"Pee? Anywhere you want. You gotta poop, there's toilet tissue in the spare room upstairs."

"Anywhere?" Carmella looked around.

"God don't care and neither do I."

Later they ate a salad dressed in vinegar and oil.

"Have you seen any people come through here?" Carmella asked as they sat on the porch.

Maggie speared a slice of tomato and plunged it into her mouth. "No." She chewed. "Not since the Blobs carried the people away on the trucks. I'd hear the trucks morning noon and night for months. And then it just stopped." Maggie stopped chewing and stared off into the distance. "I hid. They come through here looking. But they couldn't find me. I guess they thought the place was abandoned. They ain't been back. Didn't have the manpower to check a place twice. Man power." She laughed. "Why didn't you go with them?"

How could she even ask that? She stared at the old woman. "Because I'm a human and this is my home. And no fucking alien is going to come down and force me away from it!" She placed her hand on her belly and thought about Micah and Jody. They were buried here on earth, and here is where she would stay.

Micah ...

# Adaptation

Her breath hitched in her chest. They'd killed her baby, and the rest of them could believe their lies but she wouldn't. She knew their purpose had been to take the humans. It had been their plan all along. The Blobs. That name was a kindness they didn't deserve. They were a scourge that brought the ultimate genocide against the entire human race. And after the mass death and suicides, what was left was carried away to Earth 2.

But there was no Earth 2. There was only Earth! The other was only an alien world, and she would kill anyone or anything that tried to take her from her world!

She stayed with Maggie while she healed and was expected to stay on. It was unsaid. Humans who had found each other would naturally gravitate to each other. Maggie, however, could not tolerate having her things touched. She had allowed Carmella to stay but hadn't given her a space. When she had tried to move some things into the hallway and out of a spare bedroom, Maggie had gone into a tirade.

"Where is my cat? I can't find my cat!" Maggie searched hours for Kitty, the cat that Carmella had inadvertently allowed to escape the week before. Carmella carried her gun and went out searching for the cat, not wanting to admit to what she'd done. And despite being deathly afraid of wolves, she searched for hours, never finding Kitty.

When she had gone back to the farmhouse, all of the items that Carmella had moved out of the spare bedroom had been returned—*and* more.

"I can't *find* anything when you move shit around!" Maggie screamed. "Just leave it all alone! Don't touch my things!"

Carmella had said nothing, and the next day Maggie had calmed although still distraught about the missing cat. She left a can of tuna sitting out on the front porch and wrung her hands.

"Kitty will be all right, Maggie," Carmella said. "Animals adapt to the wild, even when they're domesticated."

Maggie picked at the lice in her hair sullenly.

# Adaptation

"Maggie," Carmella said, broaching a subject she knew had to be discussed. "When was the last time you bathed? Honey, your hair needs a good scrubbing. You have things living in it."

"Fuck you," Maggie said, turning cold eyes on her. "You let my cat out, didn't you? Admit it! You let her out!"

"She—I didn't know you had a cat and—"

Maggie flew at her with her hands clawed, going for her face. If Carmella hadn't fallen the woman would have gouged out her eyes.

"Bitch!" Maggie screamed. "Bitch! You let my baby get away!"

Maggie was stronger than she looked, and it took all that she had to keep Maggie's gnarled hands from her face. Carmella had to knee Maggie in the stomach to end the attack.

"You're crazy!" Carmella screamed. "I didn't mean it! It was an accident!"

She ran into the house and grabbed her satchel. She didn't want the clothes because they were probably infested with lice, but she needed her satchel and her guns. She hurried down the stairs where Maggie was waiting for her with a knife.

"You're insane." Carmella raised her hands to show that she wasn't holding a weapon. "I'm leaving, okay? Don't worry. I'll be out of your hair."

"You're not leaving me, too! You're staying!"

Carmella's heart began to pound in her chest. "I'm not a pet, Maggie. You can't keep me locked in the house like I'm some damned animal!"

Maggie looked confused, dropped the knife, and shook her head. "I'm—no no no. You can stay. I won't ..."

Carmella relaxed. "I can't live like this. I'm sorry." She rushed past the woman, who grabbed for her with strong hands, but Carmella easily shook her loose. She ran for her bike, tossing her satchel over her shoulder. She had to kick-start it with her injured leg, and it would hurt but she soon forgot about that when she saw Maggie come rushing out of the house holding the knife and yelling like a wild woman.

## Adaptation

Carmella cursed and kick-started the bike. She gunned it into life, almost flipping it when she added too much gas.

Maggie shrieked and brought back her arm, stabbing down as Carmella took off in a cloud of dust.

# Chapter 2
# ~Wolf~

**Carmella sat in her kitchen** eating her dinner. Her time with Maggie had caused her to garner certain habits. She washed daily and kept her dreadlocks neat and tidy. She kept her farmhouse in immaculate condition, sweeping, dusting, and mopping on a regular basis, maybe even to excess. She never allowed her trash to accumulate, and once a week she carried the unusable portion to the pit.

But not on Sundays.

On Sundays she had her bath, cooked Sunday dinner, read some, and sat out on the porch hoping that Wolf would come by to visit. She always saved the chicken butt for him, and if he didn't show up, she placed it in the icebox until he did come. Then she'd warm it up on her cook stove and put it in his special bowl for him and the pups.

She smiled to herself. She'd finished the paperback book by the time it had grown dark, and with a sigh she ambled inside and lit the kerosene lantern. Maybe Wolf would come tomorrow. She thought about Maggie and she thought about Kitty, whom she had carelessly released. The cat had probably never returned to the woman, unlike Wolf. He always returned home. That was another difference between the two women. Carmella hadn't kept Wolf a prisoner.

It had taken her several months after leaving Maggie's farm to find her new home. By then she was on the Kentucky side of the

# Adaptation

Ohio River. The farm had evidently served as a horse farm though the horses had long since left by the time she had arrived. The barn was the deciding factor. She had an unreasonable fear of wolves. and the barn was large enough to house the animals she wanted to keep locked away at night. The house itself was simple from the outside, but inside the prior inhabitants had spent a great deal of money making it a nice home. There was a chicken coop, a pen for pigs, and a large garden that was sadly overgrown.

And Carmella loved it.

Many of the chickens were still present, and a horse once showed up and took off, but Carmella had to find the cows—which attracted the bull, a goat, and some wild turkeys. It was a lot of hard work. The wolves kept picking off the chickens and killed the goat in the middle of the day. Although scared, she got her rifle and guns and went out hunting. It was early spring but still cold, snow covering the ground. It was her first winter there, and she assumed the bitter cold was what made the wolves desperate enough to approach the farm during the day.

It wasn't hard to follow their tracks so she was thankful for the cold weather. The trail of blood helped as well. After a few hours she came to a cave. Damn! Even a fool knew better than to go into a cave with wolves. But she didn't have to worry. Two scrawny wolves came out, baring teeth and growling aggressively. Carmella didn't think, shooting and killing them both. She didn't need their pelts. She could easily go to Macy's or Wal-Mart or any number of department stores up in Cincinnati for all the clothes her heart desired. But it was a shame to waste the fresh meat. As she prepared to butcher one of the animals, she heard a sound that made her heart slow.

It was the sound of a wolf puppy crying.

Carmella cursed as she looked at the gaunt animal carcasses. Damn, a family of wolves. They had been trying to feed their babies. It was stupid, she knew, but she crawled carefully into the cave and saw a ball of fur whining in the corner. Just one. Carmella reached out, and the pup sniffed her hand, crawling to her without hesitation. Something in Carmella's chest seemed to open up and

15

flare to life. She picked up the little pup and held it by the scruff of its neck while she examined it critically. Shit, he was a little boy who pissed and whined, but he was adorable. Carmella placed it into her coat and followed her tracks back home. She didn't have the heart to eat his parents.

She named the pup Wolf. She didn't want to give the little one a real name because she hoped not to become too attached. But Wolf became a welcome distraction from her tedious life. He was so cute, and his antics caused her to laugh often. She bathed him and brushed his fur, and to keep Wolf from crying all night, she let him cuddle against her in bed. She carried him up and down the stairs until he learned to do it on his own. He once jumped at a mouse and cowered in the corner, whining for her to rescue him. He hid under the bed whenever he left a mess on the floor. And if she couldn't find him, she knew to search for his mess. She took him with her while she hunted and taught him how to corral the animals without killing a chicken.

As he grew to full size, Wolf continued to be as gentle as ever and still tried to climb into her lap for a nap or into her bed to fall asleep against her warm body. She knew that she was every bit Wolf's mother as the one she had slaughtered, and he had become her child. Not that she missed Micah any less. But having Wolf allowed her to stop thinking about her own lost child, and for a while her hatred receded.

One day when they had gone out to corral the animals, Wolf became distracted and sniffed the area. He threw his head back and howled, the sound making her skin crawl. Carmella had never heard him make such a sound. It took her a long time to get him to come back home, and that night he was restless. Carmella wouldn't let him out, and he whined at the door all night long. As soon as she went out the next morning to milk the cows, Wolf dashed out and went running at full speed into the field.

"Wolf!" She ran after him with only a pistol in the waistband of her jeans, but it didn't take long for Wolf to disappear from her sight. All she could do was scream out his name. "Wolf!" When she thought about Kitty and what she'd done to Maggie all those years ago, she began to cry hysterically as she apologized over and over.

Wolf didn't come home. She sat out food in his special bowl. She had even slaughtered a chicken and stewed it up especially for him. But even when the sun set, Wolf had not returned. This was the first time that he'd spent a night without her in the four years that she'd had him. What did he know about the wilderness? He was just a baby …

Each evening she stood on the porch and stared out into the distance waiting for Wolf to come back. Six months went by, and one evening she heard familiar scratching on the door. Carmella sat up straight in bed and turned up the lantern. She listened and heard scratching and a soft whining. Carmella jumped out of bed and dashed to the door. She flung it open without thought, and there was her baby!

"Wolf!" She grabbed him and hugged him around his furry throat as his tail thumped back and forth.

He licked her face even though he knew he wasn't supposed to do that and for once she didn't chastise him. She began asking him where he had been. He was thin and she stood and led him into the house but he wouldn't come.

"What's wrong, boy?"

Wolf looked behind him, whined, and walked in a circle. He let out a sharp bark, and another wolf came out of the darkness. Carmella peered out into the night. The second wolf stared at her with strange eyes, watching her as if she was some curious abomination. After a few long moments, the second wolf came forward and crept up the stairs, warily keeping Carmella in its sights.

"Wolf? Is that your … wife? Did you go get married, boy?" She chuckled to herself. "Now you're bringing her home to meet your mama?"

Carmella went to the kitchen, trusting that Wolf would keep his woman in her place. She pulled out all the chicken butts she had been saving and placed them in a skillet on the cook stove to warm up. She filled his water bowl and set it out on the front porch. They both drank from it, and when she brought out the chicken butts, she placed them in one bowl and set it in front of her boy. Wolf sucked them down in appreciation while the female bared her teeth at Carmella's proximity before she joined him.

"Bitch," Carmella muttered. It was exactly what a bitch would do—come to your house, eat your food, and then roll her eyes at you.

After the chicken butt appetizer, she filled his bowl with a mixture of hard and canned dog food. They scarfed that down as well. Poor baby, he was so hungry. She made to move outside, but the bitch growled at her, stopping her in her tracks. Wolf snapped at his wife, who quickly retreated as Carmella came out on the porch and sat in her chair. Wolf sniffed the porch for a few minutes before curling at her feet. She reached down and stroked his fur while his wife stood in the yard watching and looking agitated.

Carmella thought about shooing her away but didn't. She was Wolf's wife, after all, and since wolves mated for life, she and Wolf's wife would have to get used to each other.

They stayed that way throughout the night. She thought Wolf was asleep, but he was content to lie at her feet. As the sun rose, Wolf sat up, sniffed the porch, he looked at his Mama, and darted down the stairs and into the woods, his wife trailing closely behind.

It was so difficult after that. It was as if Wolf had visited to tell her goodbye. Carmella cried for two days after that.

Wolf returned several months later.

This time he had his wife and three little furry pups. Carmella picked up each puppy in her arms and carried them into the house. This time Wolf followed and so did his wife. She still gave Carmella the stink eye, but it didn't matter. Carmella was holding Wolf's pups, and there was nothing that could have made her happier.

Carmella prepared a feast for the family and played with the babies for the rest of the day instead of tending to her chores. Wolf sat in contentment nearby, looking out at the horizon in a way she had never seen before, his ears perking if he heard an errant sound. She realized that he was watching, protecting them all in a way he had never done before. What had he experienced in the year that he'd gone out and made a family? She thought she understood why he sniffed the porch so carefully. Wolf was making sure that nothing had been at the house in his absence.

Wolf was torn between his mama and his family. He kept coming back to keep watch over Carmella. Over time, the children grew bigger, and it sometimes looked as if a pack of wolves had come for her, but she recognized each of them. Each wolf took to her except the wife. That bitch never liked her and had once snapped at her when she reached out to pat her in a show of friendship. But Wolf didn't play that shit, and he nipped her back, causing her to whine and go outside. Wolf kept his children under control when they were in the house. Sometimes Carmella would cackle at their antics, even when they knocked over and broke things and went hiding in shame. She loved them intensely.

Wolf had more pups, and the older ones stopped coming around. But every few months Wolf would return home. He never stayed longer than a day, but she knew each time he left that he'd soon return.

# Chapter 3
# ~The Blob~

**Carmella had milked** the cow and was returning to her house with the frothy pail humming some made-up tune when she saw it.

Partially concealed by a large oak tree several yards away, the Blob stood very still looking every bit like an octopus. Carmella had never been this close to one before. When they had first come, Jody had wanted to go to one of the fairs to see them. He'd taken Micah ...

Carmella shuddered. What was it doing here? After all this time, what was it doing here? They couldn't still be collecting humans after *ten years!*

Carmella was seventeen the year the mother ship had appeared in the sky. Days before there were frantic news reports of a strange mass approaching earth. NASA did extensive studies using satellites and the Hubble, but there was no official word of the findings. The leaders of the world held extensive meetings. The mother ship appeared in the sky over the Atlantic Ocean amid mass suicide and killings as people thought it was the sign of the end of the world or the fulfillment of some prophecy.

The greatest scientific minds of the world tried to find ways to communicate with the mother ship, but if it ever happened, no one was the wiser. There were conspiracy theories running wild, made worse by the fact that the mother ship hovered unmoving in the sky for  months.

# Adaptation

Half of the world thought it should be shot from the sky, but since it was the size of a small country that had been overruled, especially since there was no idea of the repercussions of such an act. She and Jody also had different opinions. She was among those who thought the ship should be destroyed, but Jody thought that they should study and befriend the aliens.

By this time Jody and Carmella were friends but too shy to admit that they liked each other a bit more than only friends. They found reasons to be together even if it was only to study ... or pretend to study. Jody was a nerdy white kid who played trumpet in the school band, and Carmella was a nerdy black girl who was more mean than nice. It should have been a death sentence for their friendship, but soon their opposing attitudes and styles seemed a magnet that attracted them to each other.

They sat in a café together, a regular hangout away from school and family, watching one of the big-screen televisions that constantly stayed tuned to news coverage of the hovering mother ship. It had been hanging over the Atlantic for six months, and interest mounted with each passing day.

"I'm going to Atlantic City after graduation."

Carmella's head turned in his direction.

"Well, there are all these parties going on up and down the coast—"

"Parties?" she interrupted. "You don't even do parties here. You're going all the way to Atlantic City to party?"

"No. I mean, not for the partying. I want to go to show support to the aliens. We just want to welcome them."

Carmella rolled her eyes. "If this was a movie, the aliens would eat you supporters first!"

Jody drummed his fingertips along the table nervously. "I was going to ... um." He cleared his throat and glanced away. "I was going to ask you to come." His eyes darted to hers quickly, his face bright red. "I know you don't like the idea of aliens, but, well, I thought it would be fun."

Carmella stared at him and felt new emotions well up inside of her. Soon school would be out, and they would go their separate

# Adaptation

ways. His trip to Atlantic City was testament to that. Beyond that was the knowledge he wanted to be where the aliens were at the same time she was desperately afraid of them. She wasn't excited about their arrival or the sharing of knowledge. She felt they meant harm to them, and she didn't want Jody anywhere near them.

"Don't go, Jody." She reached out and grasped his hand on the tabletop. "If you stay here ..." She swallowed, leaned forward, and placed her lips on his for the first time. When she pulled back, his eyes were glazed.

He gripped her hand gently in his. "Okay."

Carmella and Jody's love bloomed in a new age where the speculation of aliens and world domination and doomsday prevailed. And still they found joy in their budding romance amid the chaos and fear that formed a cocoon of security around them.

The doors of the mother ship opened one day when Carmella's belly was full and stretched with their baby. Strange signposts appeared all over the world from the most desolate tribal villages in the deepest rainforest to Trafalgar Square in London and Takeshita Street in Japan. No one saw them go up, and even cameras didn't capture the event, which helped to fuel the rumors of world government conspiracies. Later, the world would know of an international government conspiracy, but by then it was too late and the trials and executions for crimes against mankind were too little too late. By the time there were repercussions, Jody and Micah were buried for years, and Carmella no longer cared.

The signposts appeared with security cameras aimed at them and concealed by structures manned by government officials. They couldn't be removed or destroyed. A year later, the Blobs began to communicate from inside the mother ship.

But even that was a lie.

They had been communicating all along.

The Blobs blew the lid on the subterfuge that had been pulled by world leaders, and this led to mistrust that would finally destroy society.

Carmella felt it was their plan all along.

22

# Adaptation

At first, the communications were almost childlike in their simplicity: "We are friends. We come from far away. We mean you no harm. We want to learn and to teach. We want to meet you."

Scientists spent a great deal of time interpreting messages and questions, but ultimately there was nothing of importance that the visitors ever communicated.

Or at least nothing that was revealed to the masses.

Several months after the posts appeared and three years after the arrival of the mother ship, the aliens finally revealed themselves. They were introduced with worldwide broadcasts. The first sight of them caused another wave of mass suicides although the Blobs made assurances to the public that they were not here to fulfill a prophecy or to take any humans with them.

Micah was only a baby, and Carmella had put him to sleep before the broadcast. She and Jody had sat on their secondhand couch and watched the broadcast—he in excitement, she with trepidation. The aliens looked like gray Blobs of slimy flesh. Their bodies had no legs, arms, or head. They had protrusions that could elongate and were called sensors, but they looked like tentacles. When not in use, these tentacles retreated into their bodies, the only indication of their existence a slight swollen area. They had eyes, but they were concealed beneath their skin. They had a disgusting ability to elongate like an engorged slug, and if they chose they could form appendages that looked like arms and legs. They moved like inchworms or slugs, but without the use of slime, and they could move fast when they wanted to.

There was no discernable skeleton, and the difference in gender was based on the difference in their tentacles. The males had probes that could burrow into the female. The probes were not purely sex organs but also their way of communicating.

Then the purpose of the signposts became apparent—connecting to it was the way they communicated with their mother ship.

# Adaptation

**Carmella knew** that the Blob was aware she'd seen it. They could move fast, but she was closer to the house. She dropped the milk pail and darted across the yard with her heart thumping in her chest, afraid that it would be right at her heals with tentacles reaching for her neck. She bounded up the stairs and with a squeak she slammed the door and secured the locks.

Locks? What good were they when there were windows all throughout the house? She grabbed one of the rifles. She kept one loaded beside each door in case something chased her into her house. She was breathing hard when she eased toward the front window and moved the curtain back to look into her yard. She was sure the thing had followed her up onto her porch, but her porch was empty. She tried to see through the trees edging her yard but couldn't make out the form of the Blob. She shook her head. Could she have imagined it? No. She might one day lose her mind from solitude, but she wasn't there yet. She'd seen it standing behind the big tree.

How she wished for Wolf because she couldn't stand the idea that there was nothing but her and it. Carmella gnawed her bottom lip, not feeling the skin crack and not recognizing the salty taste of her blood. She hurried to the kitchen, checked the windows, and made sure the door was locked. Then she grabbed cartridges for the rifle.

She was not going to be a prisoner in her own house. And if that thing wasn't after her, it meant it was going off to rat out her location. She had to go after it and kill it before it could get to one of the signposts.

Despite her decision to do this, she didn't feel fearless and brave. She was terrified. But long ago she'd had to face unpleasant things because there was no one else she could call on to fight her battles for her. She had no one else to turn to. She'd had to enter darkened stores and face the corpses of the long dead.

And she had survived until now.

Before she could lose her nerve, she pulled back the front door and stood in the entrance scanning the yard. She knew where the nearest signpost was located in the middle of a field several miles away.

Her eyes tried to take in everything at once as she hurried to her motorcycle. She had long since replaced the one she had when she was with Maggie. This was a comfortable, well-used Harley, and while there were probably bikes better suited for her, the Harley was what she wanted.

With her rifle strapped across her back, she threw her leg over the bike and heard the unmistakable sound of shuffling. Instinct told her to duck, even if it meant that she and the bike would hit the ground — and she did.

But so did the monstrous Blob.

It was on her, its elongated tentacles circling one leg while she was trapped beneath the heavy motorcycle. With a scream she scrambled back and kicked with all of her might.

It was disgusting the way her foot sank into its flesh. It was almost like kicking Silly Putty with a tough yet pliable outer skin. If she hurt it she couldn't tell. Its tentacles kept reaching. Its mottled skin and black disc like eyes that appeared beneath its translucent skin revolted her.

She kicked and scrambled as several more tentacles appeared, all grabbing for her.

"Stop."

She heard its distinct command-request — she didn't care which. She had heard them speak on television broadcasts and later when they gathered the humans for transport to Earth 2. They spoke with voices that reminded her of synthesized sounds. Since they had no need of voice boxes, they communicated through a complex system of sensors. They recognized the modality of their explanation, but it was so far removed from how humans interacted that it always sounded vague.

Blobs had no skeleton, vocal cords, or ears and yet they could speak and hear.

They also had stingers.

They tried to explain that the stingers were their natural defense, like a human forming a fist. But Carmella didn't buy that.

# Adaptation

She knew their stingers carried poison that could kill. Blobs said they didn't kill with them. "It renders the victim immobile," they said, but that was another lie ...

The Blob's stinger appeared, and Carmella knew this moment would mark the end of her life. The Harley had impaired its movements, but now both of them had cleared it. She remembered the rifle strapped to her back, and with a fluid motion that would have impressed Clint Eastwood, she pulled it forward and fired pointblank into the "face" of the beast.

The Blob made an ungodly sound and recoiled into a ball the same time she saw the bullet exit the Blob in a spray of brackish dark fluid. All of its sensor tentacles drew back into the mass of its body.

Carmella scrambled to her feet and barely registered the quivering mass as she turned to run. But then she stopped. She had to end this ...

She turned in time to see it slithering away, this time leaving a trail of that disgusting dark fluid in its wake. Swallowing back her disgust, Carmella shot again and again with the rapid-fire rifle.

The Blob emanated a distressed sound before curling into a tighter ball and remaining motionless.

Carmella backed away, panting and shaking until she almost tripped on the porch stairs. Was it dead? She was afraid to take her eyes from it, but she had fired at it about eight times and it didn't flinch. Her eyes darted to the barn. Kerosene!

She stared at the unmoving Blob and darted to the barn, giving the Blob a wide berth. Her mind pictured it reaching out with its stinger for her, but it didn't move. Adrenaline caused her to sprint the distance without tiring. She grabbed two partially full kerosene lamps and ran back to her farmhouse. A stitch had begun to build in her side, but she didn't slow. Her eyes scanned the yard, but even before she reached the farmhouse she saw that it was empty.

The Blob was gone.

# Chapter 4
## ~Micah~

**All that remained** was the ink-like fluid that had soaked into the ground, a scattering of bullets, and a trail that headed back into the woods. Carmella reached for the bike and noticed that one of the bullets had punctured the gas tank.

"No no no!" she screamed. She couldn't drive the damned truck into the woods! Why didn't she have two motorcycles? Carmella forgot about the stitch in her side. She ran as fast as she could, following the Blob's bloody trail.

How could it move so fast after being shot eight times? She knew it's nervous system was not localized in one spot but spread out within a matrix of that inky fluid, but eight shots *should* have done it in. Unless she hit it's brain or heart, it probably would be able heal itself. Her lips formed a grim, yet determined line.

*Let's see if this bitch can survive being burned.*

In her haste, Carmella didn't consider other dangers that might be awaiting her in the woods. She carried two of the kerosene lamps in one hand and a nine-millimeter in the other. The other gun was in her waistband for easy access. Her eyes were mainly focused on the black trail. It had to deplete itself at some point. It was a huge Blob, but eventually it would have to run out of that fluid.

She knew it was heading for the signpost and began jogging in that direction, her eyes still on the alien's trail. The chase made her remember the reason for her hatred, the reason that she was alone, and the reason that the world was now devoid of humanity. Now the chase was less about making sure that it didn't bring back others but about dishing out some payback. Just a little bit, on behalf of all mankind.

"I'm gonna kill you," she muttered. "Kill *you!*"

An unwelcomed memory caused her eyes to water. Micah's laughter. God, it was so crystal clear, as if it was twenty years earlier and her toddling baby boy was right there. She almost stumbled to a stop at the idea of him, a memory that she did not relish. A memory of Jody was one thing but not Micah.

Thinking about her baby hurt, even twenty years later.

**Micah was born** nearly two weeks overdue. He was a big pink baby with a head full of ink black hair. She cradled him in her arms in surprise because he was white. How did she have a white baby when she was nut brown? I mean, yeah Jody was white, but …

Jody kissed his son's forehead and then kissed her, a look of awe on his face. "Is … is he going to turn brown?"

She grinned in relief. Yeah, okay so she wasn't the only one wondering. When Mama came into the room to meet her first grandchild, she examined the baby's ears, his little nails and scrotum, and pronounced that he was white. She predicted that he might get toasty if he played in the sun, but that was it. For a moment an unpleasant thought flashed through Carmella's mind — if he doesn't look black, will he accept the fact that his mother is? Will he wish that he had a white mother? Will he accept his multiracial heritage?

When she kissed his silky curls, nuzzled his cheek with hers, and felt his responding yawn, those thoughts disappeared and never returned. Her focus was on loving her baby, and whether he would have ever had those feelings about his heritage would never be known.

He only lived to be two.

Jody was one of those fathers who happily wore a baby sling or pushed the baby carriage whenever they went out. He

# Adaptation

talked to Micah, he sang and told stories to his son, and he showered love on his new family.

"We should go to New Foundland."

Carmella's head had whipped around. "What?"

She likened it to a zoo, where aliens — or Centaurians, thusly named because their origins were from the Alpha Centauri star system — could interact with the humans in a controlled environment.

Jody always frowned at any derogatory comments made against the aliens. He completely believed the Centaurians would usher mankind into a new age of technology. He didn't like the term "Blob" and likened it to the 'N-word', which he also wouldn't dream of using.

"Why do you think we should go there?"

Jody had matured and didn't shy away from conversations that might create a difference of opinion. "I want Micah to grow up knowing that the Centaurians are a part of his life. As he gets older, he might want to visit the starship. Hell, I want to visit the starship."

"God, you nerdy guys," she had muttered. "I don't want my baby anywhere near those aliens. They are ugly, and I don't trust them."

Jody smiled. "They aren't ugly. There is beauty in the Centaurians, just as there is beauty in sea creatures." He rubbed her arms.

She tried to roll her eyes but found herself listening to his impassioned beliefs.

"Honey, they are the first step in creating a new existence of star travel. With their technological know-how we can leave this galaxy and explore new ones. We will learn what the Centaurians have seen. This is so exciting!" He calmed when he saw that she seemed less than thrilled. "And it's scary, yes I admit that, but they have made no threats against us. Mankind needs this, Mel. We need to move into the future."

She knew she couldn't continue pushing her fear off on him, so she reluctantly relented and agreed to visit New Foundland.

# Adaptation

They planned for the trip the way people made plans for Disneyworld. It would cost them a lot, but Jody's excitement couldn't be ignored. She wouldn't back out if it was this important to him.

Each continent had several places similar to New Foundland where humans could visit the aliens and see them up close. She'd seen them on television many times. A Blob had even been in an action movie. They were a part of pop culture. Songs and stories were written about them, and late night TV hosts referenced them often in their monologues.

Carmella wasn't alone in her distrust. There were many hate groups formed whose purpose was to rid the world of the alien menace. Terrorists groups rose up attempting to close down visitation centers. The world was a mess because of the alien visits.

But six months after she relented, the family visited the aliens for the first time.

She remembered Micah's pudgy fingers pointing at the display area beneath them where two Centaurians roamed. "Bubbie!" he yelled in excitement.

Jody had bought him a Centaurian stuffed animal so that he would feel comfortable at the sight of them. It was fondly named Bubbie. Carmella watched the excitement on her son's face with trepidation. She was afraid, and maybe it was strange to be. Looking at Jody, all she saw was excitement, and it was mirrored in the faces of the others who had waited hours for their turn to be ushered through the observation area.

The Blobs were with human guards. Yes, the guards were armed, but you couldn't see the weapons. That day there were two Blobs, and they were in a green "natural" environment where they moved around easily. They didn't ignore the throngs of humans and often waved tentacles or approached the borders of their "display" area. There was no glass barrier or cages, but you couldn't move easily from the observation deck down to the display environment. If you did, you would fall into a moat that would surely cause shattered limbs.

# Adaptation

"God, they're amazing." Jody had said with wide, excited eyes.

Carmella looked at the gray Blobs and saw only a terrible life form that frightened her.

Even Micah was bouncing with excitement in his father's arms, reaching for the aliens, wanting to go to them.

"Daddy, down!" he demanded, and one of the Blobs seemed to look right at them.

Carmella clutched Jody's arm, her body breaking into a cold sweat. "No."

Jody looked at the cold fear in her eyes, and despite wanting to stay and watch them for hours, he moved them out of the observation area.

In the summer of 2013, only three months after that visit, the World Health Organization (WHO) announced a pandemic outbreak of a new virus called H1Z similar to the pandemic outbreak in 2009 of H1N1. Instead of a swine-based virus, it was a strain that had unknown origins and could adapt to the host. As a result, it tricked the body into accepting it and couldn't be combatted by the body's natural defenses or any antiviral medications. Because of that, the H1Z virus caused the death of nearly 70 percent of the world's population. Billions succumbed to it in a matter of months.

Once H1Z appeared, so-called "scientists" committed atrocious crimes against humanity similar to the Nuremburg experiments. People who were resistant to the virus disappeared, imprisoned so scientists could conduct experiments on them, their blood rumored to be sold on the black market to the rich.

And while the virus was taking its first victims, Jody had stood in the front yard begging Carmella not to come out. He had gone missing for a full day and had returned only for Carmella to throw him some clothes so he could go to one of the centers to be treated safely away from her and the baby. Barely able to stand, Jody coughed into a bloodied tissue, his already pale skin ashen.

Only when Carmella carried Micah to the front porch did Jody come into the house. He wouldn't make anyone else sick

31

because their son's pale skin was as white as snow. Micah was too exhausted to cry anymore, staring with cloudy eyes and coughing blood-tinged phlegm across Carmella's shirt before he allowed his curly head to drop listlessly down onto her shoulder. Jody had stared in misery at the sight of his sick son. He walked up to the porch, took him in his arms, and cradled his too warm body.

Jody met her eyes. "There's no hope," his eyes seemed to say. He entered the house and lay down on the couch with Micah in his arms. Carmella covered them with an afghan and then went to the bathroom where she sobbed uncontrollably.

Micah passed away five days later.

Because he was delirious, Jody never knew that Micah had died.

Jody only lived two more days.

Carmella didn't want to wait for a "death wagon" like those used back in the days of the Black Plague. She didn't want Jody's or Micah's bodies tossed into pits where they were later burned. The government advised the living to leave the dead in their houses with red signposts painted on the door with the promise they'd be disposed as soon as possible. In most cases, that didn't happen.

And later, it just didn't matter.

Carmella buried her dead in the back yard, not just Jody and Micah but her mother and brother as well. Carmella stayed in her house, broken and lifeless, for as long as she could. When her neighbors realized that she had survived when everyone else in her family hadn't, Carmella feared she would be taken. She slipped away in the night with a few mementos, mementos she had lost over the years, which she considered both a curse and a blessing.

For years Carmella hoped to die like the others around her. If she caught a cold, she lay in her sickbed until she eventually got better and cursed her resistant genes. How was it that she could keep living amid the sickness and death around her?

# Adaptation

**Carmella pushed the unwelcomed** memory back to its neat little niche where she hoped to never open it again. With bitter determination, she hunted the monstrosity that had unleashed its virulent cells upon mankind. Near exhaustion, she thought she saw it slithering in the distance.

Fuck! It had changed colors! Now it was the color of the forest around them. For all she knew, she could have been looking right at it all this time. She thought about shooting it but knew it would be a waste of her bullets. Carmella caught a flash of movement to her left only seconds before a large wolf knocked her to the ground.

With a scream she felt the piercing pain of teeth sinking into her arm. While one wolf circled her, another wolf punctured her breast while another clamped onto her wrist. Carmella screamed in pain as she realized that she was about to be killed with a loaded nine-millimeter in her waistband.

The sound of a tormented howl cut through her own pain-wracked cries, and the wolf clamped at her shoulder went flying through the air as if flung like a doll. Colorful streaks flashed in front her as a tentacle encircled the wolf holding her wrist and then jerked it away. A stinger appeared and pierced the third wolf through the side.

Carmella focused with wide terror-stricken eyes at the Blob as it heaved next to her, fluctuating between the colors of gray, green, and brown. Its inky blood still flowed in a steady stream. Its gelatinous mass quivered and rippled and seemed to form two arms.

The Blob scooped her up and lifted her from the hard ground. Her hand still held one of the kerosene lanterns, and she tried to bring it up to strike the monster, but her wrist flopped uselessly and the lantern dropped to the ground.

The Blob turned black eyes to the lantern and seemed to stare at her before another tentacle appeared from its body. The stinger protruding from it dripped some hideous, foul liquid, and she had only a second to try to scramble away before she was stung in the stomach.

# Adaptation

She had no time to register pain as the world instantly darkened around her.

# Chapter 5
# ~The Lone Traveler~

**There was beauty** yet profound sadness in a world where all that remained were the remnants of life long gone. Sometimes he would walk through houses and see decayed meals upon cobwebbed plates. Once he saw a man sitting in a reclining chair in front of a television set with a remote control still held in his skeletal hands.

Those were the worst. He wanted to explore his connection with mankind, which was the initial reason he had left the mother ship and Earth 2--in order to go on these lonesome treks. Instead he sometimes felt overwhelmed by the desolation and the complete loss. He tried to keep to places that held artifacts and memorabilia like books and pictures. His favorites were the department stores where he tried to understand some of what he saw. He ran his sensors over the clothing trying to imagine being sheathed in something so uncomfortable. Yet humans had grown accustomed to it. This he couldn't understand.

He'd once allowed his form to shift into a shape that could slip into a coat. It had stifled his senses so badly that he had felt ill afterwards.

Bilal felt like a nomad more so than other Centaurians. His parents remembered another world, a different culture, but though he wasn't a human, he still thought of Earth as his world as much as it was for the men and women born here. Earth was all he knew. He had been born on the mother ship and was six Earth years old the first time he saw the humans. Bilal grew to adulthood alongside

# Adaptation

human friends, influenced by their culture. At one point his fathers wanted to separate him from his friends, but his First Mother said that Centaurians had to adapt.

Bilal was doing only what he was supposed to be doing.

Yet that was no consolation when other Centaurians looked upon him with distaste. Bilal is the name that he took for himself after meeting a man with brown skin and hair that was twisted into long tendrils that ran down his back. He was six years old then and had seen humans with straight hair and curled hair, but he'd been intrigued by dreadlocks. The man had been equally intrigued by the smaller being. Unafraid, Bilal allowed the man to touch him and to satisfy his curiosity, and in return the man had allowed him to touch his braids and his brown skin. The brown man's name was Bilal Akunyili.

After figuring out how to make his vocal chords speak the words, he announced it as his new human name. His Second Mother did not like it, perhaps because he had already changed his name four times, or maybe because she had a difficult time forcing her mouth and tongue to form the proper shape. Whatever the reason, it was hard for Bilal to know for sure because his Second Mother found displeasure at most things Bilal did. She always faulted him for trying to be human, reminded him that he was more evolved, and scolded him for trying to emulate humans. "They should be emulating you," his Second Mother had said.

This had made no sense to him. He wasn't *trying* to be one way or another. He was only himself, and like it or not, Bilal was an Earthling even if he was not a human being.

Centaurians did not breed as often as humans did. He was the third offspring of his First Mother and only the second of his other parents. Of the several thousand Centaurians that remained in the known universe, only a few hundred had produced offspring within the last thirty years. He had met a few of them and didn't like them nearly as much as he liked his human friends. They acted and thought like his parents, and some had never befriended a single human.

# Adaptation

Bilal knew that many of his parents wished he would conform because they were important, high-ranking officials in the Centaurian hierarchy. Though there wasn't an exact word in his language for "embarrassed," Bilal knew that was what many of his parents were. They were ashamed of the way he spoke and acted because he had little interest in his own culture. It was why he was allowed to travel down to Earth for extended visits, something forbidden to other Centaurian offspring. Bilal felt that they were happy to be rid of him for a while.

Earth was hard and rough with none of the smooth edges of their mother ship, where their bodies glided without hindrance. Not many Centaurians cared to leave the mother ship for Earth, where the death of so many billions still disturbed their senses. Bilal's desire to study the anthropology of Earth mixed with his parents' shame of having a son who had no connection to his own species made the decision to allow him access to the restricted planet an easy one. Perhaps time away from his humans would help him readjust to his role in this new world order.

Bilal spent months at a time away from home going to places his human friends had told him about. He kept communication with the mother ship and his parents using the sensor signposts set up all over the world. He had a space pod he used only when he wanted to travel back home and spent most of his time combing the land and making discoveries the Centaurians had never known, could never know because they refused to immerse themselves into human culture the way he attempted to do.

Using his sensors, he collected samples of plant life, which he stored within his body until he returned them to the mother ship for analysis. Bilal once discovered a special treat, a plant that caused him to feel joy and contentment in an exaggerated manner. It sometimes caused him to do things out of character, like pretending to be human. Once he had awakened to find that he had shifted his gelatinous body into the shape of a human and had been walking around on two legs. He would never do that on Earth 2 or the mother ship. When he was a child, his human friends had urged him to form himself into a human, and when the Centaurians saw him, they became outraged. His parents admonished him never to do it again. He didn't know why at the time—though he now understood.

The first time he returned with his samples and the strange plant was analyzed, it was determined that it had the same effect on the Centaurian's system that marijuana had on humans. He was admonished never to interact with it, and he promised not to. Whenever he returned to Earth, however, he would find more of these strange plants and get stoned for a couple of days before getting down to his anthropological studies.

**Bilal was stoned** when he saw the woman. For a moment, he wasn't even sure if he was seeing what was real. In all of his travels over all of these years he had never seen another human on earth. He wasn't naïve enough to think that the Centaurians had collected every single human from Earth. Many resisted and had died of the virus for their efforts. Some were living in madness brought on by years of solitude, perhaps even going below ground to hinder detection.

He was taught that should he cross paths with a human, he was to bring them to the mother ship for processing and reintegration with other humans.

Bilal had failed to consider that if he met a human, he or she would be hell-bent on killing him. He had found himself staring at her from across the yard. He hadn't camouflaged his gray color and didn't realize he should probably hide.

He regretted his decision to consume so much of the strange plant that his movements were slow and clumsy when he tried to grab her. She should have never been able to outmaneuver him. He had never had to deal with a violent confrontation before. Yes, with wolves and other wild creatures, but never a human. It went against his grain. Violence of any sort was not tolerated on Earth 2. Humans were prone to commit violent acts against one another, and their punishment was solitary confinement. He had tried to sedate her but was clumsy, and before he realized it, she had produced a gun and shot him.

When the first bullet entered him, it had done a great deal of damage. It had rendered him immobile, paralyzing him as it cut through several important synapses. Bilal had lain quietly rejuvenating and repairing the damaged portions of his body, fully aware that the woman intended to kill him.

She had disappeared for a while, but he knew that she might return to finish the job. As soon as he could, he retreated, repairing his injuries as he traveled back to his space pod. He was shocked to find that she was pursuing him. He knew that he could outrun her, even though he was losing much of his life fluid, but he sensed the wolves. Somehow he had to make sure the wolves wouldn't take her and that she wouldn't shoot him again. Another shot in a vital area might mean the end of him.

When the wolves overtook her, he doubled back to assist her. But instead of being grateful, she tried to harm him further. He produced his stinger and sedated her, wishing that he had been successful in doing it the first time, and then neither of them would be half dead right now.

**Carmella's chest** was on fire, and for some reason she couldn't move. She tried to open her eyes, but that wouldn't happen either. Yet it didn't cause her any alarm. Instead, the gentle movement felt as if she was being carried, and the rocking motion made her feel sleepy.

Hours later she stretched and stifled a yawn and made to turn over in bed before she realized she wasn't in her bed but on her sofa. She sat up quickly, remembering wolves and a Blob that had stung her. Swiftly her hands moved to her belly, and she pulled her shirt upward to explore her belly for a stab wound.

She saw nothing.

"Shit!" she screamed, as she jumped off her couch.

# Adaptation

Blood covered her ripped shirt, but she found no bite mark. She scrubbed frantically at the bloodied flesh and saw not even the faintest mark. Carmella lifted her shirt over her chest and looked down at her right breast. Her bra was snagged and bloodied, and when she touched the area where she had been mangled, it was sore — but not as sore as it should have been. She tugged at the bra until it exposed several faint punctures that seemed years old.

Her eyes darted around the room. The Blob had to be here because it had brought her home and had somehow fixed her wounds. She narrowed her eyes and scanned every nook, cranny, and corner of the room. Her eyes spotted the dark fluid on the floor next to the couch. There was so much of it …

A smeared trail led to the front door, and she hurried to it and flung the door open without thought of her gun. Her eyes scanned her yard for several minutes before she returned to her home, shutting and locking the door behind her.

Carmella went through her house making sure that nothing was out of place or hiding and then she got a bucket of hot water and scrubbed the floor. Both guns were gone, but she had plenty more. She retrieved two before going out to spray disinfectant on the pool of alien blood in the front yard. She grabbed a shovel and covered it with fresh dirt, grimacing in disgust.

And though it wasn't Sunday, she drew a lukewarm bath and washed thoroughly, examining her healed wounds in her bedroom mirror afterwards. She was exhausted and hungry and still needed to tend to the animals. Carmella sat down at her kitchen table and ran her hand through her dreadlocks instead.

She was so confused.

# Chapter 6
## ~This So-Called Life~

**It had been** a week since Carmella had seen the Blob. She no longer liked venturing outside, afraid that it would be out there lurking somewhere. When Sunday arrived she didn't sit out on the porch reading, and she kept her ears perked for unusual sounds. Her life had been simple and predictable, and Carmella hated the disruption to her comfortable pattern. She had to be heavily armed to milk the cow and collect the eggs. She didn't tend to her garden, which always relaxed her. Her other yard work was left to multiply, and soon it would be unmanageable.

She thought fleetingly of moving but dismissed it. Wolf. How would he find her? She kept a gun under her pillow when she slept and nailed boards over the windows on the lower level of the house. There was a shit-ton of windows in the old farmhouse, and it took her most of the day to finish the task, but she felt better at night knowing that nothing could get in without making a racket and alerting her to it.

After a week of being on hyper alert and obsessively staring through cracks in the boards, Carmella knew she couldn't maintain that level of stress. She slept poorly, and her so-called life became a tedious wreck. Day after day she roamed her house and peeked out windows. When she thought she might finally be able to relax, convinced that the alien creature had either died of its wounds or had no interest in her, Carmella decided to remove the boards from the windows as the sun hung low in the sky.

# Adaptation

As she pried away the first board, she saw movement in the yard.

A Blob had moved swiftly from one tree to hide behind another, its ability to camouflage itself a split-second too slow.

Carmella panicked and nailed the board back into place. She stared out the slit between the boards, eyes peeled to the partially hidden alien. What do you do when you are the only person left in the world and there is something lurking in your yard that scares the hell of you?

Carmella dashed for her rifle. There could have been several more out there circling her house, ready to snatch her and take her to some alien world — or worse. She had hurt one of badly. Maybe she'd be punished. They wouldn't take her, and this she swore. There was a wine cellar in her lower level, which also included a cement and steel bunker. She'd retreat there if it turned into a stand-off. Carmella peeked out the window into the darkening night. She could no longer see the Blob, but her body knew that danger was just outside her door.

When total darkness fell, Carmella did not light any candles. She brought a chair closer to the window and peered through the boards out into the night. When the sun rose, she didn't go outside to tend to her animals and barely tended to her own needs.

Why was it here?

**It had been** three days since the woman had come out of her house. Bilal was certain she had seen him, and he chastised himself for being careless. He had moved dangerously close to the house in an attempt to see inside. It was stupid. But she had put up the boards, and he could not see inside to get a sense of her.

Maybe she was sick ...

He shuffled in consternation, his flesh rippling and changing from the camouflage of greens and browns to nearly black.

# Adaptation

**That fateful night,** he had been healing his own damage and hers as well. The wounds to her breast had been too much for him. It had taken nearly all of his strength, and he needed enough energy to make the long trek back to his pod. He'd done the best that he could, ashamed that he couldn't completely remove all evidence of the injury. He certainly had the ability. Bilal's tentacles shielded fine filaments that could join with objects for the purpose of exploration and understanding. He understood each cell and neuron and found its pattern. He could detect and repair any anomaly. His kind had long since eradicated human diseases such as cancer, Parkinson's, and AIDs. It was part of being processed on the mother ship before being reintegrated with humans on Earth 2.

He had worried about her as he had carried her injured and bloodied body back to her home. She was in shock and was losing a great deal of blood. Despite this, he was curious about her. She had long dreadlocks and he formed a tentacle for the purpose of examining her hair. Now that he was an adult, humans generally shied away from him unless they were his friends. He knew that humans didn't like to be touched by Centaurians, and he understood. They didn't like the feel of his cool, smooth flesh.

But Centaurians had to touch. They didn't see well with their eyes and saw with their sensors, which were confined within their tentacles. They could taste, see, hear, and sense things with the fine, sensitive filaments. Once exposed, the filaments didn't have to be connected to an object to "observe." But it was the preference of Centaurians. Humans called them touchy-feely. He found it interesting that humans considered that a bad thing.

Bilal had placed her on her sofa and had connected a tentacle to several different areas of her body. She was a strong female, healthy despite her self-imposed exile. He found a vertebra that needed straightening. She probably had some pinching in her neck because of it. He didn't have time for that, though. Bilal concentrated on her injuries, tackling the smaller ones first in case he ran out of "juice" and had to leave them unattended. He liked that particular human euphemism. "Juice" was a good interpretation for what he needed to use to facilitate the woman's healing.

He allowed his filaments to go beyond her injuries in order to collect "samples." He stared at her dreadlocks and her brown skin while he should have been concentrating on his task. He could tell that she was right around forty Earth years old. She was tall and what humans called "shapely." He determined that she had carried a child to term, and his flesh rippled. She lived alone because the house only had one human smell. He understood from Earth 2 that the loss of a child was the most devastating loss that humans had endured during the epidemic. Many humans never recovered from it even twenty years later. He wondered if the offspring she had lost had been a victim of the disease or had been taken to Earth 2. He thought it was the first. The most resistant humans joined with the Centaurians sometimes for the sake of their children.

His body turned black. How could she live like this—alone?

He completed his task and withdrew from her body. He had felt as close to death as he ever had and wondered if he had finally gone too far. He thought about his parents and friends and wondered if he met his end on Earth would anyone truly care. Bilal hunkered into a ball and shivered knowing that if he retreated completely within himself and passed out, the human would likely awaken and cover him with kerosene and torch him. It would damage him in the way that a bullet really couldn't. As long as his filaments retreated and coiled into a ball within the mass of his body, then he *might* survive being burned alive.

Not wanting to take that chance, as soon as he could, Bilal sluggishly left the house. He didn't know if he could make it back to his pod, but he had no choice. It took a day, but he made it, programmed the pod to return to the mother ship, retreated into himself, and lost consciousness.

# Adaptation

**Upon awaking, Bilal** had found himself surrounded by his four parents, their tentacles pressed into his body. His eyes focused on his First Mother. Her skin was mottled black and red because she was angry, yet a tentacle formed to caress his face. He formed a tentacle and intertwined it with hers. It was akin to a human hug and kiss.

A First Mother's bond was strongest because she had carried him. Bilal had two mothers and two fathers. Their DNA had been mixed in order to create him before he had been implanted into his mother. It was the most efficient way to coexist on a mother ship that traveled through space for years on end. The limited space meant that one family consisted of multiple parents. Offspring generally lived with their parents until it was time for them to reproduce and to form their own family units. Parents went through a great deal to negotiate the best match. Certain traits possessed by a Centaurian were more desirable than others. But that was not the only consideration. Social standing also factored in.

Mina, his First Mother, had been highly desired despite being much older than his other parents. She was a high-ranking official in the Centaurian hierarchy and was one of the few Centaurians who had only one mate like in the old days. Her first mating had occurred long before her new mates had been born, and unfortunately her original mate had died of old age. A short time later it was negotiated that she would join a newly formed family. When it was time to create a child, she had demanded to be First Mother. Perhaps that was why there was some animosity between Bilal's mothers. His Second Mother, Baba, had argued that Mina had already given birth to a child and it was her turn. Mina had never bonded with the family because of her previous mating, and the fathers thought that if she bore the child then it would help her.

It hadn't, and once Bilal had become an adult, she moved into her own home.

His First Mother had gone against tradition when she had formed her own separate house away from her partners, a luxury only now possible since the formation of Earth 2 and the extended living space afforded to them. She had then invited Bilal to live with her, which he had done happily. It had deepened the animosity with his Second Mother, who didn't even like him. It shouldn't have ever mattered, but it caused a huge scandal within the Centaurian community. Some tried to pass laws against it fearing the collapse of Centaurian family units, but it was more unpopular to pass such laws than to allow an unhappy partner to leave. Because Centaurians were so rooted in tradition, not many considered doing such a thing.

Baba removed her tentacles from Bilal, and he gave her a weary look. Here it comes …

"Child, what have you done to yourself this time?"

Child? He was an adult. His body formed into a ball, and he reached out a tentacle to communicate without words. "Mother-baba, I was attacked."

"Attacked?" his fathers asked, listening to his conversation through their own tentacle connection. "By what?"

"Wolves." He lied. Why was he lying? He prevented his skin from turning yellow in shame.

"You were nearly dead, Bilal," his Father-Tom spoke. Centaurians had selected simple names that were easy to form with their foreign mouths and tongues.

"There were a lot of wolves Father-Tom. I dispatched them but not before I lost much strength."

"What if you had died?" Baba asked.

*Then you would no longer be ashamed of me, would you?* Bilal thought. He reached out a tentacle to wrap around hers. "But I didn't."

He rested with his First Mother and was thinking about the brown woman when his two best friends entered the set of rooms allocated to him. His rooms were "human-friendly." He had chairs and couches and utensils for eating and drinking. He didn't lie to his mother that the things were for when his friends visited

# Adaptation

him. He didn't have to. His mother understood that he liked having manmade items around him.

"I heard you got your ass handed to you by a pack of wolves," Lawrence said with a broad smile.

Bilal stretched out on his bed, elongated, and came to a standing position. "And hi to you, too. Yes, I'm fine, thank you very much."

His other friend, Raj, rubbed his body until it formed a tentacle that intertwined with his arm in pleasure. "Are you okay, little buddy?"

Lawrence came over and rubbed him until another tentacle formed to wrap around his arm as well. "I'm fucking with you, Bilal. You are okay, aren't you?"

He regarded his two friends. They didn't mind when he touched them in this way. They didn't think it was like a snake wrapping around their bodies. He could see in their facial expressions and postures that they cared about him.

"I'm fine." He released them.

Lawrence went to get something to eat from Bilal's cabinet. "Did you find anything interesting down there this time?" he asked while examining a piece of fruit that had seen better days.

Bilal's body began to ripple, and Raj cocked his head. "What's wrong?"

"I did find something interesting."

Lawrence bit into the fruit and studied his friend. Lawrence was twenty, had blue eyes and blond hair, and was strong and sturdy. Raj watched Bilal curiously as well. He was smaller with a compact yet toned body. He was forty and had the golden brown skin and slanted eyes of an Asian. He was Korean but had lived his life in America before the end of days.

"Well, show us," Lawrence said while chomping away. "You always find some good shit. Tell us what you found, and we'll explain it to you."

"I can't. I left her on earth."

"Her?" Raj asked.

"A woman. One last human woman."

# Adaptation

"Fuck … me …" Lawrence said.

**Bilal watched the silent** house and worried. Maybe she had killed herself. Humans did that kind of thing when they were afraid or confused.

Bilal had shuffled back and forth before cursing to himself. He had to go inside, and that had not been his intention. He wanted to watch, that's all, to make sure she was okay. Okay, no, that wasn't it. He was curious. He wanted to indulge his curiosity. He liked looking at pictures and roaming through dead towns for a semblance of the life humans had once lived. And now here was a human right before his eyes. How could he not indulge his curiosity?

He lifted a tentacle and raised it, searching the air for any signs or sounds. Bilal turned swiftly. A wolf was coming up on him, stalking him, and he'd been so preoccupied that he hadn't realized it. It was only one wolf, but it was a big healthy one.

Bilal withdrew his stinger just as the wolf leaped and went for him with lethal teeth bared.

# Chapter 7
# ~Wolf and the Alien~

**Teeth sank into** Bilal's flesh, piercing the protective outer skin but not enough to cause his fluid to escape. There was pain, but it wasn't bad. He had no bones, tendons, or muscles, and bites could do little damage. If the beast managed to take a chunk of flesh, however, that could be a problem. Bilal wrapped a tentacle around the beast's neck and speared its underbelly at the same time he flung it through the air.

The wolf came down on all fours with a pained yelp, but he scurried for Bilal. Wolves generally retreated in the face of the strange alien with flesh that gave instead of ripped and a stinger that could stab. This wolf was different. Bilal raised his stinger again, and this time it was filled with poison.

"No! Wolf, no!"

Wolf spared his mother the briefest look before leaping at the alien. Bilal was surprised at the human's sudden appearance. She had darted out the door and was running across the yard toward them screaming at the top of her lungs.

In the brief moment that Bilal dropped his attention, the wolf sank its teeth into his flesh, this time shaking his head back and forth and tearing out a great hunk of flesh. Bilal sank his stinger repeatedly into the beast, and the human was finally upon them, slapping him and screaming until he released the limp beast.

Bilal watched in confusion as she gathered the wolf into her arms and rocked his lifeless body. "You killed my baby! Wolf!"

# Adaptation

Bilal shuddered. The wolf was hers. He wrapped a tentacle around the hysterical woman's neck and pulled her free from the dead animal. She nearly went mad with fear and grief as she kicked and fought. Bilal formed three more tentacles to wrap around her to keep her still. She soon resembled a wild-eyed creature encased in a strange cocoon.

"If you want this creature to live, then you will have to stop fighting me!" he snapped.

After a moment, she quieted, her struggles lessening.

Bilal dropped her unceremoniously and allowed all but two tentacles to retreat to his body. These remaining two attached to the animal.

The poison would stop the wolf's heart, but he could restart it as long as it hadn't been too long without oxygen. His sensors entered the animal and sought the organ that pumped life throughout its body.

Carmella watched with her hands pressed against her mouth. She was shaking and crouched near her baby. He was dead. Tears streamed down her face as she watched the alien's tentacles begin to burrow into Wolf's body. She thought about how the Blob had healed her. He could heal her Wolf, too. He had to.

"Please," she begged. She rocked on her heels and watched this hateful monster dig its dirty tentacles into her Wolf.

But then Wolf kicked. Oh! His legs began a rapid running motion as he lay on his side.

Carmella reached out and stroked his soft fur. "Please, baby boy," she crooned. "Wolf, come back to me."

Bilal turned to her. "He lives."

She blinked at him. "You brought him back?"

"Yes, but he will sleep for several hours."

Carmella focused on the area that must be the creature's face. It had eyes, two holes where nostrils should have been, and a hollowed out mouth that seemed to float over a smooth, gelatinous mass of gray. It looked much like an octopus with wart-filled tentacles. She found it hideous to look at and was disturbed that it was not as tall as she was but definitely wider. Something this ugly should not be bigger than her.

She pulled Wolf into her arms and tried to lift him, but the alien elongated its body and two tentacles appeared and wrapped around her wolf. She panicked until she saw him lift the hurt animal from the ground and cradle it carefully.

"Where should I carry it?" the alien asked.

Carmella pointed to the farmhouse.

The alien shuffled off.

Carmella was about to follow when she saw two eyes watching them from the woods. Carmella narrowed her eyes. *The she-bitch. She watched her man get attacked and did nothing. It will be a cold day in hell before I let that good-for-nothing bitch back into my house!*

**Bilal carried the wolf** into the house and placed it on a couch the woman first covered with a blanket.

She knelt beside the couch and buried her face into Wolf's neck. She was still for a long time before she lifted her head and looked at Bilal. "He'll be okay?"

"Yes."

She watched him with suspicion. "Why did you come back?"

Bilal expanded briefly as if sighing. "I'm ... I wanted to make sure that you had healed properly."

Carmella touched her shoulder. "That's it? You're not going to try to take me?"

*She said "try to take me,"* Bilal thought. *I like this human's spirit.* "No." He didn't like the idea of her returning with him to the mother ship and Earth 2. Somehow, this place was right for her. It went against everything that he had been taught. Humans had to be cared for. If the Centaurians didn't do it, then humans were destined to return to their old ways of war and violence.

"You're not going to take me?"

Bilal regarded her silently.

# Adaptation

"You ... stung Wolf and it killed him. I'm pretty sure he was dead. But you stung me, too, and it just put me to sleep."

Bilal seemed to sink into himself as he formed a smaller ball. It was his "relaxed" position. "We don't generally poison living beings. It is against our way. We only want to share information, to help."

Carmella frowned. "Way to do that by ending the lives of seven *billion* humans. You need a pat on your fucking backs for that one."

He fought to keep his skin from coloring yellow. "It was not our intent. We had no idea that our ability to adapt would somehow invade your human cells and try to adapt within you." He was quiet for a moment.

Carmella glared at him. "Not your intent. Right."

"We are sorrier than you can ever know. We want to make things right. We realize that we have a debt to repay to mankind, and perhaps it can never be paid. But we will try."

"Will you just ... leave? Leave my house. And don't come back." She glanced at Wolf. "You helped me and you helped Wolf. But if you hadn't come here, we would have never needed your help. You do understand that, right?" Her eyes narrowed. "It's only when you show your ugly face that we need your help! So just get *out! Get out!*"

Bilal's body elongated and he retreated, not taking his eyes from her. His skin began turning black.

Carmella began to sob. "You took everything and ... you think that you can make it *right?*" Carmella's hands formed fists. "You can't magically bring my husband back. My *child* back! You can't give me my mama or my brother or that fucking postman who refused to deliver the mail because the neighbor's dog broke out of the gate!"

Bilal backed out the door to the porch, surprised at the woman's sudden and complete turn. She had followed him out the door with a look of pure hatred that caused him physical pain. He had never been witness to human hatred at its worst. Most humans were happy to be on Earth 2 where they could live in comfort and security with no fear of the disease that had taken almost everyone that they knew. Yes, there were those who hated the Centaurians, but he had been protected from it by his parents and friends.

Bilal turned and moved down the porch stairs and away from her.

"Help me? Help me! Bring my baby back. Give me my baby. Give him ..." She couldn't finish. She dropped to her knees and gave in to the grief of all that had been lost. She cried all the tears for all the men, women, and children who had ever lost anyone. She cried for those who were dead and could no longer do so. She cried out her hatred and anger — and her loneliness.

Bilal was in the woods before he turned to look at her again. The woman lay on the porch curled into a ball as if she had been physically harmed. She cried harder than he had ever seen or heard anyone cry.

He turned and continued to his pod.

*Physical harm has been done to her and to all mankind,* Bilal thought. *By my kind.*

# Chapter 8
## ~Righting a Great Wrong~

**"There you are.** Have you been hiding?"

Raj had found Bilal in the glade behind his mother's home. Bilal liked being there despite grass and stones dotting the ground that were not friendly to his skin. He enjoyed the ways the sun filtered through the leaves of the trees and transformed everything. He huddled in the shadows and hoped to become so small that he would eventually disappear.

Bilal didn't answer, and Raj sat next to him. Bilal wanted to be alone, but if anyone was going to interrupt his poor mood, then he was happy it was Raj. Bilal cared deeply for Lawrence because he was funny and upbeat and liked adventure enough to be best friends with an alien and a forty-year-old man. But he disagreed with Lawrence's idea that if anything bothered you, you should "just get over it." Unfortunately, life did not always cooperate.

"What's wrong, Bilal? You've been acting weird every since you returned from your last Earth visit."

"I saw the Earthling again."

Raj frowned. "You said that you wouldn't bring her. It's why you didn't tell your parents or anyone else about her. Did you change your mind?"

"No. I just wanted to see her."

Raj pulled out a pack of cigarettes and lit one. Bilal didn't understand smoking, but once a month he linked with his friend through his tentacles to make sure Raj's lungs stayed clear and healthy.

# Adaptation

"We have a word for that. It's called *stalking*."

"No. I'm not stalking her. I wanted to see how she lives. How is that stalking her if I've only seen her twice?"

"Then why are you mooning over her?"

Bilal had not heard this expression. "Mooning? Like when humans show their asses?" He remembered Lawrence explaining what mooning was by dropping his pants and showing his pale butt cheeks.

"No, it means that you like her and can't stop thinking about her."

"Ah. Yes. I am mooning over this woman. But she hates me. She hates all Centaurians."

Raj nodded. "I see. Not every human wants to be friends with you, despite how cool you are, Bilal."

"I know that!"

Raj reached out and rubbed one of Bilal's rough patches until a tentacle formed.

Bilal allowed the tentacle to encase his friend's hand and wrist. "I'm sorry," he said. "I never saw anyone cry with so much pain. I can't stop thinking about it. I know that I am not directly responsible for the loss of human life, but she made me feel that way. Centaurians always talk about making things right, but no one has made things right for her. We aren't doing enough!"

Raj looked around and put out his cigarette. "Bilal, be careful. There are ears everywhere."

Bilal shuddered and turned a miserable black. "Yes."

Raj stood. "Come on. We'll listen to some old music and get high."

"Okay." Bilal got up and followed his friend.

He had the house to himself. His First Mother would be gone for a few weeks to take care of business on the mother ship where the Centaurians still presided over everything that mattered within the universe.

# Adaptation

**If he could** singlehandedly right the wrongs of each human who resided on Earth 2, Bilal knew that he would.

But that was impossible.

He could, however, help one, but he needed the mother ship's direct link to do so.

He weaved as he moved to the mother ship and his pod. If they knew what he was intending to do, they would put a stop to it, but he visited the mother ship often enough with his plant samples not to raise suspicion.

The mother ship was a living organism. It consumed what Centaurians did not use. It adapted to what they needed it to be. It provided nourishment and housing. When needed, the ship also stored, analyzed, and manipulated the data fed into it. Without the Centaurians, the mother ship could not live, and it was because of the ship that the Centaurians had thrived. Now it processed the humans, who also kept the ship nourished.

Once aboard he determined the location of his parents and avoided those areas. The last thing he wanted was for his parents to see him while he was wasted. He knew that he should not have indulged so much, but he felt better even if he had consumed twice as many dandelions as he had ever previously consumed.

The yellow caps of the dandelion were a narcotic for Centaurians, and as far as Bilal knew, he was the only one who had ever figured it out. He was definitely the only Centaurian to be indulging in it. It wasn't as if Earth 2 had weeds.

Bilal unsuccessfully tried to move gracefully so he wouldn't draw attention, but he decided he was being paranoid. He had every right to be on the mother ship. He had several samples that he needed the ship to process, and no one knew it was for his own purposes.

Bilal went to a level where the ship's receptors were located. There were several other Centaurians connected to the ship for various reasons, and he ignored them. Bilal slipped his body into one of the niches and extended his tentacle until he was linked with the ship. The ship felt warm and comforting, the familiar humming undercurrent putting him at ease.

# Adaptation

Bilal allowed his filaments to push from his tentacles and communicated his needs. He retrieved several samples he had stored within his body and passed them to the ship. One of them was some of the ovum he had collected from the human female. She was a bit older but still of childbearing age.

Bilal knew that he could not procreate with a human. Not directly …

He located Raj's sperm cells, fed them to the ship, and monitored every step as it performed the relatively simple task of impregnating the egg. Once the cells began to multiply, Bilal extracted samples of his DNA and spliced it into the developing egg. It aborted immediately, which is why he needed the ship. He programmed the ship to make his cells adapt.

That was the ship's purpose. It hadn't been the Centaurians that had created the end of mankind. It had been the mother ship. The Centaurians in their ignorance had no idea that it was happening until it was too late and someone had programmed the ship to stop adapting. By that time, however, most humans had been infected by the alien cells, which had been carried through the mother ship's connection to the earth — the signposts.

The alien cells lay dormant in humans, and they needed to be reprocessed annually to confirm that the cells did not come back to "life." If that happened, it would wipe out the remaining humans. It meant that the mother ship could never leave the humans. The Centaurian's nomad existence had come to an abrupt end in an attempt to pay their debt to mankind.

Bilal waited anxiously for the ship to adapt his cells to that of the humans. When the fertilized egg began to thrive, he marveled at the new life form. It multiplied rapidly as human eggs did, but because of his alien DNA, it happened at an even greater pace. He had known that his cells would dominate, but he didn't want that. He slowed the rate and manipulated them further until many of his traits remained dormant.

It only took a few days. When it was completed, Bilal retrieved the egg and stored it. He wasn't sure how long it would be viable outside of a mother's womb and wasn't exactly sure why he had done this in the first place. Now that he was no longer wasted, it seemed like an extreme and potentially dangerous thing to do. But each time he marveled at the life form that he had created, he knew that it was too late to undo it. He was incapable of turning off the life he had started.

But he would if she didn't want it.

He would destroy what was created if she wouldn't accept it.

# Chapter 9
## ~Decisions and Consequences~

**As Carmella lay** curled on the porch, eyes glazed in grief, she felt something soft and warm rub against her legs. The tears had stopped some time ago, but she was still unable to pull herself together. The depression ran so deeply that she couldn't stand.

Her eyes moved to the sight of a wolf lying against her legs. It wasn't Wolf. The she-bitch? She looked at Carmella and whined. Carmella reached out her hands, and the wolf licked them. Carmella felt her eyes sting with renewed tears, only this time it wasn't because of grief.

**When Wolf awakened,** he groggily ignored the chicken butts as he stumbled out the door and began sniffing around the yard. It was a long time before he was satisfied that the alien was gone. He marked the porch with several smelly streams of piss and tried to mark inside the house, but Carmella drew the line and wouldn't let him. Only then did he drink and eat.

Carmella could see by Wolf's panting that he was exhausted. Wolf came to where she was rocking in her porch chair. He whined tiredly and then rested his head in her lap.

"Poor baby." She rubbed between his ears as he sighed and fell into an exhausted sleep.

Wolf and his wife stayed for nearly a week, longer than he had ever stayed before. It was nice having him help her herd again.

# Adaptation

At night he slept on the porch and watched the fields and woods intently, and every day he circled the house and barn repeatedly marking his territory. Carmella wondered at his endless supply of pee, and soon the yard began to take on a strong musky odor.

He took great pains to mark the yard and to make sure his was the dominant smell. Whenever the she-wolf peed, he would immediately pee over hers.

Carmella cackled. "He's a chauvinist, isn't he, girl?"

Carmella truly cared for the she-wolf, and she named her Girl. Sometimes it took pain to bring family closer, and she guessed she had proven herself to the female.

Running low on dog food, she decided to make a run into town. Both wolves climbed into the truck. Girl was skittish, but Wolf stuck his head out the window. Girl followed suit and began to relax and enjoy the ride.

In town, Carmella got some supplies and decided to hit the Harley Dealership for another motorcycle. She didn't know much about motorcycles or "hogs," but she selected one that wasn't too big and hoped that once she gassed it, it would run. She rolled it up a metal ramp into the back of the truck while the wolves chased down some squirrels and had a quick snack. Afterwards, they returned to the farm.

As she pulled the truck to its position on the side of the house, Wolf gave her a swift lick in the face. He jumped to the ground, sniffed the air, and headed for the woods. Girl looked from her mate to her mother-in-law indecisively.

Carmella held her breath. Would she stay?

Evidently Wolf knew that she would follow him because he didn't look behind him. After giving Carmella one last look, Girl followed her mate.

Carmella grimly went about her task of putting away her supplies, unloading the motorcycle, siphoning out any old gas, and cleaning everything well before she filled it with fresh fuel. She climbed onto the bike and started it on the first try.

She triple-checked that her guns were loaded and then checked the animals. When that was done, Carmella returned to the house and sank onto her couch. She stared into the empty space before her, lowered her head into her hands, and wept.

**A few nights** later Carmella had a nightmare.

She dreamed she was sleeping in her bed and had heard the sound of her front door opening despite being securely locked. She reached for her gun, but when she looked up a shadowy figure was in her doorway. She screamed and fired off a shot, but the shadow moved quickly and pinned her to her bed.

That was all she remembered of the dream. The next morning she awoke and cuddled comfortably in her bed, the memory of her nightmare fading as the sun shone through the windows.

"Damn!" Carmella jumped out of bed. She had overslept. She had to milk the cow and collect the eggs. The animals needed to be fed—

She rubbed her side when a dull ache bloomed in her belly. It wasn't time for her period. She would take some ibuprofen later. Carmella made up her bed and splashed her face, brushed her teeth, and used the slop bucket. After dressing, she decided to save breakfast for later and went about her chores.

Carmella had an odd feeling while she did her work. She looked over her shoulders often. She couldn't understand why it felt as if someone was coming toward her even though she neither heard nor saw anything. She thought briefly of that alien, but the alien no longer scared her. It certainly would have killed her or taken her by now if that was its plan. She shrugged off the feeling and continued with her chores.

Back in the house she cracked two eggs to make scrambled eggs, but the gelatinous yolks made her ill and she threw them out. Instead she made a cup of hot tea and nibbled on day-old bread. She didn't feel like baking today. Oversleeping had completely screwed up her schedule. She was supposed to do laundry but didn't feel like doing that either. She didn't even feel like reading. Carmella climbed the stairs wearily and decided to take a nap.

When she woke, she felt better and was ravenously hungry. She opened a can of Spam because the stuff never went bad and made herself a fried Spam-wich with the last of the bread. She felt tons better, and the queasy feeling in her stomach went away.

**"Did you just** return from Earth, Bilal?" First Mother asked.

Bilal resisted turning yellow. "Yes."

His First Mother followed as he headed for his living quarters. "You have been going there quite a lot."

"I like Earth," he said. "And there is much to discover."

"Bilal, your fathers and mother and I have become worried. You seem preoccupied. And also ..." A tentacle appeared, and she held dandelion caps in them.

Bilal's body turned black. "You've been in my quarters?"

"I was worried. Bilal, you promised that you wouldn't use this again. Is that what you do on Earth?"

"No! I mean, yes, but I don't do it all the time. Mother-Mina, you had no right to invade my personal space."

"Yes, I did. I had every right."

Bilal relaxed his body. "Throw that away, Mother. I haven't consumed any of it in months."

His First Mother sighed.

"Do you want to check me? You can. I'm not lying." It had been three months since he had last indulged on the night he had created the embryo. Now it was a fetus; *he* was a fetus. Bilal had created a boy. He felt pleased and resisted turning red with pleasure. He didn't need to have his First Mother suspicious. As much as he wanted to share his news, he couldn't. His family would shun what he had done. Maybe it was wrong, but when he was doing it, it had seemed right. Even now when he was again thinking straight, it still didn't seem completely wrong.

"You're forbidden to return to Earth," his First Mother said.

Bilal tensed. "What?"

She formed several tentacles that waved in the air like snakes. "Your fathers have decided and I agree. You return hurt, you are indulging in this poison, and you have been moody and difficult to communicate with. You have let your commitments at home fall by the wayside!"

"Mother, no! You don't understand. I have to go back to Earth!"

"Even now you only care about that planet, when I am telling you that your behavior has been poor. You should be focusing on your attitude and behavior, Bilal!"

"I will. But give me another chance."

"Bilal! You speak like a human! It is done. You, above all should know that decisions like this are not arbitrary. I cannot take it back. It has been decided. You will focus on your position as a dignitary within our own kind."

Bilal knew her words were true.

He had fucked up.

**"What is the** problem Bilal?" Lawrence asked. "Man, I gotta tell you that you've been stranger than normal lately."

Bilal, Raj, Lawrence, and Lawrence's girlfriend-of-the-week were in Lawrence's house.

Bilal shuddered and gave Treya a long look until the human female made an excuse to leave. She didn't like him anyways. Bilal wished that Lawrence would date Lydia again. She was friendly, touched him without fear, and allowed him to touch her. Treya once threw up when he'd wrapped a tentacle of greeting around her wrist. He didn't like her.

"I have a problem and it's huge."

"Uh oh," Raj said.

"I'm banned from returning to Earth."

"Dude, I'm not surprised," Lawrence said. "You've been going there every two weeks. I have no idea how much alien pod-ships cost to refuel, but I'm imagining that it's not cheap."

"Why did you get banned?" Raj asked. "You didn't get caught with those dandelions, did you? Bilal, you really have to watch that shit. You could turn into a Centaurian junkie, and I'm not doing the whole intervention thing with you."

"Um …" Bilal's skin turned black. "I did something …"

Raj stood, his face pale. "Did you do something to that woman on Earth? Fuck, Bilal."

"No!" Bilal shouted. "I mean, yes, but …"

Lawrence looked horrified. "You didn't rape her did you?"

"No! I mean, maybe. I don't know."

"Oh my God," Raj said. "What did you do, Bilal?"

"You don't even have a dick," Lawrence said.

Raj gave Lawrence a withering look. "He can form a penis the way he forms tentacles."

"*No!*" Bilal shuddered. "I didn't do that! But I did make her pregnant."

"You did *what?*" Raj roared, his bronze skin red with anger.

"I didn't want her to be alone so I made her a baby. I know, yes, it was not well thought out. I was stoned."

Lawrence smiled.

Raj was less than amused. "How did she react?"

Bilal remained quiet.

"Bilal, please don't tell me that she doesn't know."

"It's not like I could tell her! She carries a gun and she would just shoot me."

"Oh wow," Lawrence said. "Even I know that's fucked up."

Raj closed his eyes as if he was meditating. When he opened his eyes he looked at Bilal. "How far along is she?"

"Eleven weeks, but she is much further along in Centaurian terms. In human terms she is more like fourteen weeks."

# Adaptation

Lawrence frowned. "Human, Centaurian ... What the hell are you talking about? Ugh, um, Bilal ... No. You didn't."

Raj stared at his friend. "You impregnated her with *your* ... sperm, DNA—whatever?"

"Not exactly," Bilal said. "I don't have sperm. I needed a vehicle to host my DNA."

"Dear God," Raj said, turning a brighter shade of pale.

Bilal felt horrible, but he had to confess what he had done. "I used yours, Raj."

Raj staggered. He bent and placed his hands on his knees while he tried to catch his breath.

"I'm sorry Raj. I was wasted when I did it, and I'm not sure what I was thinking. Somehow it seemed right, but I know it's wrong."

Raj spun around and punched Bilal—not that it did any harm. It was like punching a bucket of Jell-O. Raj then stormed out of the house.

Bilal's body formed a small ball.

Lawrence stared at him, shaking his head. He reached out and rubbed his friend's mottled black flesh. "Bilal, man, you gotta know that you just did something horrible. You hijacked your friend's sperm. Although I'm not quite sure why you chose his over mine. But regardless, you mixed two species together. It's like mixing a dog and a cat. You can't do that kind of thing just because you know how. What's worse is that you didn't even ask her, *and* she doesn't know she's carrying a monster inside her!"

Bilal's form lengthened. "He's not a monster! He's my son."

Lawrence grimaced. "You are nuts, and you have to tell your parents."

"What? Why?"

"Because you need to get back on Earth, and you need to tell that woman what you did. You need to take it out of her."

"I can't, it's too far along."

"Bilal, yes you can! And you will." Lawrence's blue eyes narrowed. "You created a genetic mutation that will think and speak, and that is a horrible thing to do. You *will* un-create it."

# Adaptation

After a moment, Bilal nodded. Lawrence was right. And he would have to tell his parents why he had to return to Earth.

*And after I tell them,* Bilal thought, *they might want to un-create me.*

# Chapter 10
## ~Mutation~

**At first** she thought she was just picking up a bit of extra weight. Lately she was insatiably hungry. She couldn't stop the hunger pangs, and her clothes didn't fit so well anymore. Fried green tomatoes never tasted so good. She had to ration her intake of tomatoes to two a day and even then she had run out. She had driven to nearby farms in search of abandoned gardens in the hopes of finding more tomatoes.

Also she couldn't get enough lemon pudding. She found boxes of the mix and made lemon pudding every day. She could barely tolerate eggs and hated wasting them, so she found creative ways to bake with them. Lemon meringue pie became a daily indulgence. She made cheese and ate it in handfuls. She drank glasses of chilled milk, now preferring it cold.

When her period stopped coming, she realized there was something going on much worse than weight gain. Her breasts hurt, and she sweated during the night. Was it menopause? But how could she be going through that when she wasn't even forty?

One morning she climbed out of bed and felt something strange and more frightening than even the idea of menopause.

Something fluttered in her stomach.

Carmella froze and gasped. She pressed her hand to the flutter and waited, but it didn't reoccur. She kept pressing her stomach and felt a lump that wasn't fat. She shook as she pressed and prodded then stripped out of her nightclothes and stared at herself in the mirror.

# Adaptation

Her belly was slightly rounded.
A tumor.
Dear Lord, she had cancer.

**"Child, if your** reason for calling this meeting is to convince us to change our minds," Mama-Baba said, "then you are wasting your time and ours."

Bilal pulled himself up until he was tall. "I'm no longer a child. I'm an unmarried adult."

Mama-Baba's skin flushed yellow. "Of course."

"Why did you call this meeting?" Father-Nile asked.

Bilal had practiced but still had a difficult time getting the words out. He reverted to Centaurian, which did not use words but waves. He explained about finding the female human, about the attack on her, and how he had repaired her. No one interrupted him, which surprised him. He explained about returning to make sure she was okay and how she had broken down in grief and accused him for her loss.

"Humans can not accept responsibility for their own self-destructive nature," Mama-Baba said, "and yet we are the scapegoats for all that has gone wrong with them."

"Well, in all fairness, we are responsible their end," Father-Nile said.

"Yes, we are, Nile," Mama-Baba said. "But they were in sad condition before we ever arrived, and now they aren't. Do we ever get credit for that?"

"Please continue with your story, Bilal," Mother-Mina said.

Bilal's body expanded as he explained about the dandelion tops and how he had consumed so many of them that it sounded like a good idea to give the human a child to take the place of the one lost to her.

# Adaptation

Father-Tom became agitated. "You should have brought her here, Bilal. Had you brought her here, then she could have mated properly. I am very displeased with you."

"I'm sorry, but there is more. I used Raj's sperm without his permission. And I ... spliced my DNA into the fertilized egg."

There was absolute silence.

"That is impossible," Mother-Mina said.

"No, Mother. The mother ship helped me to adapt my DNA into theirs."

"And you successfully implanted the embryo?" Father-Nile asked.

"Well, yes." They weren't angry? "She is in her second trimester."

"And the child is healthy?" Father-Tom asked.

"Yes, but I haven't been far from the human for long ... until now."

"I see," Mother-Mina said.

"You will bring her here," Mama-Baba said.

"There is yet another problem. She doesn't know she is pregnant. I failed to tell her."

There was quiet.

"What you did was unconscionable," Mama-Baba said. "The human has never been processed and has been living alone on earth for over twenty years. She obviously hates Centaurians, and in your wisdom you decide to impregnate her with one? Did you want to become a human so badly that you tried to create one?"

Mother-Mina stopped her with a tentacle. "Bilal was wrong in the way that he carried this out, but not for what he did. We adapt. That is what we do. When our cells merged with humans it caused their deaths. But this—"

"Madness!" Mama-Baba interrupted. "You always take his side, even when he does something like this!"

Father-Tom placed a reassuring tentacle on his partner. "Baba, please ..."

"No!" Mama-Baba pulled away and moved across the room. "We should not mix with humans. Why would we want to combine with a lesser species? We should aspire toward higher life forms and not lower ourselves!"

Mother-Mina quivered. "You've made your dislike of humans quite evident. Your dislike clouds your reason. Adaptation is not based on personal preference but on necessity. Humans can procreate easier than Centaurians can, and they are highly evolved. They are the most intelligent species that we have found."

"I think that it is time that Bilal is told about the origins of the mother ship," Father-Nile said.

"Of course," Mama-Baba sputtered. "Tell him. Why not?"

Bilal looked at him curiously, ignoring his Second Mother. "Tell me what?"

"Do you know what the mother ship is?" Father-Niles asked.

"A living organism. We sustain each other."

"Yes," Mother-Mina said. "But there is more to it than that. Many centuries ago our world began to die."

Bilal knew this story well, so why was she giving him a history lesson?

"Needing a way to travel to other worlds, we began to develop the mother ship," Mother-Mina said. "But what you don't know is that the mother ship is a Centaurian who allowed himself to adapt to our needs."

Bilal froze. "What?"

"The ship is one of us," Mother-Mina said. "A Centaurian made the supreme sacrifice to adapt for our needs. And because he did, he saved the life of thousands."

"But ... how?"

"We helped it to become something that could meet our needs, and then the most daring of us joined with the Centaurian who is now our mother ship."

Bilal was bowled over. He could have never known that such a thing was possible. He looked around and ran a tentacle along the familiar walls. "But why was I never told?"

# Adaptation

"Because it is possible—though not advised—but we can adapt to be whatever it takes to meet our own needs," Mother-Mina said.

Bilal's tentacles explored the interior walls of the mother ship. "But Centaurians have a lifespan. The mother ship has never died. How is this possible?" It would be three times older than the oldest Centaurian.

"We keep it alive," Mother-Mina explained. "So you see, young one, adapting is what we do."

"You will have to return to Earth and bring the human to the mother ship for processing and monitoring," Father-Tom said.

"Why?" Bilal asked.

"Why?" Father-Nile would have sputtered if he could have. "We can't leave her on Earth with a child as important as the one she carries. She may do it harm."

"Maybe he can take the child from her body and bring it to the ship," Father-Tom suggested.

"It might endanger the child," Father-Tom said. "Best to bring the mother along with the child."

While his parents discussed this, an idea occurred to Bilal. He cleared his throat to get their attention. "I want to go to Earth, and I want to study the human and the child. If this adaptation is to be successful then at some point it will be necessary to reintroduce mankind to Earth. Earth Two can only handle a portion of the growing human population, and there is no reason not to utilize the resources that are already in place on Earth."

"But monitoring the humans will be impossible," Mama-Baba interjected. "They need to be monitored."

Everyone agreed except Bilal. "How can we form a true opinion unless it is researched? Since I began this I would like to see it through. And besides, the human knows me. She is older in age, and I don't think the stress of a move and reintegration will be good for her or the child."

"I agree to allow Bilal to study the human and child on Earth," Father-Nile said. "Of course he will need to provide regular reports."

"Agreed," Father-Tom said.

"Yes," Mother-Mina said.

Bilal's joy soared, and he suppressed his pleasure as much as he could.

"But the study must have a time limit," Mama-Baba said. "I won't allow my son to be lost to humans. He will return home in five years."

Bilal was about to object when Mother-Mina stopped him with a tentacle.

"Five years is plenty of time to study the human," Mother-Mina said. "You will transmit reports once a year, and on the fifth year you will return home. We will take your advisement into consideration but will form our own opinions on whether or not it is in the best interest of all concerned to breed with man. As always, this discussion and decision is not to be discussed." She frowned. "Your human friends do not know of this, do they?"

"No. I have not discussed it with them."

Bilal had become a good liar, a fact that did not make him happy. But this was one lie he had to tell in order to protect his friends. Further, he would *have* to discuss this with Lawrence and Raj again. He needed to express to them the importance of not telling anyone else. He didn't want to think the worst of his parents, but deep down he knew that in the grand scope, his friends were not as important as the secret of the mother ship. Bilal shuddered to think what could happen to his friends if others suspected that they knew. Even Mother-Mina, who was the most reasonable of his parents, did not place as much value on the human species as she did on her own.

But Bilal was not like that. He saw no species as more important than any other.

**Bilal returned to** Earth 2 for his personal belongings.

# Adaptation

At least that is what he told his parents. Instead, he contacted Lawrence and told him that he would meet him at his house and asked him to bring Raj.

When he arrived, Lawrence was alone.

"Where is Raj?" Bilal asked.

"He won't come. He's really pissed."

Bilal was quiet for a moment. "I'll be away, for several years actually."

"What the fuck? Are you going to jail?"

"No, I'll be on Earth."

Lawrence frowned. "Why? What happened when you told your parents?"

"Lawrence, listen to me. I don't want to be secretive and I don't want to lie to you, but there is a lot that I can't tell you right now. When I return to Earth 2 then I'll tell you everything. But you have to promise not to tell anyone about what has happened."

"Of course. Do you think that I want everyone hating you and the Centaurians more than they already do?"

Bilal shuddered. "Raj hates me, doesn't he?"

Lawrence nodded. "He'll get over it."

"I know that I had no right."

"It's more than that. Raj does not want to procreate, and he feels helpless knowing that a child of his ..."

Bilal formed two tentacles and slithered around Lawrence's body. "Tell him that I am so sorry, and tell him not to tell anyone. It is now a matter of national security. Do you understand? If it leaks out—if there is even a hint of it—then suspicion will turn to you two, and I cannot express how bad that will be for you two."

Lawrence nodded solemnly.

There remained an underlying fear of the Centaurians among humans, and Bilal knew that. He knew that Lawrence would do what was necessary, but Raj ... Bilal wasn't sure about Raj.

"I have to go," Bilal said.

"But when will you be back?"

"I'll be gone five years."

73

# Adaptation

Lawrence ran his hands through his longish hair. "Fuck, Bilal. You're not going to stop the pregnancy are, are you?"

"You know that I can't tell you anything right now."

"Bilal, just be careful. And I'll talk to Raj. He won't say anything."

"Thank you, my friend. I'm sorry. Please forgive me." He turned and moved away.

"Wait? Forgive you? Why should I forgive you? What have you done to me?"

"Keep the secret, and you both will be okay," Bilal said.

Bilal entered the pod while Lawrence watched him in confusion. He returned to the mother ship and headed straight for the lower level. This time there were no others around. It would be too late to stop him by the time they realized what was happening.

His parents had given him the idea when they told him the mother ship was a Centaurian who had allowed himself to be mutated for the needs of the others. Bilal formed a tentacle and linked to the ship. He fed Lawrence's and Raj's DNA strands into the ship, extracting what he wanted to be dominant and what he wanted to suppress. When he was satisfied, he gave his final command.

"Ship, turn adaptation on. I want you to make me human."

Adaptation

# Chapter 11
## ~Bilal Resurrected~

**Bilal felt a strange** sensation against his skin and it was the first thought he'd had in a long time. He opened his eyes, and the world came into focus. A pain developed between his eyes, and he closed them to block out the sharp, bright images.

"He's awake," someone said.

Mother-Mina? He felt her tentacles and tried to form his own. Nothing happened. He groaned, and the sound reverberated throughout his body. "What?" He tried to speak but it hurt. Everything hurt. He felt a sharp stabbing pain followed by throbbing aches. He opened his eyes because he was unable to expose his filaments to sense what was around him.

Bilal looked down at his form. His head began to swim, but he blinked in surprise. He had legs, arms, and a torso! His parents were connected to his nude body. He felt them repairing him, helping to complete him.

"Lay back," Father-Tom said. "You are weak."

He ignored his father, reached out with an unsteady hand, and ran it over his new skin. Human skin felt strange but in a good way.

"Why did you do this to yourself?" Mama-Baba asked.

"Not now, Baba!" Mother-Mina said.

"Then when?"

"Not now when we have worked so hard to keep him alive."

"You are a stupid, stupid boy," Mama-Baba said. "You nearly died."

"*Leave!*" Mother-Mina shouted. "Get out, *now!*" Mother-Mina's tentacles waved wildly about her head, and Baba retreated. No one wanted to make Mother-Mina into an enemy.

Mama-Baba left the room without another word.

"Sleep," Father-Nile said. "You have more healing to do."

"I don't have time," Bilal whispered. "I have to return to Earth."

"Sleep."

Bilal had no choice. His parents triggered his sleep and then he knew no more.

~\*\*\*~

**Bilal was alone** in a room the next time he awoke, this time without pain. He actually felt good. He sat up slowly and noticed he was dressed in loose pants and a tunic. After swinging his feet to the edge of the platform, he studied his feet and toes. He felt a smile tug at his lips and reached up quickly to touch his mouth.

*I have lips.*

He laughed and marveled at the sound of his own voice. "I am Bilal Ayunkili. I am a human Centaurian hybrid. My son and I are the only two in existence." *My son and I.* Bilal felt pride at those words.

He stood, and his knees nearly buckled beneath him. Walking on legs was a skill he had mastered in private, but walking with bones was a different matter.

~\*\*\*~

**Carmella picked at** her meal listlessly. She had no appetite these days but kept eating anyway. She had to. When the food had magically disappeared, she looked at her empty plate and poked at her swollen stomach with her finger.

"Happy now?" she asked.

# Adaptation

She used the slop bucket and then carried it outside to dump. She walked across her front porch and watched the fall leaves as they swirled around her feet. Later she would sweep. Soon it would be winter, and then what would she do? She sighed and walked down the porch stairs.

She nearly walked right up to the man standing in her front yard. She stopped in her tracks and stumbled backwards, nearly falling on her ass.

The man reached out and righted her.

"What the? Where did you come from?" Her hands flew to her mouth. Oh God, what was it? She thought he was a man, but … Carmella backed away. "What are you?"

"Please," he said. "I just want to make sure that you're okay."

She threw the bucket of slop at him.

Bilal ducked, the slop flying harmlessly over his head.

Carmella stumbled up her stairs and into her home where she slammed the door shut and locked it. She backed away from the door and darted for the front window.

The man still stood in the front yard.

From a distance he looked like a man, but up close she had seen that his eyes were black orbs with no whites. His skin also had a strange translucent quality. It reminded her of Dr. Manhattan from that *Watchmen* movie. His skin didn't glow blue, but an undercurrent of color moved subtly from darks to reds to yellows.

The man seemed to know where she was located within the house because he looked right at the window. She ducked out of sight and peeked from behind the curtain.

He appeared to be Asian with long, sleek black hair that hung past his shoulders. He was quite tall with a toned physique and broad shoulders. He wore a white long-sleeved tunic and loose fitting pants, but she could tell that he was fit.

She knew — she had no doubt. It was that Blob, the one that kept coming back. But how? How did he make himself … human?

She took a deep breath before standing in front of the window. "What are you?"

# Adaptation

He heard her clearly through the window though she spoke in a normal voice.

Carmella saw his lips move but was unable to hear him. She unlatched the window and opened it.

"I am Bilal Ayunkili, and I am a Centaurian, human hybrid," he said.

She closed her eyes and swallowed. Remembering that Centaurians moved fast, she opened her eyes and found that he hadn't budged. "Why are you here? Haven't you done enough? Can't you just leave me alone?"

Bilal clasped his hands in front of him. "I cannot."

She was too tired for this confrontation. "Why did you do this to me?" She pressed her head against the windowsill and closed her eyes. "I know what you did. You raped me that night I thought I was having a nightmare. When my stomach kept getting bigger I figured it out. I've been pregnant before. Then I found the bullet from where I had shot at you."

"No. There was no sex. But I did place a baby inside you."

Hearing it made it more real and made her feel less crazy. "Why? Why would you do this?"

His skin color shifted subtly to an undercurrent of green. "Because I felt bad for you. I felt bad for your loneliness. I felt bad for your loss."

"Really?" she snarled. "You did this for me?"

"Yes! But I had no right to do that, and I understand that. But that night when you told me to leave, I saw how much you hurt. I just thought maybe I could make your pain go away a little."

"By impregnating me with an alien creature?"

"The sperm I used was of a man who looks like I do. He is human and my friend." Bilal took a deep breath. "But yes, my DNA is there as well."

Carmella's hand tightened on the windowsill. "My baby has two fathers?"

"Yes."

She felt sick and angry and afraid. She couldn't find the words to tell the alien in her yard how devastating this was to her and how much she hated it for what it had done to her. This was no favor. This was no gift. This was only a monster growing in her belly.

"How much longer before it's born? It's not like a normal pregnancy. Everything is moving faster." She calculated that she should only be five months along, but she was already huge.

"You are correct. A Centaurian gestation is only about thirty weeks."

Carmella knew she was twenty-two weeks. She had two more months to carry it. She stared at the alien. Would he leave when the baby was born? He said he wanted to make sure she was okay. Would he try to take her to the ship to have the child?

"I'm not going to your ship or back to your fake Earth."

"No, you won't. You may remain here." His gaze was intense. It would have rendered her a nervous wreck if she wasn't so angry. "But I will remain here with you."

Her body stiffened. "I don't want you here."

"You won't be able to do this alone."

"Don't you touch me again! Do you understand me? Don't you ever touch me!"

"I understand," he said. "What do I call you?"

"You don't call me anything." She shut and locked the window.

**The next morning** the human did not come outside to tend to her animals. Bilal knew her routine. He had watched her often enough. After returning to her home to eat, she would then do a wide variety of chores outdoors. Sometimes she washed her laundry, sometimes she mowed her grass or took care of her garden, and sometimes she repaired fences and cleaned the barn.

It was obvious that she hadn't taken care of her chores in several days. Bilal felt guilty for not being here. That night he slept in the barn, but sleep would not come. The smells assaulted his nose. The animal waste in the barn was in piles knee high! He had not processed smell in the same way in his old body. His belly was also becoming empty, and hunger was not a pleasant sensation. His skin itched, and he felt cold.

Yes, humans needed more in order to keep their bodies comfortable. Luckily he had human friends and knew much about human needs.

When the sun rose, he went to the woman's garden and ate lettuce, cucumbers, and onions. They were good, and soon he felt strong again. Being human took some getting used to. He didn't understand the pressure building in his belly until he realized he had to urinate. Urinating was nice, though. He liked having a penis and liked the way it felt in his hands.

After finishing his business, he went back to the yard and stared at the house, locating the woman's whereabouts easily. She was awake and in one of the lower levels. She was preparing food. Good. As long as she ate then things should progress nicely.

Bilal returned to the barn and retrieved a clean pail. He had seen the woman doing this several times and had even tried it once when she wasn't around. Milking the cow was not an easy feat since the cow's udders were full and she was skittish and kept stepping away. He used soothing words to coax her into stillness and soon began filling the pail with fresh warm milk.

**Carmella darted from** window to window in order to see what the alien was doing. He came from the barn and had done something in her garden. She closed the curtain and scrubbed her hands across her face.

She could run away —

*No, stupid!*

She looked at her swollen belly and peeked out of the curtain. Carmella spent most of the morning spying on the alien, and when she saw him come up on the porch, she ran to the stairs as fast as her wobbly body would allow. She could lock herself in

# Adaptation

the bunker, but he never came inside. After half an hour, she moved to the front window and carefully peeked out.

He wasn't there.

But on the porch sat a basket of eggs, a pail of milk, and a puny green tomato.

# Chapter 12
## ~Compromise~

**Bilal was happy** to see that the woman had taken his offering. When he checked, the porch was bare. He went about the daily chores the next day while she peeked out of various windows at him. He began to hope that she would invite him inside. It was cold during the day and even colder at night.

He thought of the clothes in the many department stores that he had visited over the years. Now he didn't think he would have any problems wearing a big heavy coat. The clothes he had been given on the mother ship were simple linen pants and shirt and soft shoes. They were the normal clothing given to humans on the ship, but now they were filthy—and so was he. He washed his body a bit at the pump, but the water was cold.

That night as he huddled in the barn, he sneezed twice and swiped his forearm across his runny nose.

**Carmella scrambled some** of the eggs in the skillet with fresh butter she had churned that morning. There were too many eggs for one person to eat. It would be stupid to waste them when ...

Her lips formed an angry line. I didn't ask him to come here! I certainly didn't ask to be impregnated, so he can just take his ass back to his ship!

Carmella carried her plate of eggs and a glass of milk to the window where she had set up surveillance. She settled down in a comfortable reclining chair and watched the alien as he went about the yard work. She scowled at the way he cut the wood. He was expending way too much energy! And why was he cutting the lawn in October? She craned her neck when he went behind the barn. What was he doing back there? When he returned, he was fixing his pants. Ah, so aliens pissed and shit, too.

She ambled to her slop bucket and used it. She had been opening the window and dumping it, but she really needed to get outside to use the pump to rinse it. She also needed fresh water. Carmella grabbed an empty pitcher and peeked out the window. He was shoveling animal shit. She grinned. Better him than her. She opened the door slowly and tiptoed out onto the porch. Damn leaves were building up. She had planned to sweep before he had come. She went down the stairs, keeping her eyes on him as she headed for the pump.

She figured he would hear it when she primed the pump.

He did, turning in her direction for a moment before returning to his work. Okay, so he wasn't going to chase her down. She relaxed a bit as she filled her pitcher with cool, sweet water. She drank some and shivered at the cold in the air. It would be winter soon. Carmella went back inside with a frown on her face.

She sat in her rocker and read a book for a while then poked at her belly and felt the life inside poking back. She almost smiled, but then she remembered Micah and a sharp ache coursed through her heart. She peeked out the window but didn't see the alien. Bilal. He said his name was Bilal. Strange because he appeared Asian. Okay, he wasn't Asian. He was an alien living in some human's body. Carmella frowned. No, he was an alien and a human both. Like her ... her baby.

Carmella rubbed her face, went to the closet, and pulled out some quilts and blankets she rarely used. She opened the front door and placed the items on the porch. There. She'd done what any human would do for another being, even one who had helped kill everyone that she had ever loved.

# Adaptation

**Carmella checked the** porch at dusk. The blankets were still there, and she didn't see the alien. She chewed her lips and looked out the window until it was too dark to see. Then she made a cup of hot tea, hummed some long forgotten song, and went to bed.

That night she dreamed that the world was still present. She hurried to the window and saw cars driving down the street and kids playing in their yards. Erykah Badu was playing over the radio singing about seeing someone in the next lifetime, and when Carmella felt something nudge her belly, she looked down and saw that she was pregnant. She placed her hands on her swollen belly. Micah. Tears of joy streamed down her face. But where was Jody?

In her dream, she hurried down the stairs of the little townhouse that she and Jody had shared their first year of marriage. He was in the kitchen wearing slippers, pajamas, and a white T-shirt. He was yawning and flipping pancakes when she skidded to a stop at the kitchen door.

He raised his eyebrows, his dark hair a mop of messy curls over his head, morning stubble on his cheeks. "Mel, what are you doing out of bed? I told you I was going to make you breakfast in bed." He came over and kissed her, and her knees went weak as tears pricked her eyes.

Her arms went around his body and she clung to him. "Jody …"

He gave her a tight hug, pulled back, and smiled at her. "Get back in bed. This is my gift to you."

Carmella's eyes opened and she looked around her darkened room. "No," she gasped. "Jody?" She gripped her sheets in her fist realizing that Jody's presence was only a precious dream. It had seemed so real …

Why couldn't it have lasted longer?

Carmella rolled onto her side and felt tears slip from her eyes to wet her pillow.

# Adaptation

*Why did I have to live?*

~***~

**The next morning** before using the slop bucket, Carmella hurried to her bedroom window and peered down to the porch below. The blankets had been replaced by a basket of eggs and some milk. She smiled and went to pee then hurried down the stairs and collected the items from the porch.

The alien was at the pump splashing his face and upper body. He had removed his shirt, and the water had streamed down his torso to wet his linen pants.

He looked so human ... except that his skin was not the bronze color she would expect on an Asian man. It held an undercurrent of blues and grays. It was still obviously skin, but it was as if the alien was millimeters beneath the surface.

She realized that she was staring when he looked up and met her eyes.

"Thank you," he said as he reached for one of the blankets.

She averted her eyes and worked her lips before words would come from them. "You're welcome," she mumbled then hurried back into the house.

Carmella paced for a few minutes before looking out the window. He had dried off with the blanket and was pulling on his shirt. Her face burned and her brow furrowed as she stared at him. Long, black tendrils of hair ran limply over his shoulders, and his torso was very ... nice. She scowled to herself as her eyes stared at his wet pants. Linen pants became translucent when they were wet, and she could see that he had no underwear ...

Carmella gripped the curtains and pulled them closed.

**Bilal felt too** tired to do much of anything. He wrapped himself in two of the blankets and curled into a ball on the barn floor. He fell into a restless sleep. When he awoke, his body felt

# Adaptation

achy, whether from the cold, the hard floor and his unyielding body, or because he was becoming ill, he did not know.

Centaurians did not become ill in the same way that humans did. He would know what to look for if he was treating his friends. He would burrow his feelers into their bodies and locate the clusters of white blood cells for the illness and then remove them from their bodies.

Bilal still possessed his feelers, but now they were hidden in his tongue. He didn't need to extract them to find and get rid of what ailed him because he no longer had the capability to heal himself. His human body was not built for such things, and even though he still possessed Centaurian know-how, he was unable to do it.

He would need to start a fire. Too bad he didn't know how to do that without matches. He couldn't make himself warm internally and he couldn't heal himself, and he cursed himself for opting to make himself more human than Centaurian and stuck being useless. Bilal wrapped a blanket around his shoulders and felt a pain in his stomach. Hunger. Damnit, why did he always have to become hungry? He went to the pump for water and thought about going into town for supplies.

The human would need things for a baby, and he would need things for his own comfort. He ran his hands through his hair and thought about Raj's neat black hair. It was never greasy like his was now, and Raj never smelled the way he smelled. Raj and Lawrence had soap to cleanse their bodies, and all he had was frosty water.

The door to the house opened. The human was standing in the doorway in an oversized shirt and leggings. Her belly seemed impossibly huge. Humans carried their offspring in such a strange way, but she looked healthy. He marveled that soon there would be a little one.

"This is some quiche that I made from the eggs and milk." She held a covered dish in her hands.

# Adaptation

He didn't know what quiche was and didn't care. His empty stomach growled, and he hoped she would give him some of it.

She set the dish on the rocker, returned to her house, and shut the door soundly behind her.

Bilal climbed the porch stairs and uncovered the dish. The smell of fresh baked food hit his nostrils, and his mouth began to water—which alarmed him. His mouth had never watered before. He sat on the floor and began to eat with his fingers. It was still warm, and half of the dish was left for him. When he finished eating, he stared at the empty dish then licked it clean. Afterwards he licked his fingers and checked for scraps on the porch floor. With a contented sigh, he left the dish on the porch and went to do the chores feeling energized and one hundred percent better.

Carmella had been watching from the window. A pleased smile tugged at her lips. He liked it. Well, he was an alien. A bucket of dirt would probably taste good to him.

She went into the kitchen and thought about what she could make for dinner. It wasn't Sunday, but maybe she could make an exception and have chicken ...

# Chapter 13
## ~Wolf Comes Home~

**Over the course** of a week, Bilal and Carmella formed a routine. Routines were what Carmella had become accustomed to, and Bilal began to gauge the passage of time by the meals she left for him. Each day he would bring her milk and eggs, and a few hours later she would leave him a morning meal on the porch, often an omelet made with the fresh cheese, butter, and eggs. Sometimes it was an egg and biscuit sandwich. Bilal always ate every crumb before continuing with his chores.

At midday he would leave whatever vegetables he thought were good enough on the porch, and another meal of bread and cheese or soup would appear on the porch. It was always good, and it always made him feel more energized. While he ate, he would sometimes look up and see the human in the window watching him and eating her meal. She didn't seem to like him looking at her, and he would move out of sight and "watch" her with his other senses. He was aware that she spent most of her time in front of various windows watching him. It didn't bother him, but he was anxious for her to understand that he really did not mean her any harm.

After lunch, Bilal would disappear, knowing that the woman would not venture outside until he made himself scarce. Once he was out of sight in the barn or the woods, she would carry her slop bucket to the outhouse before pumping fresh water. She would check some of the chores he had done and then return to her home.

# Adaptation

Bilal took that opportunity to watch her from his various hiding places. She seemed healthy and looked well, but he still worried.

When the sun began to set, he received his final meal. The evening meal always contained fresh vegetables, sometimes chicken, sometimes a thick stew. He would sit on the porch and gobble it up while resting from his chores. He liked evenings because he wasn't checking the fences or fixing any holes the animals made. He wasn't shoveling animal waste or feeding the chickens or letting the cow and bull graze. He wasn't weeding the garden, mowing the lawn, or wiping the outside of the windows clean.

Once fortified, Bilal explored the twilight world around him. He picked blades of grass and studied them with his new and improved eyesight. He tasted everything from rocks and rusted nails to paint chips and dust. When he wasn't putting objects into his mouth, he ran his fingers over everything that he could, relishing the way things felt.

He sensed the world with delight. The feelers in his tongue amplified the sounds muted to his human ears. Smells were more prominent to him as a human, and the sensations his body experienced were stronger. When he had accidentally scratched himself on a bit of wire from a fence, a bead of blood appeared on his fragile skin. The pain was sharp and uncomfortable. As a Centaurian, he would have never noticed, but humans had a much more acute sense of touch.

Bilal stared in the direction of town for about the hundredth time. The air was cold and would only get colder. He needed provisions. He needed clothes as well as things for a child. He didn't know as much as he should about caring for a human child but had seen human mothers with their infants. They often nursed from their breasts or used baby bottles, and the infants wore cloth or disposable diapers. Babies were wrapped in blankets even when it wasn't cold.

He didn't want to do it, but he had to.

He was going to leave the human.

# Adaptation

**Carmella saw Bilal** come up the walkway for his evening meal. She hurried to the kitchen where she had kept her plate of food warming in the oven. She carried it to the window, settled in her chair, and waited until he was sitting on the floor before she began to eat. She wondered why he didn't sit in the rocker instead of on the floor but shrugged. Not her problem.

She noted that he seemed to like the chicken the most and nodded in approval when he cleaned his plate. She didn't like to admit this to herself, but she liked that he enjoyed the meals she cooked. When he was gone, she collected his plate and fork and then washed the dishes. As she stood at the sink, she thought about the baby growing in her belly.

What was it going to look like? Would it be Black and Asian? Would it have skin that wasn't skin but a covering that was like an alien-chameleon? Carmella rubbed her head, trying to rid herself of the headache that developed almost every evening. Because she didn't take prenatal vitamins, the baby sucked the nutrients from her body. Maybe an alien baby needed more nutrients than a human baby did. Maybe her freaking hair and teeth were going to fall out! She scowled and climbed the stairs to turn in early.

Carmella tossed and turned and fell into a restless sleep. She dreamed that her belly was full with an unborn baby. When the first dream-cramp hit her, the dream-Carmella realized she was in labor. Afraid and alone she strained and screamed in pain until the searing pain reached its epoch and the baby had found its way out of her body.

Only what came out were tentacles, long gray tentacles that waved in the air.

Dream-Carmella screamed at the sight of the hideous thing, and then the real Carmella sat up in bed soaked in her sweat with her heart thumping within her chest. She trembled so hard that her teeth chattered. She jumped up out of bed and hurried to her slop bucket where she became ill.

# Adaptation

*Please God. Please don't let this happen to me.*

~***~

**While Bilal did** not dream, his sleep was also restless. He wrapped himself in one blanket, placed a quilt on the ground, and covered himself with the other. This was it. Tomorrow he would tell the human that he would need to leave for a few days but would return. He needed to get his supplies because for the first time he saw snow flurries and the birth of the child was growing nearer. He needed to be present because a human's body was not predictable, and he wouldn't take a chance that he would not be present should she go into labor.

The next morning he milked the cow. He would tell her about his plan when he had his morning meal. He felt worried about admitting that he was going away. What if she ran away? He frowned. She would be foolish to do such a thing. And besides, whether or not she tried to run away would be based on how much she despised him. She fed him. That counted for something, even if she hated him and all Centaurians.

Bilal was so caught up in his thoughts that he didn't sense two approaching animals. The cow became nervous, and he rubbed her flank. "Its fine, girl. I'm nearly finished."

His nostrils flared suddenly, but by that time the wolves were in the doorway. Bilal scrambled from the stool only to land on his backside. He could move faster than a human but not fast enough to come to his feet before one of the wolves was on top of him.

Bilal knew there was no way that he would survive, not when he was on the ground with two wolves on top of him.

Yet the smaller wolf only stood and watched.

Bilal clasped his hands around the attacking wolf's neck, but the animal was much too strong. The wolf whipped his head back and forth with his teeth bared and dug claws into Bilal's delicate flesh, leaving ribbons of torn skin in their wake. Bilal screamed in pain, a sound he had never made before, and the pain seared through him as his adrenaline rose.

# Adaptation

As the wolf growled and barked and snapped its massive teeth mere inches from his face, Bilal gripped the animal's fur. Mustering all of his strength and with one last scream, he rolled the animal from atop of him.

It was a mistake.

The wolf found his footing on the packed earth and managed to shake loose from Bilal's grip. A split-second later, the wolf's teeth sank into Bilal's shoulder as Bilal beat uselessly at the animal. The wolf released its grip to go for his throat. Bilal's arm went up reflexively, and he felt teeth sinking into his forearm. Bilal kicked the wolf's underbelly, but the wolf wouldn't let go, his teeth clamped tight and causing bone to shatter. Bilal peeled off scream after scream.

"*Wolf!*"

Bilal saw the woman standing outside the barn door holding a rifle.

"*Down!*" she shouted.

The wolf clamped even harder onto Bilal's arm, growling in renewed fervor.

Carmella glared at her son in disbelief. No, he did not just stand there and defy her! She stormed toward him with fire in her eyes, and Wolf released Bilal's arm and backed away.

"Bad puppy! You don't bite! No no no!" She shook her finger at him, and Wolf whined again and averted his eyes, walking a restless circle until Carmella's attention focused on the writhing and bleeding man.

Carmella dropped carefully to her knees and pulled back the alien's ripped shirt. "Jesus ..."

Bilal clutched at the torn flesh of his shoulder, face twisting in pain. He rolled into a ball onto his side.

Carmella chewed her lip lightly. "Can you fix this?" she asked. "Can you, because ... this is pretty bad."

Bilal shook his head. "No," he whimpered. "I cannot."

"Fuck ..."

Bilal concentrated on his injuries. His stomach and chest burned from the clawing, but it was the blood pouring from his shoulder that would kill him. He concentrated on making the repairs, going through the steps as if he was totally Centaurian instead of mostly human. He tried to slow the heart, slow the blood flow, and repair the artery.

*The cells,* he thought. *The cells need to reproduce quickly …*

Bilal lost consciousness.

**There was nothing** but quiet, and then he realized that this was not true. There was something more than the quiet.

There was pain.

Bilal tried to block it but couldn't, and then he tried to move but his body felt strange. He was no longer himself but a human hybrid with limbs and a neck — and a shoulder that was in searing pain.

"Try to keep this down. If you throw up again I swear I'm going to let you stew in your own filth."

The words were harsh, but the voice wasn't. There was a soothing quality to it, and Bilal's eyes opened. The woman. She was close to him. She held a cup to his lips, but he didn't want anything. His stomach felt empty but queasy, and his body shivered with sickness.

She put her hand behind his head and held it up and not too gently.

He grimaced as the movement caused his torn flesh to throb, but lukewarm liquid slipped between his lips, and the taste was good. He swallowed some and then more until he was drinking it steadily.

"Good," she said. "Broth."

He didn't know what that meant and didn't care. He only wanted more in his body. Soon he felt sated and drifted back into unconsciousness.

# Adaptation

**Carmella was washing** the clothes in the washtub that she kept outside. She fantasized about the time when she could simply dump clothes into the washer. Why did she ever complain about that? Throw the clothes in, add some detergent, and press a button. Damn, how spoiled she had been back in those days.

At least the boiling water and hard work kept her warm. Laundry was an ordeal when it had been only her clothes, but now she had to clean up after the alien. His bandages had to be sanitized, and he had to be cleaned like a baby that pooped his diaper. Not that she blamed him for that. At least he was alive. For a few days she had doubts that he would make it. He burned up with fever, and his wounds became infected. She plied him with aspirin and kept the wounds disinfected.

When the fever broke, he was able to hold down food. She was more than a little relieved, though admitting that cost her a lot. She hated the alien, but he was the only one present who could help her with the delivery.

Wolf brushed her leg with his furry body and whined.

She reached down and scratched behind his ear, and then Girl wanted the same treatment. After Carmella scratched behind Girl's ears, Girl returned to her spot on the edge of the woods. She wouldn't come close to the house with the alien in it, and Wolf seemed equally distressed though he did come into the house. He sniffed the unconscious alien warily under his mother's watchful eyes.

Carmella's posture and vibe seemed to dare him to even *think* about baring a tooth at the sick creature. Wolf didn't seem interested in testing his mother's wrath even though the alien creature smelled of things that should be far away from his mother's home.

Wolf watched the creature warily. He would leave it alone—for now.

Adaptation

# Chapter 14
## ~Bilal Meets his son~

**The next time** Bilal opened his eyes, he was warm and comfortable.

He couldn't remember the last time that his body felt so relaxed. There was still pain, but beyond dull aches was the feel of soft cushions beneath his body. He took a few moments to look around before attempting to move. He recognized the living room.

He grimaced at the memory of the wolf.

Though exhausted and wanting to roll over and return to sleep, he was more curious than he was interested in resting. He sat up on the couch and looked around. It was quiet ... too quiet. Where was the human?

He placed his hand on his injured shoulder, surprised that it didn't hurt nearly as bad as it did before. He lifted the corner of the tape holding down a bandage. He peeked at the angry red wound and grimaced. She had sewn his flesh together with thread. He pressed the tape back into place thinking that she had done a fine job—and happy that he had been asleep when she had done it.

He examined his forearm next, sure that it was fractured, but there was nothing to be done about that. The bone would mend without any help from him. He also didn't bother trying to unwrap the bandage and ran his fingers over the bandages on his chest and belly. He winced slightly and felt a bit disappointed that he had allowed his human skin to become marred. He was happy to be alive, but he also had to live in this body. Though he might not live

95

to be as old as a pure Centaurian, he could live longer than the average human and it would be a shame to wreck it so soon.

Bilal pushed the blanket back and stood. As soon as he was standing he grew lightheaded and had to sit. He tried standing again, and this time held onto the edge of the couch. He took a tentative step toward the window. When he felt that he wouldn't fall, he continued until he could see out into the yard.

The human was hanging freshly washed clothes on a clothesline. His eyes lingered on her swollen belly. With a frown he wondered if she would give birth earlier than he had anticipated. He wanted to examine her but knew that she wouldn't like that.

Bilal caught sight of the big black wolf, which was lolling a few feet from her. He nearly jumped back from the window. With a frown he closed the curtain and then looked around. The fireplace held a small fire that kept the room pleasantly warm. There was a solarium with French doors beside it where he could see more wood for the fireplace.

The house was immaculate and tastefully furnished. He moved into the kitchen and saw a pot of something simmering on the stove. Curious, he lifted the lid and saw broth. His stomach grumbled. He also had to relieve himself.

He walked to the back door, worried the wolf would hear him opening the door. It was a good thing he had a penis. He could aim it and pee without leaving the porch, and if he had to, he could dart back into the house.

Bilal opened the door and sniffed the air for anything amiss. He reached into his waistband, gripped his penis, and let lose a stream of urine over the edge of the porch. He sighed, relishing the feel of pissing. When the stream ended, he shook it the way he had seem Raj and Lawrence do it then tucked his penis into his pants.

He closed the door behind him and entered the kitchen. He saw bread on the table and snatched a slice, eating it quickly while returning to the living room. He was about to head upstairs when the door opened. He swung around and saw the wolf enter the house ahead of the human, who was carrying a basket of folded

Adaptation

clothes. Bilal's knees went weak, and he stopped breathing. He gripped the banister, prepared to dart up the stairs.

The wolf growled.

"Wolf! Sit!"

Bilal saw that the wolf listened to the woman, and the wolf sat at her feet. Bilal let out a relieved breath, and the woman lowered the basket with a grimace and a soft grunt.

She reached down and rubbed the wolf's neck and pointed out the door. "Outside, Wolf. Outside!" When he didn't move fast enough, she gripped his scruff and gently nudged him out. "Sorry, boy. You can come back later."

Once the door was shut and the animal was on the other side, Bilal relaxed.

The two watched each other more curious than wary.

"I didn't expect you to be awake," she said. "Your fever just broke last night."

He touched his shoulder. "Thank you for helping. You sewed the wound close, and there is no infection."

"Not now." She folded her arms and rested them on her belly as if it was a shelf. "You nearly died. I didn't know if you would wake up."

Bilal frowned, and when she reached to pick up the basket, he rushed forward.

Carmella jumped back.

Bilal reached down and hefted the basket for her. "I'll carry it for you," he said.

She blushed. "Oh."

"Where?"

"Upstairs."

He trudged up the stairs and waited for her at the top, concerned that she seemed out of breath by the time she reached him. Was the child pressing against her lungs? Maybe it was growing too big. This was his first time creating a child, and the mother ship had much to do with what resulted. He wasn't completely sure it would turn out the way that was optimum.

97

# Adaptation

Carmella gestured down a hall lined in closed doors toward her bedroom. She watched his naked, muscled back and the way his pants hung low on his hips. She knew what lay beneath those pants. She'd had to clean him, and yes she did look. The sight of a naked man had unsettled her.

Not that it stopped her from looking.

Bilal glanced around the neat room and placed the basket on the bed. His shoulder throbbed, but he hid the pain and turned to her. "I don't know what to call you. In my mind I call you 'the human' or 'the woman.' But that's not right."

In her mind she wanted to complain that she was his baby's mama, but at the last minute she bit back the retort. She stared at him. "Carmella."

A smiled touched his lips. It was so perfect. Carmella. She was Carmella.

Carmella's eyes widened at the look on his face. She reached for the clothes in the basket and placed them on the bed to sort his from hers. She pushed some pajamas in his direction. "I found these in the house when I moved in. I just put them in the basement. I should have thrown them out but couldn't bring myself to do it. It was too much trouble, but it didn't seem right to get rid of them. They ought to fit you. There are more clothes in the basement if you want to sort through them. There's a coat and maybe some shoes will fit."

"Thank you. I was making plans to go into town for clothes and provisions before winter." He looked at her belly. "The child will need provisions as well."

Carmella frowned. "What … is it?"

"It is a baby."

"No," she said. "Is it going to be like you were before? A Centaurian? An alien?"

"No," he said softly. "I tried to give you a gift. A child. A human child. He's a boy."

She sucked in a sharp breath and fingered a folded piece of clothing that lay on the bed. She shook her head. "My son died …"

"Yes. But this child will be your son as well."

# Adaptation

Carmella's eyes stung as she picked up some of the clothes and put them away in her chest of drawers.

"And I suspect that the infant will come sooner than I expected."

She stared at him. "What? When?"

"I don't know." He looked at her belly. "I won't know unless I can examine the baby." He met her eyes. "I need to do that." He rubbed his shoulder and looked at the clothes designated as his then picked up a shirt and slipped it carefully over his head. "But first, I have to go. I have to get provisions."

"Go into town? You've been out cold for three days. And my wolf nearly killed you. There are more wolves out there, wolves that won't be talked down by their angry mother. Besides ..." She moved to the door, silently willing him to follow her.

Bilal followed her into the hallway, and across the hall from her bedroom was a closed door. She opened it and stepped inside, and Bilal followed. He looked around, his mouth dropping open.

It was a nursery. It wasn't an old nursery of cobwebs and torn wallpaper like he'd seen in other abandoned homes over the years. No, this nursery was new. He looked at Carmella. She had prepared for this baby. He felt elated as he stepped inside and studied the crib, the rocker, and the wall hangings of colorful alphabet letters and pictures. She did want this child, or at the very least, she was preparing to care for him.

"Do you have everything that a baby would need? Is there anything else that the child will need?"

For some reason she couldn't meet his eyes and the room felt too closed-in. She didn't like the feeling and fiddled with the mobile hanging above the crib. She shrugged. "I don't know if the powdered formula is any good anymore, but I got tons of it. I got bottles and diapers and ... I have everything I need." She looked into his eyes. "I was kind of worried about how sick I might be afterwards. I guess ... that's all."

"I'll be here, Carmella. I do need to check the baby. May I?"

She folded her arms defensively in front of her body and looked away. Eventually she nodded.

# Adaptation

Bilal moved to her, deliberately not making any sudden gestures as he gently touched her elbow. He led her to the rocker. "Sit, please."

She did, tensing at his proximity and watching him warily.

"I'm going to touch your belly with my fingers. Is that okay?"

She nodded.

He placed his palms flat against her belly. He met her eyes when he felt the child moving actively within her.

"It ... he moves a lot," Carmella said. "Kicks and stretches."

"Are you in any pain?"

She shrugged. "I've been pregnant before. Nothing I'm not familiar with."

He concentrated on the feel of the baby's movements. "Carmella, do you remember when I placed my tentacles against your wolf? When I was in my previous body and healing him?"

She nodded.

"Within my tentacles are sensors, filaments that burrow into the body. It doesn't hurt, and it's barely noticeable. They allow me to manipulate cell development, to heal, and to see inside."

She had known that the tentacles were doing something like that, though she had not known the extent of his ability.

"I don't have tentacles any longer, but I still have the sensors." He opened his mouth and showed her his tongue. It was pink like any other tongue.

Carmella gasped. From the tip of his tongue slipped a thin filament that waved in the air like the tongue of a forked snake. Two more joined the first, and it looked as if thin gray worms were pushing their way out of his tongue. She wanted to get up and run. It was horrifying!

He closed his mouth. "Carmella, I need to connect with you through those sensors. I need to connect with the baby."

"Uh ... what? How?" She thought about those filaments traveling up her vagina, and she wanted to bolt out of her seat.

"I only need to touch your belly. That's all."

She studied his face and nodded her consent.

# Adaptation

He knelt and lifted her shirt until her brown flesh was exposed to him. It was stretched tight, nearly too tight. He placed his hands against her flesh, fingers splayed. After giving her a quick look, he lowered his head and placed his lips against her belly button.

Carmella grimaced and gripped the arms of her rocker. He was kissing her. Oh my God! She was being kissed for the first time in years and didn't know what to think or how to feel. She stared down at his lowered head, his face obscured by dark hair. She closed her eyes to block out the sight of it. She thought about Jody. Oh God, Jody. She wanted to cry, and she wanted to scream, but she stayed as still as she could.

Bilal's lips pressed against her warm brown skin where her bellybutton had once been. It had disappeared over her stretched flesh weeks before. He held her firmly in place and pressed the tip of his tongue against her. The sensors pushed into her belly, so thin that they were barely there.

But she felt them. It didn't hurt, and strangely it was far from unpleasant.

Bilal closed his eyes and "saw" through his sensors as he allowed them to connect through her nerve endings and travel through her umbilicus to her unborn child. In this way he got to see his son for the first time since he had implanted him within his mother's womb. Bilal connected to his son, and his son recognized him. It pleased him. He tested his son's blood and found that it was rich with the necessary nutrients, and his body functioned normally though his lungs were still not fully developed. He took a few more moments to transfer information to his child before he allowed his sensors to retract and return to his own body.

Bilal lifted his head, leaned back on his heels, and looked at Carmella.

"Well?" Carmella asked.

"He is good. He is comfortable and well-fed. He is anxious to meet the world. But I told him it's not yet time." Bilal smiled. "I believe he is impatient so he may kick and toss and turn, but he is quite comfortable despite the tight confines. He rather enjoys it."

# Adaptation

Carmella widened her eyes. "Are you shitting me?"

Bilal shrugged. "No. Centaurians communicate through means other than words."

"You were *talking* to him?"

"In some ways, yes. But without words."

Carmella pushed down her shirt and covered her stomach with her hands. Somehow it made her feel strange knowing that the two could communicate. She wasn't sure how she felt about the baby, but she was sure she didn't like the idea of the two of them bonding.

# Chapter 15
## ~I am not Alone~

**Carmella transformed the** broth into a luscious vegetable stew. She and Bilal sat at the butcher block kitchen table and had it with the fresh baked bread.

Carmella watched as Bilal spooned soup into his mouth. "How did you ..." She gestured to his body.

"Become human," Bilal said.

She grimaced. He wasn't human because he had some man's body. What about that crazy skin? When he was sick it had a distinct gray undertone, and now it was purple and pink like a soft bruise beneath the more normal looking bronze.

He noted her distaste but didn't allow it to bother him. Despite her obvious disdain, he knew she would not be sitting across from him if he was in his old body. He gripped his spoon. "It's complicated, more complicated than I could explain to you. But essentially I linked to the mother ship and allowed it to alter my physical makeup."

She let her mind digest that for a while. "So, can you become Centaurian again?"

"No."

She spooned soup into her mouth. "Why? You changed once."

"The part that was Centaurian is gone, not suppressed." He eyed the bread before reaching for another slice, chomping on it before continuing. "Imagine a human male undergoing a sex-change operation. The parts that are gone can never return."

"Ah ..." She nodded. "So, do you ... miss it?"

"I did when your wolf was attacking me."

She grimaced. "That shouldn't happen again."

"And it's been cold outside at night. I cannot regulate my body temperature in this human body." He met her eyes and thought he detected some guilt. He didn't know why since none of this was her fault. "But I have no regrets, at least not about my body." He returned his attention to the soup and finished it. He leaned back in the chair and rubbed his eyes. "How are the animals? I should check on them." He stood.

Over the weeks that Carmella had watched Bilal in his human form from her window, she had gotten used to him. She didn't acknowledge this, but Bilal had become the focal point of her life. He had become her entertainment as she plopped down in her armchair to watch him each day. She relished cooking again and seeing him enjoy the meals she prepared. She wondered about his intentions, his thoughts, and why he seemed so human. Other than his chameleon skin, he didn't seem much different from any other person. She had lost her fear of him. He was polite and handsome in a nerdy Asian way, but she could also sense that he really did not mean her any harm. Besides, he'd done all of the chores for weeks without complaint.

She shrugged and waved her hand dismissively. "I already took care of it. Besides, if you even think about lifting anything, you're going to open up that wound in your shoulder. You also just woke up after being unconscious for three days."

Bilal blinked.

Carmella frowned. "Who do you think has been doing the work out there before you showed up?" She pointed to her stomach. "This isn't going to stop me." That wasn't quite true. She couldn't cut the wood or shovel or haul anything. For some reason she didn't want to admit that.

Bilal didn't know how to respond, so he kept his mouth shut.

She pulled herself up to her feet and gestured for him to follow her. She led him down the stairs to the lower level and a

# Adaptation

fully finished basement now used mostly for storage. There was a big screen television and nice sectional sofa. Once upon a time a family used to gather here for something like Tuesday movie nights. Bilal's imagination tried to picture what human life must have been like in a house like this, but all he could think of were re-runs of old television sitcoms. He knew enough humans to realize that real life was nothing like sitcoms. He longed to know firsthand, but he only seemed to experience life from the outside looking in.

Carmella opened a box on a side table and began pulling items out of it. "You can see if these will fit you." She handed him some of the clothes.

"Thank you, Carmella," he said as he examined a pair of jeans. They might be a bit big, but he could make it work.

"Whatever you can find in here you can keep. It's all men's clothes." She reached for another box.

Bilal pulled it down from a stack and placed it on the floor. They stood side by side as she dug through it and pulled up a nice parka.

He smiled. "That will do fine."

She stared at his smiling face. For the first time it struck her that she was in the presence of another person, uh, a semi-person. She was talking and being talked to. She almost couldn't grasp the concept of it.

*I am not alone.*

Carmella felt overwhelmed and looked at anything but him. "Um, this is pretty comfortable down here. And winter here can be brutal, so if you want you can crash down here ..."

"Crash?"

Carmella cleared her throat. "You can *sleep* down here."

Bilal raised his eyebrows.

"Soon it will be too cold for you to sleep outside," Carmella said. "It's too cold now. Besides, I can't let you die before you can help me deliver this baby."

"You are being sarcastic," Bilal said.

Carmella looked away. "Sort of."

105

# Adaptation

"Thank you, Carmella. Thank you for the room and the clothes, and thank you for helping me to get better."

There was a cold glint in her eyes as she headed back up the stairs. "Don't thank me. My motivation was purely selfish. I need someone here to help me deliver. If not for that, your ass would be wolf shit right about now."

"You are being sort of sarcastic again," Bilal said.

"Not this time."

He watched her disappear up the stairs. *It is good not to be wolf shit,* he thought.

"The couch pulls out into a bed," Carmella called out. "Get some rest. You look tired."

Bilal smiled. *She needs me,* he thought. *She wants me to rest. He looked at the couch. I will sleep well tonight.*

# Chapter 16
## ~First Bath~

**Carmella sat on** the edge of her bed staring at the floor. She was trying to figure out how she had gotten to this place. She was pregnant, and an alien was in her basement …

She rubbed her face. Had she made a mistake? No. There was nothing that she would have done differently. She would not have allowed her wolf to kill him, and she couldn't allow him to go hungry when she had food to spare. And she definitely would not watch him freeze out in the barn.

So then why did she feel so unsure? She closed her eyes and let her mind drift. A long time ago she had known a young man named Jody, and Jody believed the Centaurians were travelers who wanted to share knowledge. He never believed they meant humans any harm. Bitterness filled her that he was taken from her, but then the bitterness disappeared. Jody had never hated anyone or anything in his short life. If he was here and she was long dead, she believed Jody would study this alien as much as the alien apparently wanted to study her.

She smoothed the wrinkles from the covers of her bed and went downstairs. No matter how much she disliked them, events were moving in a direction she could not control. And as much as she hated to admit it, she needed the alien to be here. His presence was security. He did the chores that would be difficult for her, he understood the life that was growing inside of her, and he seemed to be intelligent, non-threatening, and conscientious of her fears. He didn't Bogart his way around her.

107

# Adaptation

She went to the top of the basement stairs. Bilal scared her, but her fear was no longer because he was an alien. She feared him because he was another intelligent being, and it had been a long time since she'd had someone else for company. When there had been no other voice, no other face to gaze upon for years upon years, just about anything was welcomed.

She sighed and peered down the darkened stairs. "Bilal?" She felt strange about giving him a name other than "Blob" or "Alien."

"Yes, Carmella?" He came to the foot of the stairs.

"I need to know something."

"Yes?"

"How long are you going to be here?"

His mouth formed a grim line, but his eyes didn't move from her face. "I will be with you and the child for five years."

Her mouth parted. "What?"

"My intent is not to interfere with your life. Once the child is born I can go away and leave you to your life. But I won't be far away. I can't go far."

"Why? I mean, why are you doing this?"

He took a deep breath. "Because it was the only way that I could rectify the mistake I made." His eyes moved briefly to her belly. "Carmella, please believe that my intention was never to rape you. Raj says that what I did was rape. I am truly sorry. At the time my intentions were good, but ... "

"But what?"

"But ... I was stoned and I didn't know what—"

"Wait," she interrupted. "Did you just say you were *stoned?*"

He rubbed his hands across the leg of his pants. "Yes. At the time I was under the influence of a mood-altering drug, and I could not stop thinking that you were alone and had lost a child. I wanted to make it right for you. I couldn't stop thinking about how you were alone."

# Adaptation

"You ..." She closed her mouth and pursed her lips. "You are much too stupid to be intelligent enough to do what you did." She turned and walked into the living room and out the front door.

Bilal's head fell forlornly. He had been stupid, and he was sorry for the hurt that he had caused everyone.

But now there was a child and that was something that he could not feel sorry about.

**Carmella shivered as** she returned to the house an hour later carrying the last of the laundry. She had been too mad to return to the house to pick up a gun and shoot the ... Bilal. Instead she collected some kerosene for the lanterns inside the house.

When she opened the door she saw that Bilal had folded the couch blankets and was standing at the bookcase reading. He closed the book when he saw her and hurried to her aid.

"Let me take that, Carmella." He took the basket from her hands and carried it up the stairs while she returned to the porch for the kerosene.

When he returned to the main floor, he studied her eyes, noting that she was trying not to look at him. He felt bad about that but knew that he would have to allow her to work it out. He was happy. He was close to her and liked looking at her even if she hated him. Maybe she would stop hating him, and one day they could be friends.

He thought about Raj and Lawrence and felt a stab of regret. He was selfish and stupid, and he had a lot to learn about being a human before he could expect to be a good friend to one.

"Carmella, is there anything that I can do for you?"

She stared at him as if he was a roach.

He almost took a step back at the dislike in her expression. *Well,* he thought, *I now know what the human expression "back to square one" means.*

# Adaptation

He returned to the lower level and lay down on the couch, not bothering with the pullout bed. The sofa was comfortable. His body was tired even though his brain couldn't turn itself off, and he had a hard time processing all that had happened. Soon fatigue took over, and he fell asleep before realizing that it was happening.

Carmella refused to talk to Bilal for two full days.

Bilal refused to go outside because Wolf was out there waiting for him. He would stand at the window watching the animal in the same way that Carmella used to watch him.

Carmella went out and did the light chores like milking the cow and collecting the eggs while he dusted and swept the floors and kept the sink free of dishes.

One day she stormed into the house and stopped in front of Bilal, who stood at his normal spot at the window. "Okay, you stink!" she yelled.

"What?" he asked.

"You need to bathe!"

He looked down at himself, aware that he was dirty. His clothes had stains because sometimes the spoon spilled their contents down the front of his clothes even though he tried to be careful. Also he itched in places where it would be rude to scratch.

"Carmella, I've never had a bath."

"Aliens don't bathe?"

He scratched his greasy hair. "No. Why would we when we don't have skin the way you do?" His cells multiplied so rapidly that he continued to renew himself. Dirt was turned inward and then expelled. Centaurians carried no true odor, and they had no hair or crevices that captured dirt. "I've never needed to bathe until I became human."

She rolled her eyes. "Let's get one thing straight, Bilal. You're not human. Just because you have a human body doesn't make you human!"

His eyes moved away from hers. "I know this. I know that I am not human."

She felt a stab of guilt, but she swallowed it. "You do have a human ... form," she conceded.

He looked at her. "Yes. Yes, I do."

"So it needs to be kept clean. Look, I can't live in the same house with filth. I tried that before and it doesn't work for me. You're going to have to bathe."

He nodded eagerly.

"Okay, so what we're going to do is boil the water. You'll have to carry it upstairs to the bathtub."

"You want me to go outside — with the wolves?"

"They won't hurt you. They're well trained."

"I'm not willing to take that chance."

She blinked at him. "Are you planning to stay in the house forever?"

"No." He looked out the window. The big wolf watched him. He always watched him. "I'm hoping that he will go away. And when he returns I will fire a gun the way I saw you do — up in the air … at first."

"Well, I'm not sure that Wolf will leave as long as you're here." She was very aware of where he said he would place the first shot. If he thought a subsequent shot would go into her baby boy, then he would definitely find one in his own half-human brain! "Wolf and Girl have never stayed this long." She rather liked it but realized that Bilal didn't. For now, Bilal was needed, and the two — make that three — would have to get along. Although Girl mostly kept her distance, Carmella feared Girl. Wolf would do what Carmella wanted, but Girl might not.

"Let's just do this." She reached for the doorknob.

"Uh, I would like to have a gun."

She shook her head. "No. You get no gun."

His posture changed and his feet seemed to plant themselves in one spot.

Carmella rolled her eyes and looked around. "Okay, you can have … a big stick." She moved to the kitchen for the broom. She thrust it into his hands.

He examined and handed it back to her. "No."

She took it from him and slammed it against his head.

Bilal yelped and rubbed his sore head.

111

# Adaptation

"See? This can be a very effective weapon. And I didn't even hit you as hard as I could have. Look, you can't stay inside forever, and you can't kill my wolves — or I'll kill you. So you'll have to try to get along with each other. Or else you'll have to leave."

He glanced out of the window. "Carmella," he said without looking at her. "If I die then my people will come for you." He looked at her. "And I don't mean that they will come with the purpose of integrating you with others. They will come to experiment on you and the child. I am the only thing that is keeping that from happening. I am your protection from them just as you are my protection from those." He gestured to the wolves with his head. He moved toward the door. "I'm ready."

She absorbed Bilal's words. She was not a stupid woman even though she might be a little crazy. So she decided to rethink her plan to introduce Bilal to the wolves. She had him wait in the living room while she dug through the closet to find a leash and a collar. She waved the leash in the air. "Wolf will hate this, but it's probably the best way."

She went outside and sat on the porch stairs. Wolf came up to her and plopped his head into her lap, waiting for a neck rub. Carmella indulged his wishes for a few minutes before slipping the collar and leash around him. "You need to be on your best behavior, boy. Do you hear me?"

Wolf watched her intently.

"You be good. Be a good boy!" She stood and led him into the house.

Girl watched from the yard, her ears perked.

Bilal had moved to stand behind the couch.

Carmella kept a tight grip on the leash, but Wolf wasn't pulling at it though he did watch Bilal warily.

"Come over here, Bilal. Just move naturally but slowly. No need to be afraid. He can't bite you while I'm holding him."

Bilal resisted the urge to rub his shoulder. It still ached, and the wounds on his belly offered a nagging discomfort. But he did as Carmella requested until he was standing next to her.

"Hold out your hand slowly and let him smell you."

112

Bilal did, moving as slowly as possible.

"Wolf, this is Bilal. Don't hurt him. Do you understand? He helped you once, boy and he helped me. You be good to him." Carmella continued to croon softly to the wolf, who sniffed at the offered fingers. He sat down and turned his head away as if he didn't want any part of the alien.

Bilal waited, and with encouragement from Carmella, Wolf sniffed the fingers again. His ears moved forward and then back.

Bilal didn't know what to make of it.

"Wolf," he finally said. "Please do not bite me again. I never did anything to you. Wolf, we have to get along." He spoke as if the animal could understand his words.

Carmella realized Wolf might be able to understand Bilal. If Bilal could communicate with the unborn baby, maybe he could be understood by Wolf, too.

"I'm going to let you go, Wolf, but you behave," Carmella said, unhooking the leash and removing the collar.

Bilal could do nothing but stand there trusting that the wolf would do nothing more to harm him.

Wolf avoided Bilal and walked to the door, scratching it to be let out.

Carmella let the wolf out. "I guess he has no interest in you."

Bilal didn't believe that in the least, but he followed Carmella outside.

Wolf had joined Girl at the edge of the yard and watched without showing aggression.

Carmella went about making a fire in the large fire pit. A metal grate covered the hole, and she slid a huge pan over it.

She looked at Bilal. "Now start filling buckets with water from the pump and dump it into the pot."

Bilal did as he was told, and when the water grew warm, he dunked the buckets into the simmering water and carried them upstairs, dumping them into the tub.

He yelped once when he burned himself with hot water that had splashed his legs, but that happened only once and he made sure it didn't happen again. It took many trips to get the tub half full.

When it was filled to Carmella's satisfaction, she handed him a fresh bar of soap, a wash cloth, a fluffy towel, and shampoo. She spent a few moments telling him how to use each, and he nodded in excitement about his first bath. As an afterthought she left the bathroom and returned with a toothbrush still in its wrapper and a brand new tube of toothpaste. She gave him instructions on how to brush his teeth and told him to do it every morning and every night for the rest of his life.

Bilal nodded solemnly.

Carmella left him alone to take care of his business and waited anxiously in her bedroom.

Fifteen minutes later Bilal came out of the bathroom with the towel wrapped around his body.

She saw him standing in the hallway looking like a drowned rat. He had soap everywhere, and his hair stood straight up.

She suppressed a smile. "Are you finished?"

He frowned. "Why does it itch?"

"Okay, get back in the tub."

He returned to the bathroom, dropped the towel on the floor, and climbed back into the tub. He wasn't the least conscious of his nudity.

Carmella almost stumbled, and her eyes nearly popped out of her head. She focused on his face, but soon he was sitting in the tub.

He looked at her expectantly for further instructions.

She had seen him naked when he was unconscious, but now that he was conscious—and he looked good walking naked through her bathroom—she had to calm her nerves. She stuck her hand into the water. It was still warm. She picked up the last bucket of simmering water and poured it carefully into the tub.

Bilal shivered and seemed to enjoy the warmth.

"Close your eyes," she said.

Bilal closed his eyes.

# Adaptation

She filled the bucket with some of the bath water and carefully rinsed him from the top of his dark hair down to his toes.

He gasped and rubbed his eyes.

"You still smell like cheese," she commented while picking up the shampoo. She poured a hefty portion into her hands and applied it to his hair, working up a good lather. When she was finished, she rinsed his hair with a bucket of water.

Next she picked up the washcloth and rubbed soap into it until it foamed, and then she ran the cloth over his neck, back, and shoulders taking care around his stitches. She wrung out the washcloth and scrubbed his face and ears. Bilal sat there without comment, but she could tell that he enjoyed it. She washed his arms and his pits, scrubbed his back, and ran the cloth lightly over his torso. When she met his eyes, she noticed his look of pleasure.

"It is nice to be clean," he said.

She smiled and nodded. With a slow swallow she told him to stand. "One of the most important places to wash are your genitals."

He stood, and Carmella handed him the soap and washcloth. He mimicked the motion of sudsing up the cloth and ran it down his pelvis.

Carmella looked down quickly and then away.

*Dear God,* she thought. She felt her body vibrate as if a chord had been struck inside of her. Her skin felt alive, her breasts seemed to fill, and her nipples ached.

And the space between her thighs seemed to come to life.

Bilal was concentrating on his penis and testicles. He ran the soapy cloth over them and realized something that he had never experienced before. He could become aroused. Bilal had not thought of sex. It was the least of his thoughts. Centaurians did not have a sexual nature. Procreation did not create a pleasurable sexual sensation. It was only a means to create life. Sex for pleasure rarely occurred, and he likened it to being tickled—it was nice but not something he strived for. Bilal had enjoyed the feeling of wrapping his tentacles around friends and loved ones more than he had ever enjoyed sex.

# Adaptation

He'd seen humans and other animals engage in sex. It did not arouse him, but it did intrigue him. He had never thought to do it. Humans almost seemed ridiculous when it came to their sexual desires. It seemed that they chased every small pleasure.

But the sensation that was engulfing his penis was surprisingly pleasant and different from anything he had experienced so far. He watched his penis thicken and lengthen as he rubbed the soapy cloth over it.

Carmella coughed.

Bilal looked at her and noticed her skin looked strange. A blush of red showed through her brown skin. He liked that look on her face—her eyes big and her lips parted.

Carmella abruptly turned and headed toward the bathroom door.

"I think you can handle it from here," she said. "And don't forget to wash your ass!"

# Chapter 17
## ~These Strange Feelings~

**Bilal wanted to** call after Carmella and explain that he wasn't pleasuring himself. Though he was not human, he had grown into adulthood around them. He knew that men did such things but only when they were in private — unless pornographic movie was playing. Then it might be acceptable to do so in front of others. At least Lawrence had seemed to think this way, though Raj — who surely became aroused, too — frowned on the practice of self-pleasuring around others.

Bilal felt a bit confused on the protocol, but he knew he would never do that in front of Carmella. He was, however, certain he would explore the sensations his penis caused him later. It had been one of the things he had planned to test out but had been sidetracked by being sick and staying warm.

After Carmella closed the bathroom door soundly behind her, Bilal looked down at the wilting penis resting in his hand. He wondered what it would be like to place the penis into Carmella the way that men did in movies. Suddenly it began to rise again. He shivered and focused on washing the rest of his body.

When he felt and smelled clean, he stepped out of the bathtub and brushed his teeth. Now his mouth felt clean, and that strange bad taste had disappeared. He watched the blackened water run down the drain in satisfaction.

Bilal left the bathroom with the large towel wrapped around his wet body, the door leading to Carmella's bedroom closed, the hall empty. He went down into the basement and found clothes to wear. After slipping on his own shoes, he looked down at himself, pleased he had taken his first bath.

**Carmella paced back** and forth in her bedroom. What had possessed her to allow this *man* to live in her house? Yes, he was an alien, but he was a man, too.

He wasn't dangerous.

Carmella stopped pacing. *Either kick him out or deal with it. But stop this. Stop it!*

She opened the door to her bedroom and went downstairs. "Bilal!" she called from the top of the basement stairs.

"Yes, Carmella?" He appeared at the bottom of the stairs.

*He cleans up nice,* Carmella thought. "Look. We're going to have to get some things straight if you're going to live here."

He walked up the stairs. "Okay."

She backed up to allow him space — or at least that is what she told herself. She clenched her teeth then steeled her resolve as she led him into the kitchen where they held most of their conversations. It seemed she was most talkative when they ate.

Bilal sat down in his usual chair, and Carmella sat in hers, frowning and narrowing her eyes.

*She is angry,* Bilal thought. He was used to it, though, and didn't think it was because he had done something wrong. Carmella was just an angry person.

"I need to know what your intentions are," Carmella said.

"I intend to take care of you and the child."

Carmella's eyes popped. "Take care of us?"

"You'll have an infant because of my actions. There is much that you will not be able to do. I will do it for you. You will have to tell me what to do to help you."

She took in the man with the strange pink glow to his skin. "Are you going to take this baby when you leave?"

"No. Not unless you want me to do that. I meant for you to have the child."

118

# Adaptation

"Are you going to force me to go with you when you leave?"

"No. I won't force you. Carmella, you have nothing to worry about. I'll never do a thing to hurt you."

Carmella sighed. "But what do you want? I know you want something. I know that you aren't doing this for me. And I can't trust you until you tell me what you're getting out of this. What is it that you want?!"

"I want to be human," he said.

Carmella didn't see that answer coming.

"I want to know what it's like to be a man, okay?" His brow furrowed and his skin turned pale purple. "I want what a human wants, except that I'm not supposed to want those things because I'm Centaurian. I'm supposed to want to be a dignitary, a lawmaker, a leader. My peers were humans, not Centaurians, so I never learned to want what my own kind wants. I learned that I was a human inside but an alien—a Blob--outside."

Carmella placed her fists on the tabletop. "You can't force me into the role of your wife or girlfriend or whatever the fuck you think I'm supposed to be! I'm not going to be that!"

Bilal shook his head. "No. I don't expect that."

"Then what do you expect?"

"I don't have any expectations. I'm happy that you allow me to see how you live and to let me be a part of it in some small way." He sighed. "I don't fit in. I *know* that. So I come to Earth and try to absorb a world that I was never meant to be a part of." He shook his head. "I don't have a world. I don't have a place. But when I'm here, when I'm on Earth, I feel at home. Even though I'm not human, this is *my* Earth, too."

Carmella rubbed her face. "Okay. This is hard because I don't remember how to share my life. And I'm not sure if I want to. But I don't have a choice. You're here and you aren't going anywhere for a long time."

"It doesn't have to be horrible," he said softly.

# Adaptation

She clenched her lips. "When someone takes *your* choices away from you, then you can speak to me about it. In the meantime, just ... move into your new room."

"My what?"

"Upstairs. There are no lights down in the basement at night, and I don't want you burning up the house with a kerosene lantern. And I don't plan on walking down those steps each night just to check on it! So you can move upstairs into one of the spare rooms. And later you can get up with the ... the baby at night."

"Yes. I will do that." He nodded enthusiastically.

Carmella showed him to a nice bedroom upstairs. It was nearly as large as her master bedroom. Bilal liked it much better than the basement because there was plenty of sunlight and a real bed. Carmella helped him put fresh sheets on it and tried to dust and clean before he shooed her out and suggested she lay down and nap for a while.

She gladly took his suggestion. She had skipped her midday nap and was exhausted, and the life inside of her was restless and kept moving. This pregnancy felt much different than her previous one. Her belly was much bigger, and she was much more tired. She lay down with a yawn and was asleep before her body had completely relaxed.

Carmella knew that she was dreaming because she was still on the outskirts of sleep. She was aware of her body relaxing in bed at the same time her dream self was in the bathroom washing Bilal's body with a soapy washcloth.

Bilal pushed his wet hair behind his ears and sat with his arms wrapped around his knees in contentment as she washed him. The washcloth moved over his toned body, and she marveled at the sight of tendons and muscles beneath his skin.

Carmella dropped the washcloth and allowed her fingertips to touch his warm skin. Skin, the touch of another ... She sighed softly then plastered her hands onto his back. Bilal looked at her, meeting her eyes. She couldn't take hers from the sight of his slanted lids which slightly obscured the dark orbs of his eyes.

# Adaptation

She reached out and ran her fingers along his cheek and felt a rugged growth of beard. God, how she missed rubbing her face against the fuzz of a man's beard! And not just that—she missed touching. She wanted to touch someone. She wanted to be touched.

Carmella awoke with a jolt. The sun had dropped low in the sky, and though she would have sworn she had only been asleep a few moments, she knew it was more like a few hours. She rubbed her fingertips over her thumb as if she could still feel Bilal's phantom skin from her dream. She climbed out of bed, left her bedroom, and went to Bilal's new room but he wasn't there. She went downstairs and heard sounds in the kitchen.

He had already washed dishes and was staring at two cans of soup. "Carmella?" he asked when he saw her.

She didn't answer. She walked forward until she was a foot in front of him, reached out slowly, and touched his cheek. She exhaled in anguish then raised both hands and cradled his cheeks while looking deeply into his eyes. "You're ... real? You're not a dream?"

Bilal placed his hands gently over hers. "I'm real."

Tears fell down her cheeks. "Okay. Will you touch me? Please?"

He nodded and used his thumb to swipe away her tears. He closed the space between them, gathered her into his arms, and held her tightly against his body.

Carmella shuddered but soon the shudders became quakes. She was shaking like a leaf while tears streamed down her face. She clutched Bilal, clinging to him desperately. Bilal felt his throat constrict. He squeezed his eyes closed and tried to breathe. It was hard to do because his chest felt tight and his skin felt hot. Tears slid from his eyes and down his cheeks.

He was crying.

Bilal was stunned. He had never cried before. Centaurians couldn't cry. But it was unmistakable. His body shuddered, and a horrid croak escaped his throat. It was horrible and hurt his heart. How did he make it stop?

What was this feeling?

# Adaptation

Adaptation

# Chapter 18
## ~Asking for Help~

**Carmella pulled back** and wiped her eyes. She was about to apologize and blame it on her hormones when she saw tears sliding down Bilal's face.

*He's crying,* she thought. *Is he crying for me? Or did he ...* Carmella staggered backwards as it all became clear to her. He had emotions that were no less heartfelt than hers or any other human's. Bilal was hurting, and it was because of her. Dear God, she had humanized a wolf but couldn't see that a talking, thinking being was worthy of the same consideration. Though Bilal was not born a human, he had the capacity for compassion and for pain and for ... forgiveness.

Bilal had ducked his head and turned his back to her as he swiped the tears from his eyes.

Carmella reached out and placed her hand on his shoulder. "I'm sorry, Bilal. I'm so sorry. I've been wrong in how I've treated you, and I feel horrible about it."

"Carmella? I don't understand."

"I've treated you badly, and you didn't deserve it. Will you accept my apology?"

Bilal didn't expect to be treated in any way other than the way he'd been treated. He had never perceived himself as being mistreated because he understood that Carmella hated him, and rightfully so. He had been a disruption to her life. Centaurians had disrupted her entire world.

# Adaptation

He shook his head slightly. "You don't need to apologize to me. You've done nothing wrong, Carmella. You've reacted to me based on everything that you've lost."

She grimaced. His kindness was unfathomable. It would be nice having him around, and that lifted her heart and made her smile.

He stopped talking as he watched the display of emotions cross her face. Human emotions were so easily displayed by a slight shifting of muscles beneath the skin. Centaurians showed their emotion through the change of color within their skin. He'd been disappointed to see that his skin wasn't the same color as other humans and that beneath it anyone could see his "emotions." But now he didn't care because he knew that his face could be as emotional as hers was. His lips pulled up into a smile, not because he made it do so, but from the sheer pleasure of watching her contagious smile.

"Friends?" she asked, not sure why she felt nervous.

"Do you want to be my friend?" Bilal asked.

"I haven't had a friend in a decade. Yes, I would like very much to be friends." She shook her head. "It's so much easier than being enemies."

"I would like that, too." Bilal's smile grew.

Carmella sat on the couch with two pillows against her back and her legs crossed beneath her. She rubbed the top of her belly unconsciously.

Bilal put another log into the fireplace. "This wood won't last all winter."

"No. You'll have to cut some before the weather gets bad."

"When will that be?"

"It's hard to say. Sometimes I've gotten my first snow by Halloween, and other times it's November. But since I don't like cutting wood in sub-zero temperatures, I usually have a good stack of wood by fall."

# Adaptation

He had seen her cutting wood. It didn't look difficult, but neither did many of the things that had nearly broken his back over the last few weeks. He sat down on the couch opposite her. "Okay, so what else do you want to know about Centaurians?"

She blinked. *Jody would have loved this.* She decided she would pay tribute to her young husband's memory by asking questions Jody might have asked. "Did Centaurians come to Earth for the purpose of teaching and learning?"

"Yes. We wanted to share knowledge. We didn't think that we would only teach. We also wanted to learn."

"What did you learn?"

"Lots! We learned how dynamic humans can be. Centaurians don't express themselves in the same way."

"What is your world like? It was destroyed, right?"

"Yes, a star collided with it. We knew that we only had three years to leave our planet—many weren't able to. But our world was underwater, as you probably know. Some humans call it Atlantis, which is fine because you would not be able to speak or understand our language. There are images in the mother ship. I find them incredibly beautiful, but nothing can compare to the beauty of Earth. I've never known any other world. Earth is my home."

Her back stiffened. "Mine, too, which is why I'll die before I relocate to some planet masquerading as Earth."

Bilal didn't want her to become agitated. "Carmella, some Centaurians chose to die with our planet rather than relocate. We understand. The decision to remove the remaining humans from Earth was not a decision that I agreed with. I've fought to change the minds of my people. But they only think about what they believe to be the best for the humans."

Bilal worried even more that Carmella would change her mind and go back to hating him again. He couldn't stand the idea of being alone when being her friend was so nice.

"I don't want to talk about this anymore," she announced. She struggled to stand, and he helped her. "Get your coat, Bilal. It's time for me to teach you how to cut wood."

He didn't tell her that he already knew how to cut wood.

125

He was just happy she didn't say, "Get your coat and get out."

**Bilal found that** he was wrong about Carmella's intentions. She told him that he wasn't able to use an ax yet or he'd open up the wound in his shoulder. Instead she had a much more horrible idea.

It was horrible in Bilal's estimation.

She pulled out a chainsaw. Bilal found that he hated seeing her holding the scary, loud machine almost as much as he hated the way Wolf stared at him from across the yard when Carmella's attention was averted. He'd seen a chainsaw in use and didn't like them. It was in a movie where he'd seen a scary man chasing humans around with it. Lawrence had said it was supposed to scare the shit out of him or it wouldn't be called a horror movie. Bilal had declined to watch the rest of it and generally shied away from horror movies.

"Carmella!" he shouted over the sound of the chainsaw motor. "I saw something that I think is a generator in the barn."

Carmella let the chainsaw idle. "I haven't tried to work that diesel generator in years."

"Will it heat your home when it gets cold?" Bilal asked.

"It would if I could find diesel fuel or more kerosene," Carmella replied. "That generator sucks fuel like a fish, and diesel fuel and kerosene are hard to find around here." She pushed a dreadlock over her shoulder and scowled. "Sometimes it took me weeks to find enough fuel to last a few days. It's just not worth the effort."

"I will go out and find diesel fuel and kerosene."

"What? What about the baby?"

"I would not leave until after the birth but before the first snow. I don't believe the fireplace will be sufficient to keep the house warm enough for an infant. When I find more fuel, we can utilize the generator on the coldest days and the wood to maintain the warmth."

"You're not going to find any, not around here."

"I will search," Bilal said.

Carmella stared at the wood. "Okay, I guess." She had worried about the firewood situation and knew she didn't have enough cut, split, and seasoned. "But how will you know where to look and what to look for?"

"Carmella, I've been traveling the face of Earth for years. It is what I do."

She smiled. That made two of them.

That night when she went to bed she snuggled under her blankets and felt contentment.

Bilal slipped beneath the sheets and sighed as his body relaxed.

This was nice indeed.

**The next few** days allowed the two to become better acquainted and more comfortable with each other.

Carmella didn't like complaining. She had been doing everything on her own for so long that she didn't know how to ask for help, but as the days progressed, the pain of her belly splitting became incredibly intense. Her human body wasn't accustomed to the rapid growth of the baby, and the baby was enormous. It was as if she carried twins.

Some days she would squat to pee in her slop bucket and pain would stab up from her groin to grip her belly. Sometimes she would stand at the sink and feel as if she'd explode if she took one more breath. There were times she could barely rise from the couch or a chair.

One morning a week after she and Bilal had become friends, Carmella awoke and sat up in bed. She swung her legs over the edge, but when she tried to stand a searing pain shot across her belly.

Gasping, she braced herself against the bed and froze, waiting for the pain to subside.

It didn't let up.

A moment later she felt wetness between her legs. She reached down because it felt thick and sticky.

"Bilal!" she screamed.

Her fingers were covered in blood.

**Bilal had been** up for a while. He'd already gone out to collect the eggs and milk the cow. He kept a careful eye pealed for the wolves. He still didn't trust them. Once he'd looked up from milking the cow to see the big wolf standing in the doorway watching him. Bilal had to stand up and loudly shoo him away.

Bilal brought the eggs to a basket on the counter and poured the milk into a bowl he covered with cheesecloth. He knew that Carmella would later whip it into butter and bake bread. He loved watching her transform unappetizing items into delicious meals.

When he grabbed the water pail, he heard Carmella stirring in her bedroom. He heard her gasp and froze, cocking his head. He headed for the stairs and was halfway up when he heard her scream. He dropped the empty pail and took the remaining stairs two at a time.

"Carmella!"

He burst through her bedroom door to find her bent over and holding her belly with one hand while staring at her other, bloody hand, her gown blood-stained.

She looked at him with panic in her brown eyes. "Help me."

# Chapter 19
## ~Baby~

**Bilal didn't think** — he reacted.

He scooped her up in his arms and placed her gently on the bed.

"Is something wrong with the baby?" Carmella tried to sit up, but a sharp pain gripped her, she gasped, and she fell back onto the bed, her face twisting in pain.

Bilal's normally calm face was stitched in concern. Although she couldn't see it, his hands trembled as he knelt on the floor beside her bed and pushed up the knee-length gown. He took in the way her belly ballooned out, stretched impossibly tight. Stretch marks marred her beautiful skin, and blood streamed out of her, matting the dark curls of her pubis.

*This isn't normal,* he thought.

Carmella tensed and cried out in pain. She gripped the bed sheets, unmistakable terror in her eyes.

Bilal pressed his lips to her belly button. He was afraid as well but knew that Carmella shouldn't see his fear. The baby was not due for three weeks. His lungs were underdeveloped even though he was already as big as a baby living outside of the womb for a month.

"It's not supposed to be like this ..." Carmella knew something was wrong. What if the baby didn't make it because she had mentally distanced herself from it—him? He. Her son. Her child. Tears stung her eyes, but through them she saw Bilal do that strange thing with his mouth on her bellybutton. His hands splayed on each side of the swollen mound that was now her stomach. How could it be that only five months ago her stomach had been flat?

She tensed when he connected with her through his sensors. It wasn't unpleasant, and soon the pain began to lessen. Her body relaxed, and she let out a held breath. She watched him, his long dark hair draped over her belly in silky wisps and relaxed even more. Somehow, she knew that Bilal would make it right.

When he looked up, his face seemed calm. "Better?" he asked.

She nodded. She felt better than she had in weeks. "Is he okay?"

"He's sleeping."

She felt a smile tugging at her lips.

"It's you I'm worried about," he said.

"Me?"

"Your pregnancy has progressed far too fast and for a child much too large for you to carry comfortably." A shadow fell over his face. "This is my fault. I never considered the size of the infant in conjunction with the … with you. And neither did the mother ship." He leaned back on his heels, but one hand remained on her belly. "Carmella, I am going to have to take the baby early."

"Take him?"

"He has to come now."

"But we have another month. Will he be okay?"

His eyebrows drew together. "He may, but you *won't* if we wait another month. You will not make it."

Carmella saw the tension around his eyes and mouth. Had it always been there? Why hadn't she noticed that he was hiding his fear? "But can't you do something?"

"I stopped the bleeding inside, but as soon as you move, you will begin to bleed again. You are splitting open from the inside. Every time he moves and every time you move a wound opens. Your body cannot accommodate this pregnancy any longer."

"But … but what about people who have multiple births? Hell, I remember this lady called the Octomom who—"

# Adaptation

"But our child is not completely human," Bilal interrupted. "In three weeks he will weigh approximately seven thousand grams."

"Grams? What the hell is a gram?"

"He will weigh over fifteen pounds."

Her mouth dropped open. "What if the baby comes early? What's going to happen to him?"

"He will have difficulty breathing."

"Then we can't do it," she said.

Bilal shook his head. "I didn't give you this child to replace you."

"But you did give him to me, and I say he stays in my belly!"

Bilal stood and sat on the bed beside her. He reached over and pulled her covers over her partially nude body. "There is a way. The mother ship can fix you."

"The mother ship? I'm not getting on any alien ship! You're *not* taking me to fake Earth."

"Carmella." He rubbed a gentle circle on her belly. "I won't take you there. Please calm down."

"You fixed me and you saved Wolf."

He looked at his human hands. "I can't fix you with these. I can't do what I need to do. I don't have enough sensors." Before he could have linked with her in several places, but now he could only use the stunted sensors in his tongue. He needed to connect to her spinal column to stop the pain completely but couldn't unless he pressed his mouth against her back. And how could he help deliver the child if he was connected to her back? This was such an ill-conceived idea. He hadn't considered any of the problems that she might face giving birth. He rubbed her belly again.

"Bilal, you can do this. I'll stay in bed. I won't do anything until the baby's lungs are stronger."

"It will not be easy," Bilal said. "You are not good at doing nothing."

"Trust me," Carmella said. "I promise to do nothing. And you can fix any tears that might happen along the way."

"And when the baby comes? Do you trust that I will repair any damage that his birth might cause?"

"Of course." And she meant it.

But Bilal knew that if they did it her way, there would be much damage to repair.

## "Bilal, look."

Bilal could tell by the tone of her voice that she was okay, but he stopped everything to see what had caught her attention. This was week two of her bed rest, and he had been running the entire house. He was in the kitchen preparing the bread. He'd seen her do it often enough, but his bread never turned out as good as hers did. "I'm coming," he shouted, and he dashed up the stairs.

Wolf lay outside her bedroom door, his head raised and his ears tilted forward.

Bilal met Wolf's eyes and regarded him warily as he stepped over his prone body. There was still no trust between them, but they had developed a grudging acceptance. Once inside the room, he saw Carmella propped up with pillows in bed, a beatific smile on her face. He couldn't help the smile that spread across his face at the sight of it.

He loved her.

He couldn't tell her, of course, because she would misunderstand and think that he wanted to covet her. He didn't. He only wanted to love her and to appreciate the hard life she had decided to live on her own terms.

"I can't believe this. Watch."

He moved to the bed and sat beside her.

Carmella was dressed in something she referred to as a "moo moo," and it was hiked up to expose her swollen belly.

# Adaptation

Blankets kept her discreetly covered below the mound because it was too difficult to get in and out of undergarments.

She placed her fingertips along the top of her belly at one side and ran them across to the other side. Bilal could see the impression pushing back and following the path of her finger. She beamed at him, and Bilal laughed. The baby was playing with her! "You try it," she said.

He reached out and ran his finger along the same path, and the baby followed the movement. They both started laughing.

"He's so smart," she said.

"He is. He is my son."

"Mine, too." Carmella smiled. "You're proud of him."

"I am, and I love him and … I'm not exactly sure why. I guess it's because he is a part of me and you and Raj and of course, himself."

"Raj is the friend you look like, right?" She knew that he had used Raj's preserved sperm, though she didn't want to know where Bilal got it. "Isn't he?"

Bilal didn't respond. He'd spoken of Lawrence and Raj in passing, but it made him sad to think of how badly he had betrayed them by stealing their DNA for his own purposes. It wasn't that he looked like Raj or had Lawrence's height. He was part Raj and part Lawrence, and his  son was as much Raj's son as it was his and Carmella's.

"You miss them," she said.

Bilal nodded. "Bilal, would you like to name the baby after Raj?"

He nodded. "Yes."

"Is Raj an Asian name?"

"His name is Roger. Roger Jeung. He told me that his parents were from North Korea but they immigrated to America. He and I were able to become such good friends because he was a mixture of cultures but identified with the world in which he was raised. We are both similar in that way."

It sometimes amazed her at how good-looking Bilal was. He was at least 6-3 and extremely muscular. She wondered if that was the influence of Raj or the other friend, Lawrence. What did Lawrence look like? He wasn't African American, and that was for sure.

She sighed. "I don't care for the name Roger, but I rather like the name Raj."

"I do, too. It would give me great pleasure to call our son Raj. But I have one request. I would like it if he had my last name — Akunyili."

She tested the name a few times. Raj Akunyili. It didn't matter to her, so she agreed. She remembered a time when movie stars and singers named their children after countries and primary colors. Giving the baby the name Raj Akunyili was a good way to show Bilal how much she appreciated his kindness over the last two weeks and hopefully beyond.

Bilal didn't understand why Carmella wanted his input in naming the child, but he was happy about it. After he got her settled again, he finished the bread and returned with a tray containing a breakfast of cheese omelets, toast, fresh milk, and hot tea. He had learned that she preferred eating in his presence, and he preferred it as well.

They sat and talked long after they finished their meals, and Carmella looked forward to his visits.

After breakfast she needed to use the slop bucket, and he helped steady her as she relieved herself. She always became embarrassed, but he didn't understand why. Wolf didn't become embarrassed when he relieved himself, and neither did the chickens or the cows — and neither did he.

He then spent half an hour linked to her bellybutton, searching for tears and injuries. It was taking longer and longer to repair them as the weakened areas tore with little or no stress. He studied the infant thoroughly, marveling at how quickly he developed. He withdrew his sensors and smiled. "Carmella, would you like your son to be born today?"

Her eyes widened. "How are his lungs?"

# Adaptation

"Healthy enough for him to be able to breath unassisted. If we do this now, he may still fit through your canal. If we wait much longer, it will be harder for you."

"I don't care about that."

"I do. I don't want to cut you unless I have to."

Carmella rubbed her face. No, she didn't want to be filleted like a fish. She searched his eyes. "Okay. Okay, let's do it."

Bilal didn't waste time. He gathered several sanitized razors, boiled water, and made sure the waterproof mat covering the mattress was in place.

He reached for her hand and held it, feeling the slight wetness that denoted her fear. Her face remained calm, but he knew that she had to be afraid, if not for herself and the prospect of the pain but for the baby and the unknown.

"We talked about this. I'm going to have you lay on your side so I can connect to your spinal column and block the pain. The effects won't last for long, but when the pain grows I'll do it again. Then I'll connect through your belly button and trigger the contractions. I'll need you to relax and let the baby move through your canal, and then I'll disconnect from you and deliver him. Okay?"

He made it seem easy. Could it be that easy? She nodded. "Okay."

She grimaced when she rolled to her side and Bilal removed the pillows. Instead of lying beside her, Bilal hurried to the door and opened it.

Wolf looked at him and rose to his feet, sniffing the air before padding into the room.

Carmella smiled and reached out for Wolf. "You're about to be an uncle."

Wolf settled at her bedside.

"Are you sure you want Wolf in here?" Carmella asked.

"If you sound as if I'm hurting you, then I fear Wolf might attack me once I open the door, especially if I have your blood on me."

"Ah, gotcha."

# Adaptation

Bilal removed his shirt and settled behind her. The swell of her naked rear created a brief diversion, but he put it out of his mind. He pressed his body against her, his face close to the small of her back, and latched onto her with his lips, letting his tongue rest against her spinal column. A moment later his sensors burrowed into her flesh.

Five minutes later, Carmella sighed. "Wow, Bilal, I don't feel any pain. How did you do that?"

He placed his hands around her belly from behind. Raj was awake and pressed back against his hand wanting to play. He communicated to his son that today was the day that they had discussed and that it was time for them to meet.

Raj stretched and Bilal felt Carmella tense.

*Careful, Little one.*

Bilal felt satisfied that Carmella would remain pain-free for at least an hour and moved to her front. He met her eyes. "Are you ready?"

She nodded. "As ready as I'll ever be."

He lowered his head and pressed his lips to her belly button. Raj was eager, and Bilal had to calm him when he rolled and wrapped the umbilical cord twice around his neck. Though the cord didn't squeeze Raj's neck, Bilal knew he had to unwind it as soon as possible and before he traveled down the birth canal.

Carmella was amazed that the pain had completely disappeared. Bilal was better than a spinal block. She thought about her baby. Raj. Raj Akunyili. Her heartbeat sped up. What would he look like? She realized that she didn't care.

Bilal sat up. "I want you to get comfortable now and get into position for the baby to move down." He helped to prop her pillows until she looked comfortable and then lay down a towel beneath her hips, her legs splayed widely. It seemed strange having Bilal crouched between her legs. She didn't like it because it seemed intensely sexual, and even though sex was far from her mind, the image wouldn't leave her.

# Adaptation

Bilal used a sheet to cover her legs then placed his hand on her belly. He pressed lightly, and she felt a strange pressure. It wasn't painful, but it made her feel as if she might pop.

~***~

**Bilal had to** block Carmella's nerves through the connection he created on her back three times. Each time gave her an hour's relief. As the minutes turned to hours, Carmella worried that she would need to pee again.

Then she heard the sound of water spilling.

Bilal sighed as the liquid began to gush from her body.

*That was a lot of water,* Carmella thought.

Within minutes that strange pressure grew. "What's happening?" Carmella asked.

"I can see the head," Bilal said.

"Is there hair?" she asked.

"Yes. Black and curly."

Carmella chuckled. She didn't mind when the pain returned in small degrees because it was still manageable. She watched Bilal as he peered between her legs and had a moment when she wanted to giggle. It wasn't so long ago that she had hunted him through the woods, and now she was spread-eagled beneath him with her ass hanging out!

"Carmella, you're going to need to start pushing."

"Wow, I can barely tell."

"Push only when I say to."

A moment later he gave the command and she pushed with all of her might.

But the baby didn't progress any further.

He was stuck.

137

# Chapter 20
## ~Baby Makes Three~

"**Bilal, it's** starting to hurt really bad now." Carmella squirmed in the bed. She squeezed her eyes closed, trying not to let the pain overwhelm her. When his magical "nerve pinch" ended, it ceased completely, and the pain was incredible.

"Carmella, I'm going to have to put you asleep this time."

"Asleep? But why?"

"Because I'm going to have to take the baby."

Her mouth dropped. "But, I wanted to do it naturally."

"He is stuck behind your pelvic bone. I can't break it, and he can't squeeze through it, so there is only one other choice."

Carmella sucked in a breath as another stabbing pain hit her.

Bilal rubbed her belly. "Trust me."

"And you know how to do this? Because you've never given a woman a Cesarean section before."

"Carmella, look at me."

She stared at him.

"I created a new life form. Of course I know how to do this. But I need to put you to sleep, and I need to do it quickly because Raj is tired."

"Okay," she said. "Do it. Don't let my baby suffer."

Bilal nodded and eased her onto her side.

Wolf sensed something different because he whined and placed his head on the bed where he looked at his mother with knowing eyes.

# Adaptation

Carmella spared him a quick stroke of his nose before the pain ripped through her and she screeched. Something had pulled inside, and this time she could feel the tearing. The pain was horrible, and she tensed and squeezed the bed sheets in her fists as she felt warm sticky fluid running from her body.

"Please!" she cried out.

Bilal was in position behind her, his tongue pressed against the small of her back and his sensors burrowing through to her nerves. He was searching for the nerves that would block the pain, and then he would make her sleep. He was going to use the sanitized razors, and he couldn't allow her to remain awake while he cut her. He wished he was still a Centaurian who had tentacles that could breach her skin without making incisions.

He shuddered at the damage he would have to cause to her.

While connected, he took a moment to check the baby, who was trying to push forward even though the way was blocked. He soothed him, and a few moments later both mother and son were calm and no longer struggling. When he withdrew his sensors, Carmella was in an induced sleep.

It made him sad that he would have to take her uterus along with their child. It was too damaged to retain, and he did not have the capacity to do major repairs in his current state. This was his fault. He was about to take away her ability to have a child with a human should she chose to do so in the future. And if she returned to hating him again because of it, then it would be perfectly understandable.

He had ruined her life.

**Carmella felt tired** but refreshed though her limbs were heavy and it was hard to move. She opened her eyes slightly and groaned as the small aches returned, but at least she didn't feel the terrible pain of before. She opened her eyes completely and saw Bilal pacing back and forth near the window.

## Adaptation

He held a bundle in his arms, and his attention was on it fully.

For a moment she couldn't move as she watched him. She'd seen Jody look at Micah in the same way, and it was obvious that this *man* loved his son. She had to swallow her longing, not for sexual intimacy but for missed companionship. As she watched him, she pressed her hand to her empty belly, marveling that she missed the feeling of carrying her baby.

"Bilal?"

He tore his eyes from the face of his child and smiled. "He's healthy and beautiful." He walked carefully to the bed.

Wolf followed closely on Bilal's heels, and Carmella took a second to think how strange that was.

She swallowed, afraid and anxious and happy, as Bilal placed the heavy bundle into her arms.

"Oh my God," she murmured as she stared down at her child. The light brown baby had awakened in her arms. Black silky curls covered his head like a halo, and slanted eyes did little to conceal dark brown eyes that watched her. Pressed against his little pink lips was a tiny little fist that he tried to suckle. His eyes eventually closed as he drifted back to sleep. Carmella couldn't take her eyes off him. "He's perfect." She looked at Bilal. "He's okay?"

He nodded and smiled. "Ten fingers and ten toes. Oh, and one penis." He chuckled.

Carmella unwrapped the blanket and saw plump tan legs, a perfect torso, and a perfectly formed penis. He was perfect. Perfect. She looked at Bilal in awe. "He's brown."

"Yes. He is brown like his mother."

She peered at Raj. "And Asian like his other father. But he is Centaurian, too, like you." She rewrapped him so that he wouldn't grow cold.

Bilal sat beside her and carefully pushed aside the blanket. Raj started and woke but began sucking his fist until he went back to sleep. Bilal gently touched a patch of goose pimples on Raj's side.

"What are those?" Carmella asked.

140

"This is where his sensor will appear. But not until he is a bit older."

She searched Bilal's face. "He's going to have a tentacle growing out of his side?"

"No. It will only appear when he wills it." He was happy that his son's sensor was located in a much more useful area than his own.

Carmella's frowned briefly but made no comment.

Carmella sent him to fetch a cloth diaper and pins, a clean washcloth, and warm water. When he returned, Wolf sat in the doorway in defense mode. Bilal eyed him, and Wolf stood to allow Bilal to enter without having to step over his prone body.

When Bilal entered the room, Carmella was nursing the baby. His son was partially asleep but sucking with gusto, his little fists pressed against his cheeks while contented ticking noises issued from his throat as he fed.

Bilal's stomach twisted, his heart began to ache, his mouth felt dry, and his knees felt weak.

He realized in that moment that he would never, ever let either of them go.

**Bilal had to** leave his family briefly in order to make dinner. He let Wolf outside, and Girl growled as if upset at having been left outside alone all day.

Bilal went to the kitchen and opened cans of soup and made cheese sandwiches. He knew that Carmella had a preference for tea, which she kept in abundance. He carried a tray upstairs and grinned when he saw that mother and son were both sound of asleep. Bilal placed the tray on the dresser, kicked off his shoes, and climbed into the bed. He turned on his side and placed a protective arm over both Raj and Carmella.

He had never known this level of contentment even when he could wrap his tentacles around his loved ones or when he could lie under a tree in his glade. That couldn't come close to the feeling of lying here with his family. After watching them sleep, he allowed himself to drift off to sleep while the chilly night wrapped around the cozy house with its small little family as its occupants slept in peace and contentment.

Carmella needed to pee and clean herself when she awakened. Bilal had cleaned her up amazingly well after the birth, and luckily she had still been out of it enough not to care that he'd done that for her. She blinked when she saw him sleeping beside her, his arm thrown across her and the baby.

Instead of getting up, she settled back in bed and she smiled down at Raj sleeping in her arms. He was the most precious thing. She bent to kiss his brow for probably the hundredth time since he was born.

She felt the gentle pressure in her bladder but had lost the desire to venture out of the warm bed. Bilal had changed the sheets at some point after the birth and had gotten her into a clean gown. She wasn't bleeding much, which she thought was strange. She reached down and lightly touched the incision on her belly, and it didn't hurt at all despite nothing holding it together but liquid bandage. Yeah, Bilal had done a good job. Already the torture of childbirth was fast becoming a distant memory.

She looked at the sleeping man with his light stubble and long silky hair that he kept loose. Sometimes she wanted to touch it, to brush it and pull it back into a braid. His skin no longer seemed odd. Today it was a bright and happy pinkish because he was happy. She knew what other colors meant, too. Gray was neutral, yellow was shame, purple was emotional, red was anger, and black meant pain.

She sighed, reached out, and took a strand of Bilal's hair between her fingers. It was everything she thought it would be, silky and smooth like strands of satin. She longed to smell it and rub her face against it. Weird. She was a weirdo. She released his hair and grinned at herself.

## Adaptation

She found herself gazing at him. He was pink. He was happy. Before she knew it she was snuggling deeper into his arms until her head was against his shoulder. She inhaled his aroma that went beyond the shampoo they both used, and it was an aroma that was distinctly his own. His scent soothed her, and soon she fell asleep.

# Chapter 21
## ~Abilities~

**Bilal stared into** Raj's face. His son was sleepy but tried to fight it in order to see the world around him, particularly his father. Eventually Raj drifted off to sleep. Bilal held him for a while longer enjoying the feel of the infant in his hands then placed him in the cradle beside Carmella's bed.

She was asleep as well, which was good. The incision was nearly healed though it had only been a day since the birth. He couldn't do much with one set of sensors, but he could do that. Yet he was concerned, not for her health but for her reaction to the news he had to tell her. He had taken her ability to ever birth another child.

He moved one long dreadlock where it had fallen across Carmella's neck and positioned it on her pillow. He then went outside to finish the chores, and he was in deep thought as he did them. He was surprised to see that Wolf had left his position outside Carmella's bedroom to follow him outside. Bilal wasn't afraid of him any longer. Wolf could have harmed him, but Bilal no longer sensed aggression in the animal. Wolf even placed himself in a position to protect Bilal when he was outdoors.

Wolf walked the circumference of the yard and chased away several stray raccoons and muskrats. Afterwards he sat with Girl and watched from the outskirts of the yard. It was probably a good thing. Bilal didn't carry a gun and wouldn't know how to shoot straight even if he did. He never had use for one in all of his travels.

# Adaptation

When he was fully Centaurian, his outer skin was nearly impervious to bites and he possessed stingers that could be deadly. He was swift and could easily blend in with his surroundings. As a human, however, he was sadly inadequate. Bilal realized there were many things he had failed to consider when making his rash decision to become human.

And because of it, he had destroyed a woman's life.

When he returned to the house hours later he saw that Carmella was moving around the kitchen easily and carrying the sleeping baby in the crook of her arm.

"You shouldn't be out of bed," he said.

She smiled and shrugged. "I feel really good." She lightly patted her still swollen belly. "You did a great job. It barely hurts at all." She smirked. "You sure there's not another baby in there?"

His skin turned a strange shade of yellow.

She cocked her head at him. "I'm kidding Bilal, lighten up." She turned back to the stove. "I'm starting dinner. White chicken chili all right with you?"

"Uh, yes." He washed his hands and offered to take the baby while she cooked.

She gave her son a brief kiss on his forehead and passed him to Bilal.

He sat in a kitchen chair and decided now would be a good time to tell her the bad news. "Carmella."

"Bilal, can you grab a can of tomatoes from the pantry?"

He rose, found a can, and handed it to her. "Carmella, I—"

"We have enough supplies," Carmella interrupted, "but I'd feel better if we can go out and get more before the first snow falls."

He scrutinized the pantry and knew that with three consuming the food it would be necessary to go out for dry and canned foods. He felt guilty for using her resources.

"Carmella, I have to tell you something."

She turned to him. "Yes?"

"I should have told you this before, but I ..." He sighed. "During childbirth you were hemorrhaging badly. So badly in fact that it risked your life. I was unable to save your womb, deal with

145

the incision, and help Raj to be born. I didn't have enough hands and—"

"Wait," Carmella interrupted. "Are you saying that I no longer have a uterus?"

"Yes. I had to take your uterus." Bilal's skin turned a deep grey which edged towards black.

Carmella bit her lip. Then she threw her hand in the air and made a fist pump while whooping loudly. "Thank you, *Jesus!*"

Bilal was stunned. "You aren't angry?"

"No."

She stood before his seated figure wearing sweat pants, fuzzy socks, and a man's over-shirt. Her hair was pulled into a makeshift ponytail at the back of her head, and her eyes were twinkling and merry. He thought she was absolutely beautiful.

Bilal had always seen beauty through the eyes of the human he had wished to be. There were plenty of beautiful humans, male and female, dark and light, big and small. But even the ones who were not physically beautiful were still appealing to him for some reason. Wrinkles were meant to be explored while freckles and pimples were landscapes that intrigued him.

Carmella was not "technically" beautiful, not in the way that other humans gauged each other. She didn't have massive breasts and a tiny waist, and her hair did not look like silky strands. But to him, she stood worlds apart from any human or Centaurian that he'd ever seen.

"I am so happy to be free of that monthly nightmare," she said. Monthly? She wished that her cycle had only been monthly. Its severity and frequency made her life difficult, and that didn't factor in the number of female personal products she had to keep on hand. She had already cleared out all of the stores in her area over the many years she had lived on the farm.

Bilal shook his head. "I thought you would be angry. You won't be able to have any more children because of what I did."

"What? Children? Bilal, I never said that I wanted any more children." She glanced down lovingly at her beautiful sleeping son. "I love Raj. I love him to death." It had only been one day since giving birth and she couldn't love him more. She met Bilal's eyes again. "But I'm not having any more children."

"But, what if you meet … a human?"

"I'll never meet another human. And I'm not going to that fake Earth. *This* is my Earth."

"I understand. This is your world. But you aren't the only person on Earth. You could meet someone here."

"I don't want to," Carmella said. She had Raj to care for, and she wouldn't be quick to welcome another person into her environment. She shook her head and returned to the stove where she poured the open can of tomatoes into a pot with some leftover chicken.

He relaxed when she didn't say anything more. He was still surprised that she was far from angry about not having a uterus. He was relieved, though he wasn't exactly happy.

He looked down at his son and thought that there would not be another like this one.

~***~

**After dinner, Raj** cried for the first time.

Bilal nearly dropped the plate he was washing as he rushed into the living room where Carmella was reclining on the chaise holding the baby while Wolf barked to be let in.

Carmella smiled at and cooed to Raj, who waved his fists angrily.

Bilal moved closer to assess him for injury. "Why is he crying?"

"He's ready for his dinner."

As Bilal stood over them, he saw little tears appear in his son's eyes. It was nearly Bilal's undoing. "Please, Carmella, do something."

"He's only a little hungry, Bilal. He's a greedy one." She reached into her shirt to withdraw a swollen breast. She shoved a dark nipple into the baby's eager mouth, and Raj stopped crying

147

and began to drink hungrily. In a few moments he was asleep again.

Bilal watched the teardrop in the corner of his son's eye until it disappeared. "I didn't think …"

"You didn't think what?"

"That he would cry tears."

"Tears aren't necessarily a bad thing," Carmella said. "People cry from happiness as well as sadness. Right now, this is the only way that Raj knows how to communicate."

He reached down and touched Raj's face. "I still don't like it."

**But Bilal would** learn to understand it.

As the baby grew stronger, so did his lungs. He cried, slept, ate, and dirtied his diaper. Bilal never got used to the tears, but he realized that they didn't always appear when Raj bellowed loudly. Sometimes he cried just to hear himself, and sometimes he cried to strengthen his lungs. He even did it because he knew it would bring his mom or dad. Wolf would run in a different direction whenever he heard Raj's high-pitched cries and often darted to the front door, whining to be let out.

"You should be used to this, Wolf," Carmella said while juggling the crying baby in one arm and opening the front door to let Wolf out to join his wife. "You've had four litters already. You cannot tell me that your babies don't cry."

Bilal waved at her, and she smiled and waved back. He was on laundry duty today. It was easier to take turns so one person could sit with the baby. He never complained about the many chores he had to do outside in the cold. It was the middle of November, and winter was upon them although snow had yet to fall.

When Raj was a month old, Bilal talked about heading out for more kerosene and supplies, but Carmella did not want to stay behind. "I will go along with you," she said. "I need to get away from this place for a little while."

But Bilal seemed reluctant to bring Raj along. At one month old, he was a remarkably alert baby, following them with his eyes, cooing and laughing and interacting with them in the way that a much older infant might do.

Whenever Carmella looked into Raj's eyes, she knew without a doubt that he was aware of who she was and what was going on around him.

She jiggled him as he cried. "Are you hungry, little man?"

Taj yelled even louder.

"Okay, honey. Mommy's coming." She grabbed a book she had been reading during feedings and moved to the comfy chaise near the living room fireplace. "Shh," she cooed as she got comfortable. She released her breast, and as soon a Raj saw it, his mouth searched hungrily for it. She watched as he settled down and fed.

Carmella stared into his chocolate eyes. For the millionth time she wondered about the other Raj, Roger, his second father. How much of this stranger's personality was in her son? Did he even know he had a child? Maybe she should ask Bilal about it, but talking about his friends always made Bilal turn purple. Purple wasn't as bad as black, but it was not a good color for his emotional state.

She studied her son's light brown skin. It never changed tints. She stroked his hair and wondered if the curls would stay. She smiled at him. "I love you, son. I love you so much."

Raj stopped suckling. He stared at his mother and an instant later she felt something piercing as it stabbed through her nipple.

The pain was terrible as it tore through her and almost paralyzed her. The pain stole her breath but only for a moment, and then she screamed. Carmella's body went rigid before jerking involuntarily and curling into a ball on the floor.

Bilal heard Carmella's pained screech, dropped the clothes he had been washing, and darted toward the house, Wolf and Girl at his heels.

149

# Adaptation

Raj and Carmella were both on the floor, the baby crying softly and Carmella rocking in a ball of pain with her mouth opened in a breathless cry. Her hands cradled her breasts, and when she could, she sucked in a deep breath and screamed another bloodcurdling cry.

# Chapter 22
## ~Pleasure~

**Bilal scooped up** the baby with one hand and pressed him safely against his body. With the other hand he pulled Carmella from the floor, and sat, holding both of them on the chaise lounge.

"Carmella."

Carmella clutched her exposed breast, her eyes clenched tightly and squeezing out tears while Raj waved his hands in the air, his cries intensifying.

Bilal didn't know what to do. He looked at Wolf, half expecting the animal to give him advice. Wolf only whined, staring at him expectantly.

"Carmella." Bilal pressed his face against her neck and inhaled, searching for some injury but not finding anything. He placed Raj across his legs, jiggling them, but the baby had worked himself up into such a state that his piercing cries stole his breath as he trembled.

Bilal grabbed Carmella's wrists and pulled them away from her body. Her exposed dark nipple dripped milk, but there was nothing strange about that. He shook her slightly when her eyes stayed squeezed shut. "Carmella."

She opened her eyes.

"What's wrong?"

"Hurt," she whispered.

"Where?"

"Breast. He did something …"

# Adaptation

Bilal touched her breast, and Carmella winced. It was soft and heavy with her milk. He frowned. "Carmella, I don't see anything." He released Carmella's wrists and picked up the crying baby.

Raj's normally tanned skin had turned pink. He placed his hand on the child's cheeks and pressed until his mouth opened. He saw small sensors on the tip of his son's tongue. They were tiny, not much thicker than thread.

"Shh," he crooned. "Daddy's here." He placed the tip of his finger against his son's tongue, and the filaments retreated. Yes, his son had learned. He wouldn't be so quick to touch anyone with them again. He would need this ability as he grew older. Thankfully he was too young to have poison, but the pain of connecting his nerve endings to Carmella would have been unbearable. Raj shouldn't use them again until Bilal had properly trained him.

Bilal nodded at Wolf. "Here, Wolf."

Wolf shambled over to him.

"Lay down."

Wolf circled and lay down.

Bilal placed Raj against Wolf, cradled against his belly. Carmella had done it before to get them acquainted. Wolf knew to stay put. Bilal watched him lick the crying baby's head. Satisfied, Bilal turned his attention to Carmella, pulling her into his lap. Her hands were crossed protectively over her chest, and though she was no longer sobbing, tears escaped her tightly squeezed eyelids.

He gripped her wrist with his right hand and pulled it back. He gently held her breast with his left hand, lowered his head, and covered her nipple with his mouth. Sweet milk flooded his mouth. He had thought it would taste like cow's milk, but it was much sweeter.

He concentrated on his task, releasing his sensors and allowing them to burrow into the flesh of her nipple. Carmella whimpered and tried to pull away, but he held her securely in place. He found the trail that his son's sensors had traveled, repaired the damage Raj's curiosity had caused, and released enzymes that acted as an anesthesia.

Carmella relaxed but otherwise didn't move.

Bilal was curious. There was something else here. He stretched the filaments of his sensors and found the old injury from the wolf attack. When he had repaired her, he hadn't been able to focus on making her perfect, only keeping her alive because he was near death himself. Now he could see the scarring and was ashamed that he'd left such a mess.

Bilal stimulated Carmella's body to reproduce healthy cells and forced the scar tissue to recede and to disappear. He went over his work and made necessary repairs and several improvements.

Bilal retracted his sensors, swallowed the last of the milk, captured the last drop with a flick of his tongue, and released her nipple.

Carmella watched him with wide eyes. "What are you doing?"

"I fixed it. The injury."

"Which one?"

"From the wolf bite. Raj found it. He was trying to explore it."

She tore her eyes from his to her son, who had cried himself to sleep in the comfortable fur bed Wolf provided. "I want to see it."

Bilal glanced down at her exposed breast where milk dripped steadily.

"Not that. Your tongue. Those ... things. Your sensors."

He opened his mouth and stuck out his tongue. She saw that his tongue was longer than normal but not in a deformed way. And then thin little translucent strings pushed from its tip, stretching and reaching forward. She was mesmerized as she watched them wave in the air.

She reached up and placed her fingers in front of his lips, and the sensors touched her fingers lightly. Though she wanted to, she didn't snatch her fingers away. She took a deep breath and met

153

his eyes. "I thought you said that Raj's tentacle will come from that patch on his side."

Bilal's sensors returned to their hiding place, and he closed his mouth. "It will. But apparently he will have more than one set of sensors."

"Well, how many?"

"I don't know yet. I'll examine him again later and try to find them all. But this is a good thing. He can be more helpful if he has more areas that he can link from."

Carmella covered her breast and moved off Bilal's lap.

Bilal instantly missed her warmth.

She knelt on the floor before Wolf and gently lifted Raj, who made a face but continued to sleep. She cradled him in her arms and looked at Bilal. "He's okay? I didn't hurt him when I dropped him, did I?"

"He's pretty tough."

She looked down at her son. "He was ... exploring?"

"Yes. He loves you Carmella. He would never intentionally hurt you." Bilal suspected it went further than that but found his suspicions hard to believe because Raj was only a few months old.

It appeared that Raj had been trying to heal the old wound to his mother's breast.

**Carmella tossed and** turned in her bed that night. Raj could sleep through the night and had been moved to his own room weeks ago. With his parents' bedrooms only steps away, either could be in his room to tend to his needs in seconds.

She had been afraid to nurse him later in the evening, but Bilal sat next to her assuring her that he wouldn't hurt her again—and he hadn't. Carmella stared into Raj's eyes as he nursed and sensed his awareness and intelligence. His eyes bore into hers, and Carmella felt unsettled, wishing she could understand the meaning behind that look.

# Adaptation

She bathed him, changed him, and kissed him. "I won't baby talk to you again. No more baby talk. I don't know how much you can understand, but I know that you didn't mean to hurt me, okay? I know that. Just don't do that again, okay?"

He stared at her calmly, and she felt like a dumbass. This was a baby, only a little baby. Because one of his fathers was an alien with heightened abilities didn't mean that Raj was a little adult. She kissed him again and placed him in his crib. Wolf came in and lay by the crib. She gave Wolf an appreciative rub and went to bed.

But sleep was hard to come by. This was a strange life. She had a baby who could use his tongue to create unimaginable pain, and her baby's daddy ...Carmella closed her eyes trying not to remember the sight of Bilal's head against her breast, her nipple captured in his warm mouth. Once the pain left there was nothing but a sense of pleasure so pure that it shocked her. She hated to admit it, but it felt good. It took all of her control not to wrap her legs around him and beg him to ...

Carmella covered her face in shame. What was she thinking?! She drew in a shuddering breath and bit her lip, squeezing her thighs together in an attempt to rid of herself of the erotic throbbing there. Her memory of Bilal's hands stroking his penis while in the bath flooded her memory, the sight of it growing caused her to groan.

She had not been touched in that way in so long. She thought about the way his throat had bobbed as he swallowed her milk, the way her body pulsed, and the explosive swelling between her thighs. Her breath shot out of her mouth, and she swallowed her cry of pleasure. Oh God ... no way was she ...

Carmella rocked her hips and sighed until the pleasure ebbed away and her heartbeat stopped racing.

Bilal liked listening to his family sleep each night. No matter how tired his body was, he always made sure to listen to the soft

155

breaths of Raj and Carmella's low, even breathing. It always put him to sleep. Tonight she didn't sleep. He could tell that she tossed and turned.

Bilal closed his eyes and opened his mouth. The sensors in his tongue pushed forward and tested the air. He could "see" her through her breathing and heart rate. Bilal turned on his side and listened, recognizing the familiar sounds for what they were — self-pleasuring. Of course he knew the sound. He pleasured himself nearly every night while remembering videos that Lawrence liked to watch.

"Hey, B," Lawrence had said. "See if you can find some good porn when you're down there ..."

He understood it all now. Sometimes the remembered images helped fire his nightly masturbation session, but he always pictured Carmella in the scenes because it seemed everything was about Carmella.

He listened to her soft sighs and tasted her passion on his sensors. His hand moved down his torso and beneath his pajamas where he found his penis hard and throbbing. Bilal closed his eyes while he rubbed his fingers over the hard flesh.

He knew that his penis was impressive because he'd seen enough porn. He also he knew that he was more endowed than either of his friends. It wasn't his design to make himself that way, and he wondered if it felt so good to touch himself because there was more to feel.

He wrapped his fingers around the hard flesh and squeezed slightly, shuddering at the sensation. When semen oozed from hole at the tip, Bilal rubbed it into the head and shaft to create a lubricant. He sighed and suppressed his groans. Touching himself felt good, but it would not be good to have Carmella hear.

Bilal's fist moved rapidly over his shaft as he thought about dark nipples, large areolas, and the taste of sweet milk ...

His ejaculation was so powerful that he had to bite back his cry of pleasure.

He couldn't stop thinking about her.

# Chapter 23
## ~Turning the Corner~

**Carmella was in** the kitchen preparing lunch. It was a rare to find her without the baby propped up on her hip or asleep. Bilal was in the living room with Raj, and she considered how far she had come. She remembered once telling Jody that she didn't want her baby near one of "those things."

Now her baby was partially one of "those things."

Every so often she would have a fit of uncertainty concerning the direction her life had taken, and it usually went away as soon as she set eyes on her beautiful baby boy. When he smiled at her or kicked his pudgy feet and played with his toes, she was overwhelmed with love for him.

Carmella wondered if it was love for her son that changed her feelings for Bilal so drastically. It wasn't because she had been alone for so long. Lonely people did not resort to going out of character or departing from their true natures. Racists might be lonely and keep company with other ethnicities if forced to, but they would still be racist, wouldn't they?

Carmella decided that her change in feelings had nothing to do with her need for company but her growth and acceptance of the unknown. She was willing to accept Bilal as a man because she knew he was no more or less a human than she was.

She poured the rice into the saucepan. She was ashamed that she felt physically attracted to Bilal. He was someone she accepted as her equal, but he wasn't really a man even if he had a nice penis. Her cheeks grew warm. He was incredibly attractive to

# Adaptation

look at, and he was strong. He was intelligent and had the capacity for emotions. So what did it matter that he was an alien and the body he resided in wasn't the one he was born with?

She had no idea how old Bilal was. He had to be younger than her, and she was damn near forty. She felt her cheeks warm again. What in the hell was she thinking? He was a fucking alien, and that was more important than anything else. She rubbed her elbows and decided that she would ask him.

She opened up two cans of black beans and smiled. Bilal liked black beans and rice, especially when she took the time to dice onions and peppers into them. Unfortunately the bell peppers were all gone—

"Ugh!" Bilal cried from the living room.

"Bilal?" Carmella nearly dropped the can as she dashed into the front room.

Bilal turned to her with a scowl on his face.

Raj was on the couch playing with his toes, much of his body covered in shit.

Carmella stopped as she was hit with the stench.

Bilal's face twisted in disgust. "That is the most horrible smell. That is worse than cow and chicken feces. That smells worse than *my* feces!"

Carmella gasped and hurried to the couch where Raj gave her a nonchalant look before gurgling and concentrating on his toes again. "What happened?"

Bilal backed away from the couch. "I decided I would help by changing Raj's diaper. I didn't think it would be difficult. You make it look easy. It was a mistake. Feces began to pour from his behind." He gave Raj an accusatory look. "He began to defecate as soon as I took the diaper off."

Luckily Bilal had placed the baby on top of the afghan, but shit was all over her child. "Oh, Raj, what did you do to your daddy?" She turned to Bilal. "Put the teapot on so I can give him a quick bath."

"I need a bath, too," Bilal said. "He urinated on me."

158

# Adaptation

Carmella tried not to laugh, but she couldn't help it because Bilal looked so helpless covered in baby urine.

Bilal cocked his head at her. "Why is this funny?"

She tried to stifle her laughter. "I'm sorry, Bilal. I can't help it. You look so funny!"

He shook his head, turned, and headed for the kitchen.

"Oh Bilal, I didn't mean to laugh at you! Where are you going?"

"To put on the teapot so that I can give Raj a bath — or better yet, so that you can."

Raj looked at her curiously, smiled, and gurgled.

"You got him good," Carmella said. "But how'd you get your own shit on your shoulders?"

She undressed Raj and tossed the soiled clothing into the corner to be washed before they dried and became impossible to deal with. She carried Raj into the kitchen.

Bilal stood by the cook stove waiting for the teapot to warm up. He had removed his shirt and was wearing only jeans and boots. His long black hair fell down his back in unruly waves.

The sight of Bilal stopped Carmella in her tracks.

"The water should be warm enough now," Bilal said.

"Oh, uh, yeah." She handed him his son while she put a stopper in the drain and poured the water into the sink.

Bilal held Raj out an arm's length away from him. "You smell."

Raj gurgled happily.

Carmella shook her head and hid a grin. "You know, babies are prone to pooping and peeing on themselves — and others. Don't take it personal."

Bilal's eyebrows gathered as he passed the soiled baby back to her. "I know that. But he waited until the diaper was off before defecating."

She had another spontaneous eruption of laughter, which she tried to mask by coughing.

Bilal was far from pleased as he tested the water. "It's warm. Put him in. I'll start his wash." He returned a minute later with

159

# Adaptation

baby wash, a washcloth, and a towel, which he placed on the counter.

Raj had a bath every night. Bilal knew the routine well, and despite what he had said about the wash, he began bathing the baby.

Carmella peeked at him. He was handy and so cute with or without a shirt, but she preferred without. She allowed her eyes to scan his perfectly toned torso, which had returned to an even-tempered tannish gray. She wished everyone's moods would be as transparent. What would he think if he knew what she was thinking now? What color would he turn? She looked away.

Raj was busy splashing and slapping the surface of the water as his dad washed him. Both father and son held exactly the same serious expressions on their faces as they concentrated on their perspective tasks. Raj could sit up on his own, but so far only in the sink. She thought Raj was advanced for a two-month-old, but it had been a long time since she'd been around a baby. Maybe it was normal.

Bilal finished washing his son, swept his long hair out of his way, leaned forward, and kissed the top of Raj's head.

Carmella blinked. She had never seen Bilal do that even though she kissed Raj every day—maybe every hour. Something cracked in Carmella. Maybe it was the last straw she had clung to in an attempt to hold on to the last piece of her past. But her past only held hatred and mistrust, and it was time to let that go. She suddenly wanted to kiss Bilal and to be kissed in return. Her heart ached at the longing. Bilal loved her son, *their* son. Even when he was disgusted at having to face his poop and pee, he still loved his son.

Carmella realized that she trusted Bilal implicitly.

She leaned forward, wanting her lips to touch his sensuous ones, wanting to run her fingers through his silky strands.

Bilal's turned and met her eyes with a piercing stare.

She froze, her mouth open.

"What is that?" he asked. "Is something burning?"

"Oh shit!" She jumped to attention and hurried to the stove where smoke billowed from the pot of rice. She removed the pot and set it on the counter. The rice was ruined. "Well damn."

"It's okay." Bilal wrapped Raj in a towel. "I'll eat it."

"You'll eat anything."

He shrugged. "Yes. I probably would, but I wouldn't enjoy it." He smiled. "I always enjoy your meals, though."

Her heart fluttered. "You might not enjoy this." She tilted the pot toward him.

Bilal looked into the pot. "Rice is normally white, isn't it?"

"Maybe I can scoop off the top," she said.

His eyes scanned her face until she turned back to the stove and fiddled with the cans of beans.

"I'll put a diaper on Raj," Bilal said as he left the kitchen.

"And a clean jumper, okay?" Carmella called.

"Okay."

Bilal carried his son upstairs to his bedroom and placed him on the changing table. "Raj," he whispered, "please do not pee or poop."

Bilal figured out how to put on the disposable diaper and dressed Raj in a clean jumper. He lifted the baby in his arms and looked at him.

Raj reached out for some of his father's hair to pull, and Bilal let him until he tried to put it into his drooling mouth.

Bilal carefully untwined it from around Raj's pudgy little fingers and smiled at him. Bilal thought about Carmella and the way her heartbeat began to race when he smiled at her in the kitchen. What did that mean? No, he knew what it meant. Did his smile excite her? He shook his head and smiled again, this time to himself.

**After putting Raj** into his crib for a nap, Bilal returned to the kitchen wearing a clean shirt. The table held two bowls of black beans and the rice Carmella had salvaged. Slices of fresh baked bread were placed on the table alongside freshly churned butter and two bottles of iced tea.

Carmella sat in her usual seat. "Raj asleep?"

"He will be shortly. He is playing with his feet again. For some reason he finds his toes interesting."

She looked at Bilal. "Well, have a seat."

He took a deep breath. It was now or never time. He had a more than a suspicion, and he needed to know if he was right.

Bilal held out his hand to her.

Carmella frowned and slowly placed her hand in his.

He pulled her gently until she was standing before him.

"Carmella." He swallowed. "I get a feeling in my belly that is not like hunger or fullness. They call it butterflies, I think. Sometimes my heart races and my palms sweat. Sometimes I have a difficult time catching my breath. It mostly happens when I am thinking about you, which means it happens all of the time."

Carmella's mouth dropped open. "What?"

Bilal took a deep breath and leaned forward. He knew the feeling he had was one she shared as well. Her heart raced, her breathing became shallow, and her hands trembled slightly. If all that happened when she thought of him …

Their lips met, and he half-expected her to pull back.

She didn't.

He sighed against her lips then reached up to touch the line of her jaw. Bilal kissed her, and although he had never kissed anyone like this before, it wasn't foreign to him. He'd seen it done countless times. He closed his eyes and thought about what he'd seen in movies or while observing his friends and other humans. As he kissed her, he quickly forgot to think. He became awash with emotion brought on by the proximity of her body.

Carmella didn't try to think or reason. When his lips touched hers, she was lost. Her hands closed around his arms and held him.

Bilal's knees felt weak and his heart was pounding. His hand moved to the back of her neck, his fingers captured by her dreads. He stroked a dread lovingly and then pulled back.

# Adaptation

When Carmella felt the loss of his lips on hers, she opened her eyes. After a moment she reached up and captured a few strands of his hair, feeling Bilal shudder as if her hands had stroked him. Her heart raced even faster. "Bilal, I ..." She lightly bit her lips. "Bilal, I know how you feel ... because I feel the same way about you."

Bilal exhaled. "Carmella, what does this mean for us?"

"I don't know Bilal, but I don't think we should try to figure it all out at once. Is that okay?"

He nodded. "Yes. We must not figure this out all at once."

He wrapped his arms around her body and pulled her into a hug, holding onto her tightly. It was like wrapping his tentacles around someone he loved but better, a million times better.

"I want you to know that I want you," he whispered.

# Chapter 24
## ~The Truth~

**Carmella stiffened and** pulled back from his embrace. "What? Bilal, I think we need to take things slow. I mean, this is a lot for me. I never thought I'd ever come this far."

He raised his eyebrows. "Go slow? We are in a place that I could have never dreamed. I wanted for you not to hate me. And now you tell me that you care for me as much as I care for you. I can't ask for anything more. Slow? This is anything but slow. I'm content, Carmella. I will stay in this spot with you for as long as you need me to."

She relaxed and smiled. He wasn't thinking about sex, but she was. What did that mean?

As they ate their lunch, Carmella decided to find out more information about the man she was now living with. "So, how old are you?"

He finished chewing his beans. "I was six Earth years when we first arrived in the mother ship. To you, it was twenty-two years ago, but in actuality we were here five years before that observing and learning about your world. Your scientists knew and began communicating with us even then. When we finally arrived in the sky, you were told that it was a 'mysterious' appearance. But it wasn't. We were invited."

*So the world conspiracy was five years in the planning,* she thought. *And all we invited was disaster.*

She sighed and suppressed her mounting anxiety. "So you are thirty- two, thirty-three?"

# Adaptation

"Thirty-two Earth years."

"Good." She smiled. "I was afraid you were underage."

He inhaled and exhaled deeply. "In my culture you are not an adult until you leave your parents' home and begin your own household with your spouses."

"Spouses?"

"Yes, Centaurian marriages usually consist of two males and two females."

She frowned. "Why?"

"We had limited space on the mother ship, and out of necessity families combined. Some untraditional families have developed since we arrived that contain only one male and one female because we have more space and are adapting again. A Centaurian can live for several hundred years. So in the eyes of my people, I am still a child."

"So you still live with your parents?"

"I technically live with my First Mother. She has separated from the family unit, and I joined her. But I have my own quarters."

She couldn't read his emotions. His face was peaceful, and his skin was pink like Pepto-Bismol. She wondered exactly what pink meant. "Do you ... have a girlfriend?"

"No," he said. "Centaurians do not socialize in the way that humans do." He finished his beans and rice and got up for a glass of water. "Centaurians go to the mother ship and share with the ship, and that is entertainment, socializing, even sex."

"What?"

He sat drank, happy that she was interested in his life. "We don't experience sex in the same way that you do, and it doesn't have the same meaning. Relationships are based on forming a family unit. Procreation is considered technical more than pleasurable. How we share pleasure is by hugging."

Carmella blinked. "Hugging."

"We twine our tentacles around people we feel fondness for."

"So, when we hugged, that was very intimate to you." She felt goose bumps forming on her arms.

# Adaptation

"It's hard to explain. Intertwining your tentacles isn't forbidden or done discreetly. It's fully accepted by all ages. But I will say that it is more meaningful for us than a hug would be to you."

She cocked her head at him. "It's sex?"

He shrugged. "It's akin to sex in that it involves pleasure through contact. For example, one of my mothers would rub the nodule that would cause my tentacle to extend if she wanted to wrap her tentacle around me. Raj and Lawrence would do that to me when they said I was bummed."

"Ah, okay. I think I understand." She gathered the dishes and placed them in the sink to wash later. "You miss them, don't you?"

He looked at his hand on the table. "Yes. I'm not like other Centaurians. I find little interest in the things that they do. Because I am more interested in behaving the way a human would, I am shunned by my family and my kind."

She sat. "I'm sorry."

He met her eyes. "It doesn't mean anything to me as long as they leave me to roam. It's why I'm allowed to do what is forbidden for others, to get me out of sight."

She shook her head. "So you're saying that Centaurians don't come to Earth anymore?"

"It is forbidden. No one is allowed on Earth."

"I don't understand. Why?"

Bilal didn't answer.

Carmella leaned forward. "Humans have to want to come back to Earth. Why is it forbidden? Why do you collect us remaining humans like we're stray cats that need to go to a shelter? I mean, I'm home, I'm happy. But I have to hide from Centaurians!"

He met her eyes, surprised at how quickly she had become hostile toward him again. How much distrust still remained? "Carmella, you don't understand. The world that they remembered doesn't exist here anymore. That is found on Earth 2. There are schools and homes and jobs ..."

"So? We had that here before ..." She turned away.

# Adaptation

"We're trying to return a sense of normalcy. Humans were dying, and we were frantic to find a reason why and to put a stop to it. We did."

Carmella turned to him but didn't look up.

"Some humans were resistant to the illness. They got sick, but it didn't consume them. We manipulated and defeated the illness for those who couldn't fight it. Then we brought them to a planet that was very similar to Earth."

"Oh, for fuck's sake. Bilal, why didn't you just return everyone to Earth?"

"Because there was no way we could monitor if what we had done was good enough. We keep humans healthy. We monitor for illnesses. There is no more cancer or AIDS. A human's life expectancy has nearly doubled. We take care of the humans ..." He saw a cold look in Carmella's eyes. "What would you have us do? Return the humans to a lawless world with no sense of direction? There would have been mass havoc! Humans are perfect and yet flawed in so many ways. Even now, you hate that we gave you a chance."

"Because we are not yours to rule!"

"We are not rulers."

"Who created the rules, Bilal? Ultimately?"

"We have a committee made up of both human and Centaurians."

"Why aren't the humans returned here after all of these years?" She saw his skin shimmer from pink to black.

"Because they can't. They wouldn't survive here because of the atmosphere. In order to breathe on Earth 2, humans had to be modified."

"Oh my God!"

He reached for her hand. "Carmella ..."

She snatched her hand back and stood, her eyes dark and accusatory.

"Carmella, please listen to me. I didn't like it either, but there was no choice. When we tried to colonize on Earth, the rebels

167

nearly destroyed everything. We had no choice but to find a safe place for the survivors."

"It's funny how you remember it in that way. I remember prison camps where people were forced to comply with you!" She turned and ran up the stairs.

Bilal heard her slam the door to her bedroom.

He didn't know what to do. He was hurt by her words and at a loss for how to make this right. He understood completely how she felt and had argued this same point with his parents. But this was bigger than him.

How could he let her know that this was bigger than him?

**Bilal gave her** some time and then went to her room. "Carmella, may I come in?"

"The door is open."

He entered and saw Carmella sitting on her windowsill looking out into the world, her eyes red from crying.

"It will never be the same," she whispered through trembling lips. "I thought, somehow I thought that it would someday return. Earth is dead now."

He looked down and felt the stinging in his own eyes. "I'm sorry. I hate what has happened to Earth. I love Earth, and I've wanted so badly to be a part of a world before this destruction. But there is no way that I could have ever lived the lives that you humans lived. I am on the outside always looking in. My friends and peers were all humans. I grew up with pop culture, listening to the music and wishing I was like them and not me." He shoved his hands into his pockets.

"You're not ever going to modify me, do you hear me? Ever. I'm never going to Earth Two."

Bilal nodded. "I understand."

# Adaptation

**Bilal was in** the front yard hanging Raj's clothes as icy winds whistled around him, and he wished he had taken time to put on a coat. When he returned shivering to the house, Carmella was settling down on the chaise lounge to nurse their son.

He felt warmer at the sight of his family and stopped shivering when he saw Carmella's face, her features smoother and no longer as hostile. Maybe everything would be okay.

"I'm sorry I yelled at you," Carmella said. "You don't deserve that. I just don't want to discuss the past."

"That is fine by me. We have other things more important to discuss."

"Such as?"

"Winter is coming, and there's not enough wood. We are low on powdered juice, tea, and rice. We could also use more canned soup."

"I've pretty much used up the supplies around here. We'd have to go far away to find more. Do you know how to get diesel fuel from holding tanks?"

"No."

"Then I have to go with you."

"What about Raj?"

"We'll bring him with us. The truck has heat. He'll be fine."

"Carmella."

"The alternative is that you stay here with Raj while I go alone."

Bilal shook his head. "No. We'll all go."

Neither realized how disastrous that decision would be.

# Chapter 25
# ~Shopping~

**Carmella made a** long list of items they would need. "I think I'm pretty self-sufficient," she said. "I preserve fruits and vegetables, hunt and fish, and I think I've done pretty well without having to go into town too often. Hell, when there was civilization, I'd go to the grocery story every single week and sometimes twice a week."

"It's admirable, but there are other ways to live," Bilal said.

Carmella scowled. "Like on fake Earth."

"I don't mean on Earth Two. There are ways that you can make electricity without running a generator. Solar power is an easy conversion. There is also organic energy, which is what we Centaurians use. I can convert the house to use solar energy, and you can harvest the energy from the sun to heat your water and your house."

Carmella rolled her eyes. "Oh, sure. We'll be able to find dozens of solar panels lying around." She starred "diesel fuel" and "kerosene" on the list. "Until then, we'll need fossil fuel. My truck can use diesel or kerosene, though it prefers diesel. Kerosene makes it ping and smoke."

"Could the generator use kerosene, too?" Bilal asked.

"It did when I ran out of diesel," Carmella said. "But it nearly smoked out the cows and the chickens when the old thing decided to start." She underlined "car seat."

"I have seen them inside cars," Bilal said.

"That will be the first item we get."

# Adaptation

They loaded Carmella's idling Ford F250 Diesel while Raj was buckled securely in the middle of the front seat. Raj looked alarmed at being left in the foreign environment without his parents but smiled whenever he saw them through the windows. Bilal wedged several empty metal barrels onto the truck bed, stowing the hand pump and two eight-foot fuel hoses in the truck box mounted behind the cab.

Carmella climbed into the truck, and Bilal took his place in the passenger seat.

Wolf whined to come along.

Carmella rolled down the window. "No, Wolf, not this time. I need you and Girl to stay to keep an eye on the animals."

Wolf whined but retreated.

Carmella felt strangely excited. She, Bilal, and baby Raj were going on a family outing.

It all felt so normal.

She turned the truck and headed down the driveway that crisp December day, bulbous nimbostratus clouds drifting overhead. Snow flurries had already fallen on two separate occasions but thus far hadn't stuck to the ground.

Raj concentrated simultaneously on the movement of the truck, Raj's busy hands and feet, and Carmella's joyful expression.

"So when can you make my house solar?" Carmella asked.

"When I have all of the materials, I can do it this spring."

She glanced at him before returning her eyes to the road. "Knock yourself out, Bilal. You have five years here, right? It would be nice not to worry about freezing to death in my old age. I can't see myself siphoning diesel from underground gas tanks when I'm eighty."

Her nonchalant words hurt him more than he could describe. Carmella growing old alone was not something he wanted to imagine. He looked out his window. "I will make it happen."

As they rode down a country lane, Bilal's intrigue overwhelmed his sadness. He liked the way the scenery looked as they drove past houses and businesses. Some places had been burned down, most likely during the time of the riots when

171

humans had rebelled against those who had chosen to live instead of giving in to the illness that was killing them.

Carmella turned onto the highway, which was littered with burned out and abandoned cars, and weaved the truck through them until she slowed to a stop beside a green minivan with dark tinted windows. "I'll bet there's a car seat inside that mommy van." She opened the glove box and took out a hammer. "Go shopping."

Bilal took the hammer. "Shopping?"

"That hammer is your credit card," Carmella said. "Never leave home without it."

"I do not understand," Bilal said.

"If the doors are locked, you'll have to break a window to get inside."

"Oh."

Bilal tried the driver's door and found it locked.

"Come on, man," Carmella said. "Smash the window. There's a Target store I'd like to check out before it gets too dark."

Bilal smiled. *She called me "man,"* he thought.

Bilal smashed the window with the hammer, reached in, and opened the door from the inside. He ignored the withered corpse leaning on the steering wheel in front of him and unlocked the back door. He found a dusty yet serviceable blue car seat in the middle row, unhooked it, and brought it over to the truck.

"I don't want that one," Carmella said. "It's the wrong color."

Bilal froze. "What?"

"I'm kidding, Bilal," Carmella said. "Get in, strap Raj in, and let's go."

Bilal unbuckled Raj and handed him to Carmella, slid in and attached the car seat between them, and secured Raj into the seat. "I wish I could have cleaned the seat first."

"There wasn't a ... passenger in it, was there?"

Bilal shook his head.

Carmella smiled at Raj. "Now you can see where we're going." She continued weaving through the unmoving traffic. "The Target was ransacked during the rebellions, but I remember seeing

# Adaptation

some baby items that were left untouched." She supposed that rioters and looters didn't have babies. She certainly didn't when she had first scoured the area for food and supplies. She glanced out of habit in the rearview mirror. *As if anything might be following us.* "I want to find a baby sling to make doing chores so much easier. And maybe we can find a baby swing."

"I could take the truck out to find solar panels," Bilal said.

"Do you even know how to drive?"

He suppressed a smile. "How do you think I travel from Earth to the mother ship and to Earth Two?"

She had not considered this. "Do you have a spaceship?"

"A pod."

"I'd like to see it sometime. Where is it?"

"You can't see it. I returned it. It will come back for me in two and one half Earth years."

She squinted into the sunlight. "Oh. I thought you'd be here five years."

"I have to go back to make a report, and then I will return."

"I see." She felt relieved and then frowned. Bilal wasn't staying forever, and she would do well to remember that.

Carmella pulled the truck into the Target parking lot after dodging several red shopping carts. It still felt weird to pull up at the curb and bypass the parking spaces. The glass entrance doors were nothing but crooked metal frames, and trash and broken glass littered the sidewalk.

"There could be wild animals inside, especially since it's growing cold," she said. "Since you don't know how to shoot, you carry the baby and the flashlight and I'll keep us all covered."

Bilal appreciated Carmella's caution, but he sensed no animals larger than squirrels nearby. He didn't tell her, however. He was learning when not to speak around her. After putting the diaper bag over his shoulder, he and Raj exited the truck.

Carmella switched the safeties off the two nine-millimeters in her holsters and grabbed her rifle from the back seat. When she got out of the truck, she was pleased Bilal had wrapped Raj in a sheepskin blanket. Raj protested until his little face peeked out and

173

he was able to see the world around him. Bilal wore a parka, knit hat, and gloves, his long hair flowing down his back. The wind periodically blew his hair into his face, and Carmella had to resist the urge to reach out and push it back.

She adjusted her knit hat and scarf. The thin leather gloves she wore allowed her to pull the trigger easily, and the thick leather jacket she wore made her look like a badass. Thanks to whatever Bilal had done to her during the delivery, Carmella felt healthier than she ever had and nothing like a woman who had delivered a baby less than three months ago.

"Let's go shopping," Carmella said, and Bilal and Raj followed her into the darkened store.

Once they were inside, the looting became obvious. Overturned cash registers, mangled display racks, and several limbless mannequins made for slow going only a few feet into the store.

"Turn on the flashlight."

Although he had no problems seeing in the dark, Bilal flashed the beam into the darkness of the store for Carmella. Raj seemed to know something important was happening because he watched everything wide-eyed.

Carmella hung her rifle around her neck, rolled a cart to the center of the store, and grabbed two baby slings, tossing them into the cart. She frowned when she couldn't find a baby swing.

Bilal rolled up with Raj in the front seat of another cart. "I need shoes."

They found him two pairs of work boots, and he wore one pair immediately, leaving his tattered sneakers behind.

"These feel wonderful," Bilal said.

Carmella collected all the baby clothes she could. She picked out some underwear and also chose a cute nightie, which she shoved into her jacket pocket when Bilal wasn't looking. Bilal found several pairs of pants. While she grabbed all of the candles, Bilal collected tools. Because the canned and packaged foods had long expired, they still had a great deal of room left in one of the carts.

# Adaptation

"I guess it's time to do some Christmas shopping," Carmella said.

Bilal knew little about the human holiday other than it involved people spending exorbitant amounts of money on things they really didn't need. "Where do we begin?"

"In the toy section."

They filled the second cart with toys.

Raj especially liked gnawing on a plush, stuffed wolf.

They packed their items into the back of the extended cab. After Carmella gave Raj his pacifier to replace the soggy wolf, she pulled out of the Target parking lot.

"Maybe we should get you a truck for when you're hauling those solar panels," Carmella said.

Bilal's eyebrows rose. "My own truck? Yes, I would like that. A big diesel truck like this one."

"We'd have to get you something bigger to carry all those panels," Carmella said, suppressing a smile. Bilal's joy gave her a strange satisfaction that warmed her more than the heat barely flowing through the truck's vents.

"I would like a bigger truck," Bilal said.

"But a bigger truck requires more diesel fuel," Carmella said. "We need to go across the Ohio River to Kentucky. There's a truck stop I've used to get diesel. We can fill up the barrels and then go get your truck at a dealership somewhere. How's that sound?"

Bilal smiled broadly. "I would like that very much."

**They decided to** stop for a quick lunch before the exhausting work of siphoning diesel. Carmella had packed sandwiches spread with softened cheese she had made that morning. Homemade brownies and bottled iced tea rounded out the meal, and Raj enjoyed his mother's breast.

They sat on the back of the truck and watched the Ohio River from the Roebling Bridge. Bilal had never been more content in his life. *This is what it is to be human,* he thought.

# Adaptation

"Raj's sensors haven't come out again, have they?" Bilal asked.

"No, thank God."

Bilal swallowed some tea. "I'm going to begin training him how to use them."

Carmella frowned. "So soon?"

"Yes, he's capable of understanding how to use them. Soon he will need to explore items with the sensors, so he needs to understand how to use them."

"How old were you when you learned to use yours?"

"It is different for Centaurian infants. Parents keep a connection with their infants using their sensors almost constantly. Infants learn through that connection."

Her nipple slipped from Raj's mouth as he slept, sucking his thumb and relaxing in slumber. She slipped her breast back into her bra and put the baby over her shoulder to burp.

Bilal's eyes lingered on her before he turned back to the river. He sighed in longing to be the one suckling there. He recounted the taste of her sweet milk and sighed again.

"What's wrong?" she asked.

His face turned a bright shade of yellow. "I'm sorry, I ..." He was not good at lying. "I, uh ..."

Carmella stared at him. "Well?"

Bilal sighed a third time. "Oh well." He leaned over and kissed her.

It was swift and chaste, but she thought it was sweet—even sexy.

They both smiled, looking out to the water before them.

"We should go," she said.

He cleared his throat. "Yes."

Four miles down I-71 Carmella pulled into a deserted truck stop in Florence, Kentucky.

"Popeye's," Bilal said, reading a sign on the main building.

"My chicken's better," Carmella said.

She parked the truck close to what looked like a manhole cover set into the concrete. "You wouldn't believe how long it took me to get that thing open with a crowbar," she said, setting the parking brake. "Let's fill 'er up."

After Bilal removed the cover, Carmella fed one of the fuel hoses into the underground tank. She inserted the other hose into the truck's gas tank. "Get to cranking."

Bilal cranked the pump.

For the ten minutes.

"My truck's thirsty, huh?" Carmella said.

Once the truck's tank was full, Carmella snaked the hose into one of the metal barrels on the back of the truck. "I'm taking Raj inside to get away from these fumes, okay?"

Bilal nodded and resumed cranking.

To stay warm — and to keep from thinking about the feel of Bilal's lips on hers — Carmella gave Raj a tour of Popeye's. There wasn't much left to see. Animals had cleaned out the walk-in freezer and refrigerator long ago, and the condiment packs that littered the floor looked chewed. "This was a fast food restaurant, Raj. This is where people came to eat delicious greasy food and gain weight. I wish I could have an ice-cold fountain Coke right now." She looked out at Bilal, who was moving the hose to the last barrel. "Your daddy is working up an appetite, isn't he? Look at his muscles! I know you're going to grow up big and strong like your daddy. Or daddies. Centaurians would have to celebrate Fathers' Day instead of Father's Day, Raj."

Raj blinked.

"I know those two words sounded the same," Carmella said, "but you didn't see where I put the apostrophe. An apostrophe is a flying comma."

Raj continued to blink.

Carmella laughed. "As if the location of an apostrophe matters anymore."

When Bilal finished filling the last barrel, he wrapped the hoses around the hand pump and stowed them in the truck box.

Carmella and Raj joined him, and she bounced nervously from one foot to the other. "Once we get you a truck from a Toyota place up the road, we can pick up more supplies from a Walmart about a mile from here," Carmella said. "Then we can go home." She chewed her lip.

Bilal's nostrils flared as he scented the air. Her heartbeat had sped up and her eyes were dilated. He licked his lips. "Yes, we should be home by nightfall."

She nodded shyly.

He smiled.

She returned the smile. "Yes, by nightfall."

As she drove to Kerry Toyota, Carmella felt cocooned by feelings of warmth and love, and she couldn't stop smiling.

Bilal smiled because Carmella smiled.

Raj smiled because he had gas.

She parked near a gray Toyota Tundra Dually Diesel. "What do you think of that one?"

"I like it," Bilal said.

"We'll have to go inside to find the keys," Carmella said. "That's how I, um, purchased this truck."

Carmella decided to use one of the baby slings. She slipped off her jacket and holster as she fastened the straps around her neck.

Bilal scanned the rows of cars and trucks around them, his eyes zeroing in on the front of the building. The windows were all intact. "The windows ..."

Carmella dropped Raj into the sling, and he immediately gripped her chest with his hands. "What about them?"

"They're ... there."

"They must be bullet-resistant," Carmella said, opening her door.

"I don't think so," Bilal said. "I don't think we're alone."

"Nonsense," Carmella said.

Bilal pointed at the holster. "I would feel better if you wore that."

Carmella sighed, buckled the holster around her waist, and put on her jacket. "Are you happy?"

"Yes," Bilal said, but he still felt uneasy. "But I still sense ... something."

# Adaptation

Carmella opened her door and slid off the seat. "There's no one here but us." She stepped out into the parking lot and shut the door.

Bilal got out of the truck, his eyes trained on the building as he followed Carmella. "Carmella, I sense other people."

Raj snapped his head around and cooed.

"Raj does, too."

Carmella reached her right hand to her holster.

"I wouldn't do that if I was you!"

Carmella looked up and saw a man on the roof of the building with a rifle trained on her and Raj. Her knees nearly buckled but she froze in place. "We're only here to get a truck."

"Ain't none for sale today, lady," the man said. "Take off the holster, nice and slow, now."

Carmella unbuckled the holster and let it drop to the ground.

The door to the dealership opened. She saw a man and a woman exit. The man had a rifle but wasn't aiming it at anything. He appeared to be in his late fifties, and his belly protruded from his unbuttoned down jacket. White tufts of hair stood out in a clownish manner around his face. The woman was old and dressed in a coat much too big for her. She hobbled toward Carmella with a look of wonder on her face.

"We don't want any trouble," Carmella said. "We only came to get another vehicle, that's all."

"Is ... is that a baby?" the woman asked. She looked at the man. "Oh, Sonny. I wants me a baby. Can I have it? Please, can I have it?"

Sonny shrugged. "I ain't seen a baby in ages. Yeah, Ma, we can keep it."

Carmella wrapped her arms around Raj. "No ..."

"Kill the man," Sonny said.

Two shots rang out from the roof, and Bilal fell to the ground.

# Adaptation

"Oh my God!" Carmella screamed. She reached for the holster, but something hard hit her in the side of the head. She cradled Raj as she fell.

A moment later, something hard struck her again, and everything went black.

# Chapter 26
## ~Loss~

**Ma pulled Raj** from his sling and cradled the crying baby lovingly in her arms. Earl, the shooter from the roof, came down and exited the building carrying a duffel bag filled with tools.

Earl kicked the body of the man he had shot, careful not to step in the pool of blood around him. "What the fuck?"

Sonny put on Carmella's holster before lifting and dumping her into the back seat of the Ford. "Nice of them to get us some fuel, huh, Earl?"

"Come on!" Ma urged while jiggling the crying baby in her arms. "Sonny, you drive this truck, and me and Earl will take Earl's."

"Not yet," Earl said. "Come over here. Look at this." Earl nudged the man over onto his back.

Sonny stood over the man. "What's wrong with his face?"

Ma sighed and joined them. "He's completely ... black. Why is he black like that?"

Earl frowned. "I don't know. I ain't never seen nothing like that. Maybe when I shot him it did something, I don't know."

"Maybe he got some type of disease," Ma said.

Earl looked at her. "He wasn't black when he got out the truck." He felt goose bumps crawling over his arms. "Let's just get out of here."

Earl had done a number of terrible things over the years since the end of civilization. He'd lost much of is capacity for empathy once he no longer had to be accountable for his actions.

But this thing, killing a man in cold blood and having him turn black afterwards, made him feel as if he had crossed some line that would keep him from gaining admittance through the pearly gates.

While Earl and Ma followed behind them in a beat-up Chevy Silverado, Sonny looked into the backseat at the unmoving woman. He licked his lips. She would be his. Earl had Ma, and now he had someone and wouldn't have to think about doing bad things to animals. She was pretty, too. He was already becoming hard. He wanted to pull the truck over and ...

He swerved the wheel, nearly running into an abandoned car.

*Focus.*

**Carmella's stomach turned** before she was completely awake. She coughed back the bile that had risen in her throat and forced her eyes open. Pain stabbed through the back of her head as stars appeared before her eyes.

"She's awake!"

Carmella forced her eyes to focus on the old woman.

"See!" a man shouted. "I told you I didn't hit her too hard."

Carmella tried to sit up but couldn't move, her hands bound behind her.

The old woman held Raj, whose eyes were red. He was hiccupping as he chomped on his pacifier. When he saw Carmella, he opened his mouth and began to wail, the pacifier falling to a carpeted floor.

"Oh, for *fuck's sake!* Shut him up!"

The old woman jiggled Raj on her hip. "I can't! He wants his mother!"

"Mamamamamama!!" Raj yelled while tears streamed down his face.

*Oh my God,* Carmella thought. *He just said Mama!* Her heart nearly rose out of her chest. Carmella blinked her eyes rapidly in an attempt to see straight and clear her head. She tried to move again but couldn't. *Bilal.* No ... She squeezed her eyes shut and tried to think. Bilal was ... gone. Raj was crying for her.

"Give him to me," Carmella said weakly. "Give me my baby."

The older woman pursed her lips and frowned. She backed away a step. "No, he's mine now."

Carmella tried not to black out. "You can't have my baby ..."

Raj reached for Carmella and wailed hysterically.

"He needs to be nursed. I need to feed him."

"Give him to her," another man said.

Carmella looked at the man. He appeared to be in his late fifties but was more put together than the others. His short white hair was sheared into a military cut, and he wore camouflage khakis and combat boots. Carmella's eyes narrowed and felt her breath freeze in her lungs. This was the man who had shot Bilal.

"Well, untie her, Sonny," the old woman grumbled.

Sonny grunted and knelt behind her. He roughly yanked her arms and undid the ropes. "Don't give us no shit now, or Earl will do you like he did your man."

Carmella rolled to her knees and focused on Raj.

The old woman cooed, but Raj wanted nothing to do with her. "I don't know why you're making me give him to her. *I'm* gonna be his mother!"

"You can't feed him," Carmella said, reaching her arms toward Raj. "He's only three months old."

"Three months?" the old woman screeched. "Who in the hell are you trying to fool? This baby's nine months old if he's a day!"

Carmella shook her head. "He's always been big. Please give him to me."

"Three-month-olds don't say 'Mama,' Missy," the old woman spat. "And he's wearing nine-month baby clothes."

"Like I said," Carmella said, "he's always been big."

"Cuz you been overfeeding him," the old woman said.

Raj let out an ear-splitting bellow.

"I told you to shut him up!" Earl shouted.

The old woman handed Raj to Carmella. "Shut his ass up if you know what's good for you."

Carmella hugged him tightly, burying her face into his sweet neck. She rocked and held her son, her heart breaking as she cried for the loss of Bilal.

**Carmella nursed Raj** until he fell into a restless sleep.

Everyone watched her until Ma pulled herself from her seat and reached for Raj. "Give him to me. I'll lay him down."

Carmella bared her teeth. "No."

Earl cocked his rifle. "Give her the boy. We need to talk. When we're done talking, then we *might* let you hold him again. If you don't, this will be the last time you ever hold him."

She took a deep breath and saw her life moving before her eyes. She saw and relived the losses of Jody and Micah. She pictured Bilal being shot. "Okay." She held Raj out in front of her.

The old woman snatched Raj away. "You need to learn you some manners."

Carmella clenched her fists wanting badly to hit the woman in her wrinkled face. *But I have to keep my shit together. Raj needs me. He already lost one parent today.* She swallowed back her sadness. Now was not the time to give in to her hears. She unclenched her fists and slowed her breathing.

The old woman kissed Raj's curls and left the room.

Carmella sat back on her knees and looked up at the men assessing every possibility that she could over-take them. But it always ended with Earl and the rifle he carried.

Sonny's tongue peeked from his lips. Now that he'd seen her titty, he intended to have her as soon as possible. He wanted to throw her on the floor and fuck her right there in front of everyone.

"What's your name?" Earl asked.

Carmella glared at Earl.

184

# Adaptation

Earl took a step closer. "I'm Earl. This here is Lester but we call him Sonny. The woman in the other room is Linda, his mother. I'm going to ask you again. What's your name?"

"Carmella," she whispered.

Earl walked toward her and offered his hand.

She looked at it and saw a series of scars on his knuckles. Ignoring the offered hand she stood on her own.

Earl chuckled at the rebuke. "Have a seat." He gestured to filthy green couch.

Carmella sat on the edge.

Earl sat across from her in an armchair covered with a quilt. "I'm sure you've figured out that there is no walking out of here for you and the little man. You're smart, I'm guessing. I can make it pretty or I can make it plain. I'm thinking that you're the type who wants to cut through the bullshit."

"You're the boss," she stated while giving him a chilly look.

Earl smiled and then laughed. "I like you. Yes, indeed I do."

*And I want to smash in your faces and feed your bloody carcasses to Wolf,* Carmella thought. But her only response was a cold stare.

Earl's smile disappeared. "All right, here's how it is. There ain't that many humans left here on Earth. We've been traveling all over, and you're the first person we've seen in five or six years."

"What happened to the last person you met?" Carmella asked.

Earl squinted. "He's as dead as your man cuz he sassed me."

The response stabbed at her as purely as if she'd been knifed. "I'm sure you gave him a reason," Carmella stated.

Earl leaned forward. "Yep, I surely did. You planning to sass me?"

*I'm planning to kill you,* she thought.

Earl seemed to read her thoughts and threw back his head in laughter. "Carmella, we're gonna get along just fine. You see, you're obviously a fertile woman. We need you here with us. But if you don't go along with the program, then we'll just take your kid and continue our travels."

Carmella gripped the edge of the couch. "And what exactly is the program?"

"You just need to be nice to us."

Sonny stood. "Us? She's mine, Earl."

Earl looked over his shoulder at the unkempt man. "She's *ours*, Sonny."

Sonny stood over him with his hands on his fat hips. "You got Ma. You already got a woman. Now I do, too."

Earl's nose flared. "What do you know about it, pig fucker?"

Sonny's face turned red. "Now you hold on there just a minute." He looked at Carmella. "I ain't no pig fucker."

"Do you think I don't know what you were doing to those pigs that time?" Earl asked. "And the goat?" He looked at Carmella. "He even tried to fuck a horse, Carmella. That's the reason his leg is messed up, not because he tried to ride it."

"I did not!" Sonny yelled.

"You tried to fuck it," Early said, "and it kicked the shit out of you!"

"Shut up!"

Ma came from the back room and closed the door behind her. "What the hell? Are you trying to wake up the baby again?"

Sonny hurried to his mother. "Ma, tell him that the girl is mine! I ain't got a girl, and she's mine!"

"Of course she's yours, son." Ma glared at Earl. "What are you up to now? You know he can't live the rest of his days without his own woman."

Earl stood. "Well, I'm certainly not going to be stuck the rest of my days fucking your withered ass. I get a piece of her, too, and that's all there is to it."

Carmella wanted to vomit. She was about to be tied or chained up and turned into their sex slave, and there was absolutely no one to help her. She had to be smart and strong even though she wanted to rage and kill every one of them.

"You don't ever have to touch me again for all I care!" Ma yelled. "You think I like having you shove that thing in me?"

# Adaptation

Earl closed his mouth and inhaled. "Then I guess we have an understanding. You won't have to worry about my dick anymore."

"Ma!" Sonny yelled.

Raj began to cry from the next room.

"You dumb shit," Earl said, glaring at Sonny. "You woke that baby again. Go get him and give him to his mother before I *really* get angry."

Ma wrung her hands. "No one is going to put a hand on that precious baby."

"Give him to his mother, or I will leave you two to starve to death," Earl said.

The old woman retreated to get the baby while Lester looked at Carmella as if she was slowly disappearing.

> *ad-ap-ta-tion n.* any alteration in the structure or function of an
> organism or any of its parts that results from natural selection
> and by which the organism becomes better fitted to survive
> and multiply in its environment

Bilal's body was stiff and cold on the cement parking lot. Even the blood which had pooled from his body had stiffened in the cold. His chest no longer rose and fell, and his heart no longer beat. Only his long hair moved, fluttering in the wind above lifeless eyes that did not notice the flakes of snow drifting down. He no longer had memories of his biggest desire: to love and to be loved.

But his cells did.

One cell remembered to turn on adaptation.

The other cells swiftly followed.

# Adaptation

# Chapter 27
# ~Something New~

**The dormant cells** in Bilal's body sparked to life, regenerating enough to start his heart beating sluggishly in his chest.

He lay there without knowing or thinking until the sun fell. By the time his eyes popped open and he took in the night sky, he was covered in a fine dusting of frost. He moved his rigid arms to his chest where he felt hot blood on his cold fingers. He tried to close his eyes and sleep to continue repairs on his body, but his thoughts overruled the urge.

He opened his mouth. "Carmella …"

The sound was less than a whisper.

His heartbeat spiked as he remembered what had happened. Two men and a woman. The men had guns. The woman wanted …

"Raj!"

He tried to sit up but the pain overwhelmed him and left him on the brink of unconsciousness. He squeezed his eyelids closed, fought the pain, and looked inward. *How is this happening? How can my body be repairing itself without tentacles or sensors?*

He tried to stop his mind from charging ahead and to concentrate on making the repairs, but he couldn't stop thinking of Carmella or their son. Where had they been taken? And were they okay? He had to get up. He had to find them …

He opened his eyes and looked around. The dark didn't inhibit his ability to see, but the dark concerned him. His blood

189

would draw predators. He might be able to repair the damage caused by two bullet wounds, but he couldn't survive being ripped limb from limb by wild animals.

*I need time to heal,* he thought. *Time and shelter.*

He bared his teeth, braced, and forced himself into a sitting position. The bullet wounds pierced his body and left him lightheaded and nauseous. He fought the blackness swimming in front of his eyes by thinking about Carmella and Raj. He thought about kissing her on the Roebling Bridge while their son quietly watched. He thought about that supremely human moment as he scooted himself a few inches toward the dealership door. He ignored the trail of blood he left behind, and fifteen excruciatingly painful minutes later, he was out of breath and leaning against the glass door of the building.

He felt numbness in his hands and cold spreading through his chest. He tried to lift his hands to reach the door.

*Pull it open.*

He couldn't lift his hands.

He heard growls and snarls and looked across the street into the Best Western parking lot. Four sets of yellow eyes flitted among the burned out cars and trucks.

He smiled despite his pain. "Wolves," he whispered. "More wolves."

He fell into unconsciousness.

~***~

**Raj stared out** at his strange surroundings periodically crying out in distress. Carmella rocked him and held him close to her. Whenever Ma came close, Raj would turn his head away and scream against his mother's chest until the older woman retreated.

"I'm going out for a smoke, but I'll be back," Earl scowled. He headed toward the front door. "Maybe you should think about making us something to eat." He opened the door, stepped through, and slammed it behind him.

Sonny's eyes lit up, and he stared at Carmella with open desire, a tendril of drool spilling from his lower lip.

Carmella watched Ma leaving the room for the kitchen. *Don't leave me alone with this dumb shit!* "Ma'am!"

Ma turned and looked at her in annoyance. "What?"

"I need to use the bathroom."

The old woman rolled her eyes as she returned to Carmella. "Why? You ain't eaten nothing."

Raj shrieked when he saw Ma approach.

"Shh, Raj," Carmella whispered. "It's all right." She looked up at Ma. "I have to pee."

Ma gazed down at Carmella. "Okay. This is what we'll do. Let Sonny hold the baby, and I'll take you out back where you can do your business."

"No," Carmella said. She held Raj tightly.

"You ain't walking out of here with that baby," Ma said. "You think I trust you not to run off as soon as you have the chance? Maybe you're thinking of knocking me in the head or something. I'm not stupid. I know you won't try to run away without that boy of yours, so you hand him over to Sonny, and then you can go pee."

Carmella looked at Sonny, who had both of his hands in his pockets and a bulge filling his crotch. "Does Sonny know anything about taking care of a baby?"

"Hell no," Ma said. "Boy can't hardly take care of himself."

"So why don't you put Raj in the other room until we get back?"

Ma shrugged. "So you can bop me on the head while we're outside and come collect him through the window? I don't think so."

*Think!* "Earl's outside, isn't he? He wouldn't let that happen, right?"

"Nope," Ma said. "He'd shoot your ass." She reached out her arms. "We'll do it your way. Give him to me."

Carmella lifted Raj into Ma's arms, and Raj kicked his pudgy legs and wailed, "Mamamamama!"

# Adaptation

Ma grabbed Raj and propped him on her hip. "Oh, don't be so angry, little boy. I've been taking good care of you, haven't I?"

"It's okay, Raj," Carmella said. "Mommy's not going anywhere."

Raj's wails slowed until his small body hitched with residual tears. He looked from his mother to the woman carrying him and then opened his mouth exposing his tongue.

Carmella saw translucent strings springing from the tip of Raj's tongue. They seemed to be straining and stretching to reach the old woman's neck *He plans to sting her!* She scanned the room for a chair, a vase, a lamp, anything to bash Sonny's brains in. *What was he waiting for?* She thought while frantically watching for her son to strike. *Sting her! Sting her* ... and then she realized that Raj was forbidden to do it. *Damnit!*

"What'd you call him?" Ma asked.

"Raj," Carmella said distractedly while scooting to the edge of the couch. "It's short for Roger."

Ma squinted at Raj. "He don't look like no Roger."

Raj tried to twist his body away from the women, his chest still hitching in anguish. Luckily the old woman would not have realized that small thread-like filaments were ready to make contact and then zap the living shit out of her.

Carmella looked into Raj's eyes. "Go ahead, baby boy," she whispered. "On her neck. It's okay."

Raj's sensors lashed out at Ma's neck, his mouth locking onto her flesh giving the appearance that he was giving her a slobbery baby kiss.

Ma's face alighted with delight seconds before growing slack. Her mouth dropped open to reveal slightly greenish bottom teeth. "AHHH!" She screeched.

Sonny's eyes swung to his mother in surprise. He'd been fantasizing ...

Ma grabbed for her wrinkled throat and Carmella lunged forward to catch Raj before he hit the floor. She clutched her son to her, soothing and thanking him quietly, praising him for being a good boy.

# Adaptation

Damnit! Sonny was too far away for her to both catch her son and brain him with a blunt instrument! Instead she quickly returned to her seat on the couch to bide her time as Ma dropped to her knees attempting to scream. The woman gasped breathless, no sound issuing from her withered lips. Her eyes rolled to the back of her head.

*Hurts like a bitch, doesn't it?* Carmella thought, cradling Raj. "You done good, son," she whispered in his ear. "Thank you."

Ma then flopped to the floor, her arms and legs twitching as foam spit from her mouth.

Sonny lunged forward and dropped to his knees beside her. "Ma!"

"She's having some type of seizure," Carmella said. "Go get Earl!" *And when you do, I am so out of here.*

Sonny ran to the front door and threw it open. "Earl! Come quick! Ma's dying!"

*Leave! Run off!* Carmella leaped from the couch. But where should she run?! Out the back door? Out a window?

"Earl! Hurry! It's ma!"

Carmella heard rapid footsteps approaching the house.

*Shit!* She dropped back on the couch, out of time.

Earl pushed past Sonny and into the house, a cigarette dangling from his lips, his rifle trained on Carmella and Raj. "What the *fuck's* going on?"

Sonny looked at Earl with tears in his eyes. "I think Ma's having a heart attack. Do something, Earl!"

"God damnit!" Earl howled. "Sonny, turn her head so that she doesn't choke to death!"

Sonny hurried back to his mother and gently turned her head to the side. "Is she dying, Earl?" he looked at the man fearfully.

Earl put the cold muzzle of the rifle against Carmella's temple. "Did you have anything to do with this?"

"How could I?" Carmella asked in a shaky voice.

"She's never had a seizure before," Earl said. "Not until you showed up."

193

Carmella gave him an innocent look. "One second she was holding Raj, and the next she was foaming at the mouth. She dropped my son, and I had to catch him. I didn't touch her, I swear." *My warrior baby did, though ....*

"Put the kid on the couch," Earl said.

"Why?" Carmella was terrified.

"I'm gonna have to tie you up while we deal with her," Earl said.

"You ever have kids?" Carmella asked in a desperate rush not to lose this opportunity to escape.

"Yes," Earl said. "Two."

"You can't put an infant on a couch and not expect it to fall off," Carmella said.

Earl smiled. "Then you'll have to figure something out, won't you? Put the brat on the couch."

Carmella placed Raj on the couch. "Stay put, Raj, okay?" She stated.

Raj opened his mouth to begin wailing again and Carmella wondered just how much of this her son understood. Did he know that they were in a life or death situation?

"Put your hands behind you," Earl commanded.

Raj cried but watched intently while Earl secured Carmella's hands behind her with coarse rope.

*That's right, baby boy,* Carmella thought. *Take notes.*

She scooted next to Raj while Earl helped Sonny pick up and carry Ma down the hallway, her withered legs still twitching.

Raj pulled himself onto his mother's lap and clutched her. Carmella smiled at Raj wishing that he could read her silent thoughts.

*One down,* she thought. *And two to go.*

# Chapter 28
## ~Battles~

**Carmella waited until** she heard a door open and close before leaping up and darting to the kitchen. Her eyes frantically scanned the counter for a set of knives. Every kitchen had them — except this one.

Damnit!

She looked into the sink and found a dirty butcher knife among some unwashed dishes. She backed up to the sink and felt around blindly, her hands closing carefully around the sharp blade. Once she had it securely in her grasp, she dashed back into the living room and sank back onto the couch, working the knife under the cushion behind her.

Little man had pulled himself up on his hands and knees when he saw her leave but was now exploring the couch, rocking back and forth and gurgling nonsense words. *Good, he was being so good,* she thought.

"Blablabla," Raj gurgled. "Dadada ..."

Carmella swallowed as fresh tears welled in her eyes. He was calling his daddy. Bilal. Dada ... It broke her heart. *Fuck! Bilal ...*

She couldn't think about the loss of Bilal. It felt like a cavern in her soul that she couldn't explore. It took everything she had to grasp the impossible fact that her son was three times as advanced as the average baby — maybe even more.

# Adaptation

A door opened, and Earl stalked into the room. He roughly yanked her arm, and she went skating off the couch onto her feet. "Come on."

Raj began to whimper.

She turned to Raj. "Don't cry. Mommy will be back."

As Earl half dragged Carmella down the hallway, Raj rubbed his eyes and stopped whimpering. He crawled to where his mother had hidden the knife.

He sat back on the couch and guarded it for his mother.

**Wild dogs owned** most of ruined civilization and wolves claimed the woods, but all bets were off in the winter.

In the winter it was eat or die.

A pack of wild dogs warily watched the wolves battle for the man from hiding places under broken down cars and within abandoned building. Some of the older ones remembered the time 'of man' and thumped their tails in want of a remembered neck or belly rub. Others didn't know what to make of humans and wanted no part of them.

Two wolves were all that remained in the battle; the weaker ones having already retreated or injured too badly to be a threat.

Of the remaining two was one youthful wolf that had only seen three adult seasons. The other was much stronger but also much older. Old battle weakness opened in his neck and hind quarters and despite his desire to not only win the prey but to maintain his dominance; the older wolf was finally defeated.

The winning wolf bared his teeth at the ones that looked on or hoped to scavenge. And they quickly retreated further to the buildings that served as their hiding places. The winning wolf turned his attention to the bloody mass across the street. He scented the air and then lowered his head and eased his strong sinewy body across the street.

# Adaptation

Bilal's head swam and he fought to open his eyes. His body was renewing the recent damage that he had done to it by dragging himself across the parking lot. But he had lost a great deal of blood and it continued to pump its way through the two holes in his torso; one in his chest, the other in his abdomen. Each time he moved he reopened the recent repairs to the wound. He needed to lie down and sleep so that his body could heal, he needed to heal so that he could get his family.

His eyes were closing again when he smelled the dank musk of a wolf. His body tensed and then his eyes tried to focus. Wolves. Not just one...

He tried to reach up for the door again; in his mind's eye he was opening the door and dragging his body inside the building. In reality he hadn't moved one inch. His eyes closed again in exhaustion and his body relaxed. It would take over despite his actions to hinder the healing.

The wolf hurried to the parking lot, head low, eyes scanning the area for movement. He paused at the pool of blood; the smell of it nearly overwhelming the other smells — but not quite.

The wolf's tale curled up as he found a scent that he recognized. The wolf remembered being a pup and being introduced to this smell by his father. It was the smell of a human who was the supreme pack leader. This human lived in a dwelling that smelled of his father. When he was a pup the human would lift him in her arms and rub his neck and feed him good food. When he was bad the human would make loud sounds and put him out of the dwelling until he apologized by putting back his ears or approaching her low. She would always reward him with long rubs and kisses.

His father had taught him that she was the dominant within the pack, even if he was the pack leader. But more importantly, he had been taught that she was not food. Humans were never food.

He looked at the bloody mass. But *it* wasn't human; it smelled wrong. It was food.

# Adaptation

**Carmella stood at** the foot of the old woman's bed, unhappy she was still alive. Other than a facial tic, drooping eyes, and a cold compress on her forehead, she looked the same as she did before.

Sonny sat on the edge of the bed holding his mother's hand while Earl squeezed Carmella's arm tightly.

"I brought her," Earl said, releasing Carmella's arm and shoving her into the footboard.

The old woman's face twitched. "Is the baby hurt?"

Carmella blinked. "No."

"I dropped him."

Carmella nodded. "But I caught him. He's okay."

"I didn't hear him cry. I thought I hurt him."

*Wow,* Carmella thought. *This bitch of a woman did some serious suffering, and she still shows concern for Raj.* "He's fine."

The older woman nodded. "Bring him to me. I want to see him."

*If I put Raj in that hag's arms,* Carmella thought, *he'll sting her again and probably try to sting everyone else in the room.* Carmella eyed Earl. *But if he stung Earl first …*

"Go get my boy," Ma said. "*Now.*"

Carmella couldn't risk Raj's life like that. Raj had had enough "venom" or whatever it was to knock Ma on her ass, but he might not have enough to harm Earl or Sonny. "But you're too injured to hold him without dropping him, um, Ma," she said with a smile.

"I suppose I am," Ma said. "*Daughter.*"

Carmella stifled a shudder and looked at Sonny. "In my truck somewhere in the back seat is a baby sling. Go get it, and I'll wear it so your mom can watch him. Oh, and bring in his car seat, too."

Sonny was so used to being bossed around that he did as she instructed.

Carmella smiled at Ma. "Thank you for asking about Raj."

**198**

# Adaptation

"I'm going to name him William," Ma said. "No, Will. Don't call my son Raj again."

If Carmella's hands weren't bound behind her, she would have leaped across the bed and strangled the woman. Instead she decided she would kill her slowly. *The more pain the better.*

"You can see she's still hurting," Earl said. "You need to take care of her ... and us."

Carmella's skin began to crawl.

Sonny returned with the sling and the car seat.

"Sonny, go get the baby," Earl said.

*No! Raj would surely sting him.* "But I need to change his diaper first," Carmella said quickly. "You need to untie me so I can do that. I mean, unless *you* want to do it, Earl. He may only be wet, but his poops are legendary."

Earl cursed and untied the rope around her wrists. "Don't try any shit." He took her roughly by the arm and led her back into the living room.

Carmella scooped up Raj, hugging and kissing him as he hiccupped and made quiet whooping sounds. "I love you, Raj," she whispered. "You're not going to be someone's William." She picked up the diaper bag, laid Raj on the couch, and prepared for the worst. *I hope you left me a big, stinky present ...*

Earl looked out the window remembering a time when he'd had two children and a wife who loved them as much as this woman loved her child. But that time was gone, and they were living in a new world. He had needs that had to be met. For eight years he'd sought comfort in Linda's body, but she was old enough to be his mother and there was nothing pretty about her. He had to close his eyes and dream about his wife just to get hard.

He watched Carmella changing the boy's diaper and felt a yearning that went beyond sex. He wanted more than a family consisting of a half-dead old woman and her babied son who was older than he was. He wanted to have more children, and he wanted to take care of them. He wanted a real family again.

Carmella glanced at Earl. "I'm finished." She cradled Raj in her arms. "He was only wet this time."

# Adaptation

Earl thought the kid was cute with his curly black hair. He knew the boy was fighting sleep the way he rubbed at his eyes. His children did the same thing, and when they did, his wife and he would load them into the car and go for a ride—

*Fuck!* He had to stop living in the past.

Grimly he gestured to the other room with the muzzle of his rifle.

Ma's face lit up when Carmella came into the room with Raj.

Carmella tied on and deposited her drowsy boy into the sling, placing a pacifier into his mouth. *To keep your stingers where they belong for now.* Raj protested briefly, but when she gave him her hand to hold, he quieted and seemed to stare at everything at once.

"He's so beautiful," Ma said. "His father was Chinese?"

Carmella clenched her teeth and swallowed her pain and rage. "Korean and Caucasian." *And Centaurian …*

"Sorry you lost your man," Ma said.

"I didn't lose him." Carmella glared at her. "Earl killed him."

"We all lost somebody." Ma felt the compress on her head. "This cloth is warm. My migraine's coming back, Sonny."

Sonny picked up the cloth. "I'll make it ice cold, Ma."

Ma rubbed her forehead. "Earl, you go out and see about making dinner. I want tomato soup. I think the baby will like that."

"I'm not leaving her alone with you," Earl said.

"Then take the baby with you. You can wear that sling thing." She frowned at Carmella. "You won't try nothing, will you? Not with Earl holding that boy."

"Um, no," Carmella said.

"Ma, I don't want to leave you," Sonny whined.

"I know son, but I need to talk to her. Alone. Woman stuff." She looked at Carmella. "I haven't had a woman to talk to in ten or fifteen years."

Earl yanked Carmella's arm roughly and whispered, "You do anything to hurt that woman, and I'll put a bullet in your kid's brain. You got it?"

Carmella nodded.

Earl released her arm. "Now hold him till I get this sling off you."

Carmella patted Raj's bottom. "You be good, son." *But if you can't be good, sting Earl directly in his testicles.*

Earl untied the sling. "Give him to me."

Carmella put Raj in Earl's arms.

"Well, tie me up," Earl said.

*I'd like to hogtie you,* Carmella thought, tightening the knot. "Not too tight?"

Earl sighed. "Come on, Sonny. Let's go."

Sonny reluctantly followed Earl out of the room.

Ma patted the bed. "Sit down over here."

Carmella sat.

"I thought I was having another stroke," the old woman said. "Had one of those and couldn't speak right for weeks." Ma sighed. "I'm getting older. I'll get better, but I'm not a hundred percent sure that I want to."

*Oh, woe is you,* Carmella thought.

"My son needs a woman, you know."

"You've made that clear," Carmella said.

"But Earl wants you and means to have you." Her face twitched. "I know he don't want me no more. And I expect tonight he's going to take you, and that might just damage my family because Sonny wants you, too. Sonny can't go up against Earl." She sighed. "Earl would stomp him like a bug."

*And Sonny would be one less asshole I'd have to worry about,* Carmella thought.

"Earl's always taken good care of us," Ma said. "We just let him." She reached out and touched Carmella's hand. "If I could, I would blow your brains out right now."

Carmella's eyes flitted to the shrunken, cold fingers of this ancient, cold-blooded thief of children.

"Just to stop the pain that is about to be visited on my family," Ma said. "We had a good thing going before you showed up. You've made them want the same thing, and only one man can win."

## Adaptation

Carmella jerked her hand away. "You hijacked *my* family and yet I'm an inconvenience to *you*? You are a monster, lady. A real monster."

"You can't talk to me that—"

"I can and I will," Carmella interrupted. "Let me explain to you how this really works. I don't have to let your son fuck me. In pack terms, he's nothing but an omega. Earl is the alpha of this fucked-up 'family.' And he's already made it plain that he means to have me. I'm going to choose him. This way I'm not passed around from man to man like I'm some whore. That's the only way I'm going to survive this situation that you put me in when you set eyes on my child and said you wanted him for your own."

Ma frowned. "You're not leaving my son without a woman."

Carmella crossed her arms in front of her. "If Sonny was the head of this group, then I'd choose him. I'm sure I'd get pregnant quickly." *If hell froze over.* "I can have a whole lot of babies before I get too old. And they would be your grandchildren, made of your own flesh and blood."

Ma's eyes lit up.

"Sonny and I could have a real family, and you could help with our babies. Humans have to be packs now. We can't make it on our own. I need a pack, but I'd be a fool to take Sonny the omega as my mate when I can have Earl the alpha."

"You're going to choose the man who shot your man?"

Carmella felt hot tears behind her eyes but she swallowed back the pain as she glared at the old woman. "It's bad enough being the whore for one man. I won't be a whore for two."

"We've all been whores at one time or another," Ma said. "Before those space alien demons came to Earth, Sonny worked at the bank. He was security guard."

"Once that virus hit, Sonny brought me to the bank. We stockpiled the vault with food enough to last a few months, and then Sonny locked us in. At first I thought he was crazy and that we would suffocate, but he said that air circulated and the vault could be opened from both the outside as well as the inside. We stayed

202

holed up in the bank, just sleeping in that shiny steel vault." She shook her head. "We heard the riots, but we were safe." She cackled. "We were safe in the safe!" Ma laughed until she started coughing.

*Please choke to death on your laughter,* Carmella thought, *so I can have something to laugh about, too.*

"Time just seemed like it didn't exist anymore, you know?" Ma said. "The only way I knew time was moving at all was because we began seeing fewer and fewer people whenever we went out to find food." She sighed. "We shouldn't have stayed so long in that safe, because something happened to Sonny. He just … changed into a child again. He needed to be taken care of all over again. All he wanted to do was drink beer and eat sweets."

*And play with himself,* Carmella thought.

"One day we had to leave the bank because the fans stopped working," Ma said. "And the smell was horrible. But we weren't equipped for what we found out in the rest of the world — death, burned-out cities, everybody scared, people who would just as soon shoot you as say hi to you. And those gray Blobs were everywhere, trying to stop the rebellion." She shook her head. "We wouldn't have survived any of it without Earl. Scavenging is hard when you don't know how to shoot."

*That's why you get you a gun and learn,* Carmella said.

"Earl found us pushing a shopping cart filled with beer and soup." Ma smiled crookedly. "That was generally what we ate. Soup. He helped us with the cart and invited us back to his house. He started doing things like hunting for fresh meat. He had guns and knew how to use them. He found places for us to rest our heads and protected us from the wolves." She closed her eyes. "And for eight years I've been his whore."

**The wolf crept** closer to his prey, which hadn't moved for a long time. He stayed low to the ground and crawled within inches of his prey's feet. He eyed the tender neck. Once he sank his teeth into that neck, he would crush the larynx and twist.

The wolf leaped.

Bilal's body bowed forward as the wolf flew through the air, and two sleek, new talon-tipped tentacles shot from the holes in his chest and abdomen to impale the torso of the young wolf. The tentacles held the wolf high in the air while the talons pumped poison into the wolf's body.

The wolf writhed briefly before the tentacles retracted and the wolf's body dropped to the ground beside Bilal.

Sensors sprouted from the tentacles, waved in the air, and pointed southwest.

They had found the fading scent of Carmella and Raj.

# Chapter 29
## ~Escapes~

**Bilal turned** his head and looked at the furry carcass next to him. A moment of confusion overtook him and he reached out weakly.

"Wolf ... what did I do ... ?" He pulled the dead animal to him feeling the warmth radiate from him like a furnace. He pressed his face into the animal's fur and clutched him with stiff fingers. Without another thought he released his new tentacles as if he had always had them. In fact, reaching through them felt safe and familiar.

He remembered the last time that he'd saved the wolf; after stinging him in battle. Carmella would never forgive him if he hurt her child. His tentacles arched around the still body of the animal finding the entry points and then he latched on. Filaments quickly entered the body and sought the damage.

Bilal's awareness moved through his filaments in a familiar way. He felt comfortable but the damage he had done had been bad. He had to force the wolf's body to imprison the poison so that it could be expelled and then he had to find the trigger within the cells to make them begin healing.

His filaments thinned until they were invisible to the naked eye. Just one stem cell is all that was needed and if he could find one that was still viable then he could 'turn it back on'. If he found the trigger in time then the others would learn and adapt because that is all life was—a series of adaptations. It would be a rapid wild fire in the dead animal; but only if he caught it in time.

He 'saw' the animals body crashing like a row of dominoes, moving swiftly and turning everything grey but he also saw that there were still areas of pink; life! He allowed a filament to surge forward and bury itself into the nucleus of a bright, living cell. Other filaments did the same. As the grey closed in to extinguish the last bits of life there came the smallest spark from one lone cell. The grey of death came to a skidding halt; waiting, and soon the spark spread to the other cells and life arose like a goliath forcing the grey of death to retreat.

Bilal knew that in order to get the blood to circulate so that it could feed the life the heart must beat. Bilal worked on the animal, sapping the little strength that he had but not caring, perhaps not even realizing. Exhausted he again lost consciousness and yet his body continued its work on both himself as well as the wolf that had only moments before intended him to be its next meal.

**Ma's bedroom walls** seemed to close in on Carmella. After they ate tomato soup, Earl and Sonny hovered around Ma until she fell asleep. Carmella fed Raj and laid him in his car seat where he soon fell asleep.

As she sat in a chair in the corner, Carmella thought about smothering that hateful bitch with a pillow after the men left, climbing out the window with Raj, and running off into the night. Instead she patiently bided her time until she could take away everything that Ma loved.

Ma's eyes finally drooped and her snores announced that she was sleeping deeply.

A spike of fear rose and fell in Carmella. This was the eleventh hour. Sonny continued to hold his mother's hand, so it seemed raping Carmella was the last thing on his mind.

*But it wouldn't take much to make it the* first *thing in his mind,* Carmella thought. *How am I going to get out of this?*

# Adaptation

Earl stood near the bedroom door, his rifle slung over his shoulder, Carmella's nine-millimeters in her holster around his waist. He shifted his stance and stared at her.

*Oh, Lord,* Carmella thought. *Here we go.*

Earl stepped over to her, grabbed her arm, and snatched her up from her chair. "Come on."

Raj awoke and started to whimper, his pudgy hands reaching for Carmella. When he began to cry, Ma stirred and tried to sit up.

Sonny stood. "Earl?"

"Sit the fuck down, Sonny, and take care of your mother." Adrenaline and need coursed through Earl's body. He hadn't planned on doing it this way, but as he watched the girl sitting there, he fantasized about shoving his cock into her, into her mouth, into her pussy, maybe even into her ass. She would have full firm titties instead of flaccid sacks like Linda. And maybe she would like it. Yes, he would make her like it. He had to have her, and he had to have her *now.*

Sonny moved toward Earl. "What are you doing, Earl?"

Earl ignored Sonny and dragged Carmella out of the room and into the hallway. He had almost reached the living room despite Carmella's kicking and clawing when Sonny jumped on his back, knocking Earl to the floor and sending Carmella flying into the couch.

"Mine!" Sonny screamed, his face filled with rage as he pummeled the back of Earl's head with his fists. "She's mine!"

Earl was surprised that soft, stubby Sonny had jumped him, and some of the blows were starting to hurt. "Get off me, Sonny, or I'm going to hurt you!"

"No!" Sonny shouted. "Ma said she's mine! You got Ma and she's mine!"

Earl couldn't let the fucker beat the shit out of him, so he worked his arm free until the gun was pressed into Sonny's hip. "Get off or I shoot, Sonny."

"No!" Sonny screamed, ignoring the weapon while his fists landed on the other man more painfully than Sonny could have imagined possible.

Carmella ignored the pain in her neck and shoulders, dug out the butcher's knife from under a cushion, and scrambled off the couch. While Sonny continued to pound on Earl's back, she darted into the bedroom for her screaming son.

Ma was trying to pull herself out of the bed and had one foot on the floor but froze when she saw Carmella waving the knife.

"Don't move, bitch." Carmella snatched the car seat.

"No!" Ma screamed. "Don't take my baby!"

"This boy is *mine*," Carmella hissed, throwing up the window beside Ma's bed. She maneuvered the car seat out and reached her arm out as far as she could. "Hold on, Raj." She dropped the car seat to the ground below.

"Earl!" Ma yelled. "Sonny! Come quick! She's getting away!"

Carmella climbed out of the window and landed near the car seat. As she grabbed the handle and started to run, she heard the loud crack of a gunshot.

**Bilal's violent shivers** pulled him out of unconsciousness. Dull pain engulfed him, but it wasn't as bad as the ripping pain that had coursed through him earlier.

He tried to sit up and felt the warmth of the wolf next to him. He braced himself and looked at the unfamiliar animal, vaguely remembering hurting it and than healing it. The wolf merely thumped his tail once and allowed his ears to fall back in submission.

A frown creased Bilal's brow at the vague memory of a new set of tentacles and how he had repaired both himself and the wolf. He pulled up his shirt. It was stiff and cold with blood, but he felt his chest and abdomen as well as the new patches of roughened skin. He saw what his son had on his side, only his holes were the size of bullets.

He pulled himself to his feet, and the wolf stood. Bilal watched him warily, but the wolf waited with his tail tucked between his legs. Bilal turned to examine the dark night. The tentacles in his tongue pushed their way from his mouth, and Bilal followed the scent near the dried pool of blood. It smelled like Carmella.

Bilal turned to the dealership building and pictured the woman and man who had exited it. He relived the surprise of being shot and stared at his feet. Something had happened to Carmella right here on this spot of ground.

His heartbeat quickened in anguish. She had fallen to the ground right here. He didn't see blood. She hadn't been shot. He hurried to the entrance of the building and pulled the door open. The wolf scampered in behind him.

He crossed his arms in front of himself and tucked his hands beneath his armpits. He scanned the large showroom, his body shivering. The wolf began to sniff and investigate. Bilal moved to a bright red convertible sports car and saw a key in the ignition. Carmella said regular gas didn't work, but maybe it would since this car had been sitting inside for all these years. He got in and turned the key.

The rumble of the engine startled the wolf, who backed away from the offending vehicle and raised his hackles, thick smoke filling the showroom. Bilal fumbled for the heat controls and turned them on full blast. When his stiff fingers had warmed up enough to be useful, the engine sputtered and the car died. He climbed out of it while the wolf growled at the vehicle.

Bilal spotted a large black Toyota Tundra that reminded him of Carmella's truck. *Her truck was diesel,* he thought. *Is this a diesel truck?* Anxiously he climbed inside and started the engine. It sputtered to life but quickly died. *Not a diesel.*

*But there's one outside. We were coming inside to find the key.*

He checked several offices in the showroom and found no keys. He did find a vending machine in a waiting room outside the service area. The machine contained chips and snacks old enough to have become new life forms, but he didn't care. He needed sustenance. He pushed the machine over, the loud crash of the shattering glass and metal causing Wolf to scamper away and hide behind a desk.

The wolf looked out at the pack master, who stood fearlessly over the destruction. The human reached down and lifted the broken machine onto its side where several small packages fell out and landed among the glass. The wolf watched the man pick up one of the packages and tear it open. He greedily ate the contents and picked up a second package and did the same. The wolf watched from his hiding place, and then the pack master tossed him one of the packages. The wolf eased toward it and sniffed but didn't find anything about it particularly interesting. But following the example of the human, he ripped the bag open and found something tasty. He ate greedily and eyed the other packages.

The human tossed him a few more, and they ate. While he munched on the stalest of pretzels, Bilal found a mechanic's jumpsuit. He shed his bloody clothes and pulled on the jumpsuit, "Mike" written on the breast. Without the blood stiffened clothes he didn't feel as cold. He looked around at the service area then ransacked desks in the sales area, yanking drawers and searching, always searching—

And then he smiled for the first time.

**There were a** series of shouts behind Carmella, both male and female, Ma screaming "No! No! No!" and "Why?" repeatedly and Earl cursing up a storm.

Carmella ran around the house to her truck with Raj in his car seat. She ripped open the driver's side door.

No key.

For a moment shock froze her. *Earl has to have it!* She looked toward the front door of the house and saw Earl crouched and aiming the nine-millimeter out into the night.

# Adaptation

"Don't move or I'll shoot!" Earl shouted.

With trembling fingers, Carmella unstrapped her son from his car seat and held him tightly against her. Moving low to the ground, she darted around the truck to the opposite side and began sprinting into the darkness.

"Stop!" Earl yelled, and a shot rang out.

Pain flared in Carmella's right thigh, and she stumbled. *Please God, no ...*

Carmella didn't feel a lot of pain, but when she tried to put weight on her leg it crumbled beneath her. She rolled before she hit the ground to keep Raj from hitting the ground. She tried crawling on her knees through the dirt, but there was nowhere to go.

She had no place to hide.

She felt a kick on her side, and her breath colored the cold air.

"You stupid bitch!" Earl growled.

Carmella curled into a protective ball around Raj, covering her head and protecting her baby as Earl began raining down blows with his fists.

"You ruined it all! Look at what you made me do!" Earl gripped her by the back of her shirt and heaved her toward a stump, Raj spilling from her arms.

She reached for Raj, but Earl dragged her a few feet away. She stared at her baby. He wasn't wearing a coat, and it was far too cold for him.

Earl pinned her arms to the ground and covered her with his body. His face was swollen and bloody, his nose flat and obviously broken, one eye swollen and already turning purple.

Carmella wiggled and squirmed beneath him and Earl tried to force himself between her legs. She thrust her knee into his groin, Earl cried out and rolled over, and she scrambled to her feet dragging her right leg toward Raj.

Earl lurched to his feet and pointed the gun at Raj. "You touch him," Earl wheezed, "he dies."

# Adaptation

Carmella's life seemed as if it would crash to a halt. There would be no reason to continue if Raj got shot. "No!" she screamed. "Don't! *Don't!* I'll do whatever you want."

He turned and wiped blood from his lips. In a voice devoid of all emotion except his lust, he said, "Take off your clothes."

**Bilal grabbed a** pile of keys from the drawer of a desk, each key attached to a black fob with buttons. He pressed random buttons, but nothing happened. He read through the small tags attached to the fobs and found several marked "Tundra." He walked as fast as his body would allow to the truck outside, inserting each key into the lock.

The third key worked.

He opened the door, put the key in the ignition, and turned the key.

Nothing happened.

He looked at the floorboards and saw a third pedal. *Carmella's truck only had two, one for going fast, and one for stopping.* He pushed the third pedal toward the floorboard with his hand and turned the key.

The engine sputtered once and died.

He climbed in and pressed the third pedal all the way to the floor with his left foot. He turned the key.

The engine growled to life, and Bilal smiled. He lifted his foot from the pedal.

The engine cut off.

He pressed the pedal down and restarted the truck. He looked to his right and pulled the gearshift until it wiggled back and forth. He slowly released the pedal.

The engine kept running.

He turned up the heat, and while the engine idled, he opened the door, stepped out, and stared into the night. He opened his mouth and concentrated on the feel of Carmella and Raj. He reached for the buttons on his jumpsuit and opened the front. Gray snake-like tentacles pushed past his skin, and long and powerful filaments emerged from the tip. They moved to the left, reaching in that direction, stretching toward something invisible to the human eye but clear to the Centaurian eye.

Bilal climbed into the truck, hesitating before closing the door and looking behind him at the darkened, ruined building.

The wolf appeared amid the broken glass and twisted metal of the entrance.

Bilal got out of the truck and pointed inside.

The wolf did as he was bid and scurried up into the unfamiliar interior. He shivered in fear-laced anticipation as Bilal gunned the engine, shifted into first gear, and raced toward Carmella and Raj.

# Chapter 30
## ~Endings~

**Carmella's terror nearly** numbed her as much as the cold did. She peeled away several layers of clothing as Earl watched and Raj wailed. When she was only in her bra and jeans, her trembling became fierce. *If he walks behind me, he'll see the knife. I have to keep his attention on my front.*

"Take it off ..." Earl whispered.

Carmella unhooked the bra, shrugged out of it, and let it drop to the ground. She stood straighter and made no effort to cover her breasts with her arms. "It's cold. Please, can we go inside? My son isn't wearing a coat."

Several expressions passed across Earl's face before it turned to stone. He gestured with the gun. "The sooner you suck it, the quicker you and your boy can get where it's warm. Not back to that house; a different one. You, me, and the kid."

Carmella nodded, sliding one hand behind her to grip the wooden hilt of the knife. She dropped to her knees and suppressed a gag. *I will stab the shit out of him before I suck his dick, but I have to keep myself between the gun and Raj in case he fires.* Pain flared to life in her right thigh, and she did her best to ignore it. The longer she prolonged this, the longer she and Raj would be cold. She put both hands behind her back to fully expose her swollen breasts.

Earl groaned huskily. He fumbled at his waistband and dropped his pants where they pooled around his knees. His penis strained toward Carmella's face, thick, hard, and throbbing.

# Adaptation

Carmella stopped shaking. She had to do this right or it would be the end of her. She pictured her hand shoving the knife blade through his ball sack and impaling his cock. She pictured slicing it off and stabbing him repeatedly in his groin as he bled to death.

A shot cracked from the porch, the ground near Earl's feet exploding in a puff of dust.

Earl dropped to the ground and covered his head.

Carmella saw Ma ambling across the yard carrying a rifle.

"Linda!" Earl screamed, cowering.

Ma shuffled toward Earl. "You killed my Sonny." She fired another shot, and it whizzed wide and struck the stump.

Carmella grabbed her bra and remaining clothes and scrambled toward the truck. She scooped up Raj, who had managed to crawl her way. He was still squirming and crying, but he wasn't making a sound. *Shoot his ass!* Carmella thought. *What are you waiting for?*

Ma limped closer and drew a bead on Earl's head. "Why'd you kill my boy?"

"I didn't have a choice, Linda!" Earl shouted. "Look what he did to me! He was trying to kill *me!*"

Linda fired another shot, and this one hit its target.

Earl screamed like a baby. "Linda, no!" Earl begged as he held his belly. "Linda, *please!*"

Carmella tried to back away, but her leg felt like it was on fire. She could feel the hot blood wetting the back of her pants. She stared at the house. She had to get there …

"Don't you move," Ma said, and she swung the barrel of the rifle in her direction. "William's all I got now cuz my Sonny's gone!" Her eyes narrowed, and she returned her attention to Earl, who was moaning in pain on the ground.

Raj's body became rigid. "Daaadaaadaa!!" he cried. He kicked his little fat legs and clutched at her as if he was trying to get away from something.

215

# Adaptation

*Oh my God, is he hurt?* Frantically she felt inside his clothes. Dear God, he was burning hot! "Ma, something's wrong with the baby! He's hurt!"

Ma's head swiveled back to Carmella and the hysterical baby. She dropped her right hand from the gunstock, and the rifle butt dropped to the ground. She reached out her right arm. "Give him to me!"

Carmella saw Earl crawling toward Ma. *He's going to grab for the rifle!* "Look out!"

Ma snapped up the rifle and pointed it at Earl's face. "I see him. He's done for anyway. He's gut shot. Critters will be eating his intestines all night. Now give the boy to me."

"No, Ma," Carmella said. "We need to get him into the house where it's warm."

Linda frowned. "Where you think I'm going? It's cold as shit out here."

"But you're still not strong enough to hold him *and* that rifle," Carmella said. "Let's go inside, okay? You don't want the baby to die, too, right?"

Ma blinked and swallowed back a sob. She shook her head. "Just shut up, will you! *Just shut up!*"

"Linda!" Earl wailed in pain.

"You shut up, too, Earl." Ma sighed. "And don't you ever say my name again." She fired the rifle, and Earl's head snapped back, a neat, black hole blooming in his forehead. Ma pointed the rifle at Carmella. "Get my son out of this cold, will you?"

Carmella took a step but fell in a heap to the ground.

"Hurry up, you stupid bitch!" Ma screamed. "What the hell's wrong with you?"

"Earl shot me," Carmella moaned. She squeezed her eyes closed, and the pain subsided. She crawled and pulled herself across the dirt, her breasts throbbing with the need to feed her baby and leaking milk. Raj hiccupped and reached past Carmella, trying desperately to get out of her arms. She was alarmed to see that he was reaching in Ma's direction, little fat hands clutching at the air as he cried repeatedly, "Blaaa! Blaaadaadaaa! Dadadada!"

# Adaptation

Was he calling *Bilal?* Not much could have broken her heart more. Her baby was crying for his dead daddy.

Ma followed behind Carmella as she crawled. "Yes, baby boy. Mommy will get you all warmed up."

*Yes,* Carmella thought. *I will make you warm and safe …*

When Carmella reached the porch, the harsh light from inside allowed her to see what was causing her baby to cry out.

Snakes seemed to be coming out of his shirt.

Carmella pulled off his shirt to expose Raj's tan and pink chest and abdomen and found two gray and tan tentacles whipping around in the air. They seemed to be reaching behind them.

"What's wrong now?" Ma yelled.

Carmella couldn't let Ma see the tentacles because she was a crazy bitch with a loaded rifle. "Uh, he had a spider under his shirt." She dragged herself into the house and fumbled with Raj's shirt, pulling it back onto his body and swaddling him in one of her shirts.

She struggled to the couch where she offered Raj her breast, praying that he would take it by the time Linda entered the house, but Raj kept turning his head away.

"Blaaa, no!" Raj cried. "Blaaadaadaaa, Dadadada, no!"

*No?* Carmella thought. *He's saying "no"?* Carmella looked into the hallway and what was left of Sonny's face. *Two down, and the one I thought was down to go.*

Ma entered the house and hobbled to the couch, reaching for Raj with a shaking right hand while holding the rifle with her left. "Give him to me."

Carmella pressed her nipple into Raj's mouth.

He latched onto her nipple with an angry whimper and was soon feeding hungrily.

"I need to hold him," Ma said. "He can eat later."

Carmella shook her head. "He's hungry, Ma. He needs a warm bath, and then we need to put him to sleep." *And when you go to sleep, I'm planting my butcher knife in your skull.*

Ma's eyes glazed over. "You know, I don't need you anymore." She raised the rifle.

217

# Adaptation

*Oh my God, this bad-shooting bitch is going to fire at me while I'm nursing a baby!* "Ma, no!" Carmella screamed.

A low growl sounded behind Ma, and the old woman swung around.

Directly behind her in the doorway stood a wolf and a man.

Raj released Carmella's nipple. "Dada," he said calmly.

Ma recognized Bilal instantly. "But you're dead!" she howled. "You can't be here!"

Bilal blinked, and two tentacles squirmed into the air from his chest.

Ma backed away, her lips quivering. "Unless you're the Angel of Death come to take me!" She raised the rifle with shaking hands.

The wolf leaped, gripping her right wrist in his massive jaws and dragging her to the floor. The rifle flew for her hands and banged into a wall. The wolf released her wrist and stood on Ma's shoulders and hips, growling and snapping at her face as drool dripped onto her shirt.

Bilal stepped over Ma's legs and took in everything at once. He saw a dead man lying in the hallway with his face half blown away, Carmella sitting on the floor stunned and topless, and Raj, who had worked his way out of the swaddling of his mother's shirt and clutched at the air with pudgy fists crying "Bla Dadada!" as little tentacles reached for Bilal from his abdomen.

Bilal collected his son in one arm and Carmella in the other. His arm held her firmly, soothing her hysteria until she reached up and touched his face, assuring herself that he was really there.

"Bilal ..."

Raj's tentacles intertwined with Bilal's while his hands held his father. The two sets of tentacles moved in a strange rhythm, the son's mimicking the intricate twirls of his father's.

Bilal looked into Carmella's bewildered eyes. "I smell your blood. You're hurt."

"I saw you," Carmella whispered. "They shot you." Carmella wrapped her arms around his strong body and hugged him. "I thought you were dead."

218

# Adaptation

"I'm here." As she buried her face in his neck and sobbed, Bilal turned to the old woman watching from the floor.

Ma was going insane with terror. A wolf's teeth were inches from her eyes, and the man's black skin was turning red. He had to be the father of the baby. The baby had similar tentacles growing from his stomach, and they were twirling around each other like a pit of vipers! He glared at her with slanted, Asian eyes, "Mike" written on the nametag of his coveralls. "What *are* you?" she whimpered.

*I am a new being,* Bilal thought. "There is a dead man in the front yard with his pants down. Did he rape my child's mother?"

Carmella hugged him tighter, shivering uncontrollably and he gently rubbed her back.

"No," Ma stammered. "I killed him before he did that. I-I-I sh—shot him." Anguished tears streamed down her withered cheeks.

Bilal gestured to the dead man behind him. "And that one? Did he rape my child's mother?"

"That's my son! He killed my son!"

A talon-tipped tentacle moved toward her. "I asked you a question. Did the man in the hallway rape my child's mother?"

"No!" Ma shook her head. "And it was Earl who shot her in the leg, not me! Tell him, lady!"

Carmella turned her face to the sight of the cowering woman. "Yes, Earl shot me, but she was about to shoot me when you arrived."

"I wouldn't have done it!" Ma cried. "I swear!"

"You know, if you had killed me, Raj would have killed you." She looked up into Bilal's face. "Raj is amazing."

Ma shook her head. "His name is William, and he would never hurt me!"

"And your name is Dumb Bitch." Carmella picked up and put on a shirt. "Raj stung you, and you didn't even know he did! You tried to take everything from me, Ma, but now you have nothing." Carmella smiled at the tentacles waving and intertwining around her. "I may have a strange family, but at least I have a living one."

Ma appeared every bit as insane as she probably was, because when the devil-man's tentacle moved to caress her cheek, she leaned into it and smiled.

"Let's go home," Carmella said, her eyes half closed as another tentacle moved to twine lovingly against her neck and throat.

Bilal nodded once and lifted her carefully, transferring the baby to her arms. One long tentacle swooped down for the rifle, and the other untwined from his son and touched the wolf's neck.

The wolf backed off the old woman and followed his pack masters out of the house.

Bilal placed Carmella in the passenger seat of their truck, Raj's tentacles securely around Carmella's body.

"I don't know who has the keys," she said. "And we'll need the car seat."

Bilal passed her the rifle. "We won't ever need a car seat again." He nodded at Raj. "His tentacles will keep him safe. I'll be back."

"Be careful," Carmella said. "There are more guns in the house."

"I will be fine," Bilal said.

Raj whimpered. "Blabla! Dada!"

Bilal blinked. "Did he just call my name?"

Carmella nodded. "He even knew you were coming."

Bilal bent down and placed a kiss on his son's curly hair. "Daddy will be back. I swear it to you." He leaned in and placed his lips on Carmella's. After a moment he closed the door behind him, and he and the wolf returned to the house.

Carmella's fingers touched her lips. She counted the seconds tensely as she reached in the back for the coat Bilal had gone "shopping" for earlier and pulled it on, wrapping her and Raj in the warmth of the oversized parka.

Two minutes later, Bilal reappeared with the keys.

# Adaptation

The wolf climbed into the truck and nestled into a space in the back.

Bilal started the truck and cranked the heat.

"Did she say anything to you?" Carmella whispered.

"She asked me to kill her," Bilal said.

"I wish she had asked me that," Carmella said. "Did you?"

"No," Bilal said. "She made you and my son suffer, and now she will suffer. She will die of starvation or the cold. Is this acceptable to you?"

Carmella nodded. "How did you get here? And where did that wolf come from?"

Bilal drove past the truck he had abandoned a short distance from the house. "I was able to get one of the trucks from the dealership running, and the wolf—"

"Stop," Carmella interrupted.

"Why?"

"Stop the truck. We need to go back and get that truck."

He slowed and braked to a stop. He turned in his seat and stared at her. "Carmella, you can't drive with a bullet in your leg. You'll end up having an accident. We can always get another truck."

"We need that truck. You already got it working, and we have plenty of fuel. We have some supplies. I want that truck, and we're not leaving without it."

He reached past her and pushed her seat back.

"What are you doing?" Carmella asked.

"You need to take off your pants," Bilal said. "I am going to fix your leg so you can drive."

While Raj held on, Carmella reached down to undo her pants. When she brought her hips up, the pain intensified enough to cause her to cry out. "I'm going to need your help."

Bilal used a tentacle to lower her jeans to her knees, leaving her only wearing French-cut black panties.

She tried to turn to face him, but he stopped her.

"You don't have to move." A tentacle elongated and moved to wrap itself under her thigh.

221

# Adaptation

She tensed, preparing for imminent pain.

The tentacle, however, bypassed the hole in her thigh and moved up a few inches. She felt pressure, but considering the pain of the gunshot, it didn't amount to much. After a minute, the pain disappeared completely.

She sighed in relief. By the time he'd finished, both the wolf and Raj were in a deep sleep.

His tentacle retreated and dropped a bullet into his hand. He showed it to her as she flexed the muscles in her thigh.

She had only the memory of pain and nothing more. "Thank you."

He placed his hand on her thigh and stared deeply into her eyes. "I love you, Carmella. I will never allow anyone or anything to hurt you again. Do you understand? I will *always* come back for you."

She inhaled deeply and closed her eyes. She felt the love he had for her in every fiber of her being. She opened her eyes and looked at him. "I love you, Bilal. And I trust you. And I know you will always protect us. You'll always come back for us."

Bilal closed his eyes for a moment. "Yes."

The most horrible day in his life had turned out to be the most beautiful because the woman he loved now loved him in return.

# Chapter 31
## ~Home~

**Carmella pulled her** truck into her driveway. It felt as if they had been gone for a million years, but they had only been gone twelve hours.

Bilal pulled his truck in beside hers and got out, his wolf leaping out after him. He opened the passenger door, extended his tentacles, and extricated a soundly sleeping Raj from Carmella's grasp.

"Thanks," Carmella whispered. "He's a chunk." She stretched and stared at her farmhouse. She knew it wasn't only her home. It was *their* home. She smiled at *her* man holding *their* child.

Wolf and Girl were on the porch, alert to the presence of the strange wolf, which stood below the porch steps scenting the air and wagging his tail. Hackles raised, they moved down the stairs. Carmella was about to call out for them to back down when Wolf nipped the young animal playfully on the neck. They then rolled in the frosty grass, and Girl jumped into the foray.

Carmella smiled, laughed, and clapped her hands. She pointed happily. "That's one of my grandbabies!" She slipped her arm around Bilal's waist. "You befriended one of Wolf's and Girl's offspring."

He smiled. "I knew he looked familiar. Let's go inside. It's cold and you're half dressed." He put his arm around her, and she sighed in contentment.

While Bilal built a large fire in the fireplace and stoked up the wood stove, Carmella retrieved dog food from the pantry and set out big dishes for each of the wolves. After Bilal put Raj to bed, he saw Carmella on the front porch surrounded by the three wolves and rubbing them as if they were puppies. He smiled. Those wolves were part of her family every bit as much as Raj and he were. He joined her on the porch, and though he was more than tired, he spent time with her giving love to Wolf, Girl, and Lil' Wolf.

Afterwards Carmella went into the kitchen to put on a large pot of water to boil. She then poked around the pantry.

"What are you doing?" Bilal asked.

"I'm making you something to eat." She held up a can of beef stew and took a can opener from a drawer.

He put his hand over hers, stopping her before she could open the can. "It's okay. I'm more tired than hungry. Come here."

He opened his arms, and Carmella closed her eyes and slipped into his embrace. She sighed as Bilal stroked her long dreadlocks and hugged her tightly. She felt tears filling her eyes but was afraid to allow them to spill down her cheeks. She didn't want to lose it now, because what if she never got it back?

She slipped from his grasp, wiped her eyes, and sniffed back her tears. She picked up the simmering pot and poured steaming water into a large bronze washbasin. "Come here. I want to wash the blood off you."

Bilal looked down at his dirty hands. His nails were caked with drying blood, dirt, and oil. He stood in front of the wood stove while Carmella examining his hands front and back. She squeezed them, released them, and wiped tears from her eyes.

"Stand next to the wood stove," she said. "I don't want you to catch cold." She knelt and untied his boots.

Bilal watched her knowing that she did this for him as a way to pay tribute. He wanted to lift her from the floor and hold her in his arms but knew she had to do this in order to feel better. He kicked off his boots.

She rose and gently pulled down his coveralls, which left him nude. She helped him step out of his pants then pointed at the washbasin. "It might be a little hot."

"I'll be fine," Bilal said, stepping in.

# Adaptation

She dipped a small plastic pitcher into the water and poured it over him, steam rising from his skin. She wet his hair then dipped a washcloth into the water, lathering it with the soap she used for Raj. She rubbed the cloth over his body.

Bilal remembered the first time Carmella had given him upstairs in the bathtub. His penis had grown then nearly as fast as it was growing now. He did nothing to hide it.

Carmella's washcloth moved lovingly over Bilal's body. She knew he would take care of them, and she would take care of him. That was what family did. Bilal and Raj were her family, and she wouldn't have it any other way. She was painfully aware that she had almost lost them, but she would never take what she had for granted again.

Her hands stopped over the bullet holes in Bilal's chest. They looked like old scars with keloid impressions on them. She placed her fingertips over them and peeked at Bilal, making sure it didn't hurt him. He made no indication that it did. She pressed lightly, and it bulged back slightly.

While Carmella watched in fascination, a tentacle emerged from each hole. One tentacle twined its way around her hand and her wrist. She reached out tentatively and touched the second tentacle, the flesh smooth and gray, then held and brought it to her lips where she kissed it softly. She looked at Bilal, whose lips had pulled upward into a smile.

"You're not afraid?" he asked.

"No."

She dipped more water into the pitcher, and the tentacle around her wrist released. She rinsed him and scrubbed at the old blood on his hands and under his nails. When they were clean, she worked on his head.

Bilal leaned forward so she could work a lather through his long, silky strands. He peeked at her through the strands, and the intensity of her expression mesmerized him. Bilal reached up and placed his fingertips on her cheek. When she met his eyes, he took the pitcher from her and finished rinsing his hair. When he stepped out of the washbasin, water streamed down his body and hair leaving a puddle on the hardwood floor.

Carmella moved to get the towel, but he gripped her wrist. His strong arms pulled her to him firmly around her waist.

Carmella stared into his almond-shaped eyes, losing herself in their total blackness. He was so beautiful, from his strange black eyes and changing skin to his beautiful hair and toned body. And despite how distrustful and angry she had been, he had been beautifully caring and patient.

She slipped her arms around his neck, her body molding against him so perfectly it was as if they had been made for each other. She kissed him, her heart drumming in her chest, with the intensity of her desire for him. She needed to feel the release that came from lovemaking and not only a climax from her fingers. She wanted to feel him inside of her, to wrap her legs around him and to press her breasts into his chest.

Bilal could both feel and hear her heart beating rapidly, and his heart sped up to match it. His lips explored her mouth, his tongue tasting her, and she sucked his lower lips into her mouth. Bilal inhaled, his penis lurching to fully erection, and then he mimicked her, drawing her full upper lip into his mouth and sucking it lightly.

Carmella felt the tender warmth at her core flare to life. Her hands moved over him restlessly, not able to get enough of him. Her hand lingered on the swell of his ass, and it all became real— she was kissing him and she was caressing him.

She wanted to make love with him.

Bilal couldn't equate the pleasure of kissing Carmella to anything else he had ever experienced, and not because he was aroused. She was allowing him to hold her, to feel her touch, to kiss her lips. This woman he had violated and whose life he had invaded somehow loved him. She proved it when he felt her grip his erect penis, and the pleasure coursing through his body nearly caused him to lose his balance. He gasped, his lips parted, and his eyes closed.

# Adaptation

Carmella moved her head back in order to watch the expression of pleasure that crossed his face. His dark brow furrowed, and his skin moved from its normal gray tan to a soft red. Her fingers continued to manipulate his hard shaft until he sucked in a sharp breath.

He gripped her wrist to still her action. "No," he gasped. "I want to spill myself inside of you." He didn't ask, and he didn't wait. He lifted her easily into his arms and carried her upstairs to her bedroom.

Carmella's arms moved to wrap around his neck, and her body pulsed with wanton desire. She wanted to grip his cock again, to feel him straining over her — anything to ebb the incessant desire that had been building in her for months.

He moved surefooted through the darkened corridor. His eyes were made to see in the dark — perhaps even created for this very purpose — so that one day he might carry a woman to her bed to make love to her for the first time in a decade. Maybe everything that had happened — the world ending, him impregnating her — was supposed to lead to this.

Bilal set her down beside the bed. He looked at her face and felt her desire. As he watched her sweeping off clothes, kicking off shoes, and shimmying out of her pants and panties, his skin darkened from red to purple. Bilal's breath felt strained as he took in her beauty. With one step he closed the space between them and cupped her full breasts. He brought his lips down to one nipple and indulged in what he had fantasized about for months. He drank from her breast, her sweet milk filling his belly and curbing his hunger.

Carmella cradled his head and stroked his wet strands of hair.

When he drank his fill from the first breast, he moved to the second, drawing the warm liquid into his hungry mouth. When the flow of milk ebbed, Bilal sucked harder, drawing the milk out and gently squeezing her breast until Carmella moaned. He eyed a lone drop of milk that threatened to drip from her thick nipple and flicked out his tongue greedily, catching and swallowing it. He kissed both nipples and moved upward to reclaim her lips.

Carmella's body felt as if her breasts and nipples were on fire. When he lifted her, she clung to him, wrapping her legs around his sinewy body. When he lowered them to the bed, his cock hard between them, Carmella ground her hips against him. Her fingers buried themselves into his hair as his weight came down between her spread thighs. With insistent groans she lapped at his mouth and lips and he reciprocated, feeding her his tongue and offering his mouth.

Bilal's body knew exactly what it needed to do. He raised himself up on his left elbow and gripped his shaft, lining himself up with Carmella's opening. He moaned when he felt her slick warmth against the tip of his cock. He knew that meant that it was okay for him to push inside of her. He did and felt her hot velvety flesh engulf him. He cried out in surprise as he pumped his hips and felt the friction of her canal as it squeezed and vibrated around him.

"Carmella!" he cried.

Carmella's eyes rolled up into her head at the remembered pleasure of having a man inside of her, pushing in and out of her rhythmically. There was pain, but she remembered that the pain was unique and on this side of pleasure. The spiraling in the center of her core soon reminded her how purely delicious it was to feel a man deep inside of her.

She cried out and clutched his back with each plunge of his cock. How could she have gone so long without feeling this? How could she think her fingers could ever bring her pleasure like this? Shockwaves turned into an earthquake as her body could take no more and finally exploded. Her hips moved from the bed and met his pelvis, forcing him to bury himself balls deep into her. She buried her head into his shoulder and whimpered as wave upon wave of pleasure ebbed through her, her first manmade orgasm in over ten years.

Bilal held her, shocked by the intense feel of her clenching vagina. It was milking him the way Carmella milked the cows. He couldn't hold back any longer, and with a loud wail, Bilal released spurt after spurt of semen deep into Carmella's body.

His body tensed and seized, holding him in the throes of his own orgasm while his semen continued to flood Carmella. It took several minutes before his body would release itself from its paralysis, and with several small twitches he collapsed on top of her.

Carmella held onto Bilal's panting body. She stared wide-eyed at nothing, allowing herself to feel something she thought she had forever lost. She now knew that it had never been lost to her but had been hiding away safely until she was able to bring it back out to the light of day.

What she thought she had lost was hope.

She would never lose hope again.

**Bilal listened to** the silence of his home.

His son slept soundly in the next room, and his woman slept contently in his arms, sated from three acts of lovemaking. Had she not fallen asleep, they might still be having sex.

He was exhausted. His body told him to sleep so that it could rejuvenate, but he found it impossible to turn off his brain and allow his body to shut down.

Every second of his time was precious, and he would make every second count.

Five years and counting …

# EPILOGUE
# ~THE FIRST DAY OF THE REST OF
# OUR LIVES~

**Carmella thrashed** in her sleep, fighting the monsters of the night before. She suddenly sat bolt upright in bed with a scream ready to escape from her lips. She looked around frantically and saw that she was in her warm bed with Bilal beside her fast asleep, the covers pushed down exposing his taut belly and one nude hip. Despite the fact that he was asleep his tentacles pushed through his chest and appeared to reach for her.

As Carmella's frantic breathing calmed she watched in fascination as one tentacle gently touched her neck the other touched her cheek. This is Bilal, she thought as a warm safe feeling engulfed her. He is watching me even as he sleeps. Tiredly she settled back into bed and placed her head on his shoulders her arms going around his warm body. He didn't awaken, obviously exhausted and yet his tentacles stayed attuned to her.

She was curious about something…could they see her even without the use of Bilal's eyes? Could HE see her even though his eyes were closed? With a yawn she reached out a finger and one tentacle gently twined around it. She smiled to herself and then fell asleep with it wrapped around her finger, secure in the knowledge that none of the monsters from her dreams would ever reach her, no bad men could hurt her or her child. She was safe.

# Adaptation

The next time she opened her eyes it was daylight and Bilal was lying on his side facing her. The first thing she saw were his dark eyes staring at her and she smiled. One of his tentacles was embedded in her shoulder and she reached up to touch it but it slowly released her.

"I fixed the damage to your neck and located other things that needed fixing." His brow drew together not wanting to contemplate what she'd endured last night and all the nights before.

Carmella reached up and felt smooth skin from previous scars. How far they had come when she had hunted him down to kill him and despite that he had saved her from a pack of wolves. He could have left her to her fate but instead he carried her back to her house and repaired her even while he was badly injured from the gun shots that she had delivered.

In silent acknowledgement of all that he had done and how far they had come, Carmella hugged him tightly and kissed his lips.

"Thank you," she murmured.

"Of course."

She pulled back and looked at him. "What about you? Are you completely healed?"

"Yes."

She sat up and swung her legs out of bed. "I'm going to check on the baby."

Bilal gripped her wrist. "He's sleeping." He could hear their son's steady breathing. He would be asleep for some time unless interrupted and Bilal knew that his son needed the healing sleep just as much as he had.

Carmella looked down at Bilal's hand on her wrist; grey and tan against brown. She met his expectant eyes and smiled.

"You aren't ready to get out of bed yet?" She said with a teasing tone.

"There are things that I would like to do in this bed." He sat up. Long dark hair trailed in unruly strands over his shoulder and when the bed covers moved down below the dark thatch of hair that nestled between his legs and hinted at the delights to be found there, Carmella felt a warm jolt of electricity between her own thighs.

He reached out and drew her back down into bed. He watched the way her brown eyes darkened and listened for the increased beating of her heart and the rapid way that her breath moved in and out of her lungs. He then leaned forward and kissed her. Her responsive kiss caused his body to grow hard again and he delighted when she gripped his penis in her hand and rubbed it gently. He wasn't sure what he wanted to do more; make love to her or just lay back and let her touch him.

Suddenly he remembered that there was something that he was curious about. Sitting up suddenly he trailed kisses down Carmella's torso, not forgetting her sweet brown nipples. When he got to her belly she rolled onto her back and gave him a look filled with intensity and need.

He stroked the bush of pubic hair that covered her mound and then trailed a finger at the crease of her labia. Carmella's body began to shiver. She spread her legs and watched him as he explored her curiously.

Bilal took two fingers and spread her lips marveling at the pink, moist folds and the little pearl of pleasure that slowly unfolded from its hood. This is what he was curious about; how it would taste.

He lowered his mouth and then flicked out his tongue and collected a bit of the clear moisture that was streaming from her vagina. Immediately her body arched and she mewed. When he glanced up he saw that her head was thrown back and her eyes were tightly closed.

He flicked with his tongue again and this time her legs began to tremble and her body lurched. She gasped and caught her breath as her hands caught the sheets. Bilal watched her as he licked and sucked at the moist warm folds and soon her writhing and moans escalated until the little pearl against his tongue began to spasm rapidly. He licked it, which caused Carmella to screech and almost come off the bed. But he didn't stop. He knew that she liked what he was doing.

## Adaptation

After a moment, Carmella drew up her knees and with a breathless giggle moved away.

"Enough!" She laughed. "I can't cum anymore!"

He climbed up onto the bed and gripped her in his arms just wanting the feel of her there against his body. But she had other ideas. She kissed him and then wiggled out of his grasp and moved down the bed.

Bilal sat up on his elbows and watched as she took hold of his hard shaft. She placed his penis into her mouth and for a wonderful few seconds he forgot how to breath.

Carmella's tongue swirled around the tip of Bilal's penis. His sweet salty taste caused her mouth to water with urgency and she gobbled up as much of his shaft as she could. He was thick and hard but she was able to fill her mouth with him until he teased her tonsils.

She knew that he enjoyed her efforts when he gasped and then choked out her name.

Now Bilal understood why Lawrence always talked about and thought about sex. This was the best feeling imaginable! How could anything feel better than this? He managed to look down and the sight of Carmella's mouth filled with his penis was enough to send him over. His body seized and then he ejaculated filling her mouth with powerful jets of semen.

Yet again he abandoned all reason as he allowed his body to take over. He didn't analyze the feelings as he would have in his Centaurian body. As a human there were more emotion and sensation. He understood the passion that filled humans. And why they sometimes acted so recklessly; because there was so much more intensity. For instance, this sensation could barely be confined within himself and it was as if he was imploding into shards.

When his body finally fell from its blissful state he managed to crack open his eyes to see Carmella's beautiful face smiling down at him.

"That was … amazing," he managed.

She snuggled into his arms. "We need to get up … the cow needs milking, the eggs need to be collected, the animals need feeding-"

"Yes … " Bilal yawned. A moment later he was fast asleep.

Carmella yawned and decided that they could use a quick nap and soon she fell asleep as well.

**Much later the** two new lovers finally made their way from the bedroom and went about the task of tending to their chores. Carmella carried her fussy son on her hip. His new tentacles provided a great deal of distraction for him as he gnawed and drooled over his new limbs.

As she bathed him she examined the new limbs thoroughly. Like Bilal's his tentacles were grey and very reminiscent of a snake except that the tip held an opening, which she knew could produce a deadly sharp talon. She wondered if it was safe for him to play with it and decided that she would ask Bilal. She got him diapered and then dressed him in a set of new clothes that they had found the day before.

As she pulled on the coveralls she wondered why she had never noticed how big he had gotten. The coveralls were for nine month olds and he nearly fit them perfectly. Yes, she knew that due to her son's Centaurian DNA he was bigger than the average baby. But what she did not expect was for him to continue growing at such a rapid rate.

Carmella's head began to ache as she tried to sort through all of the things that needed to be dealt with. She'd have to talk to Bilal about Raj. Then there was the events of yesterday …

The foul memory of Sonny, Earl and Ma was one that she couldn't handle right now, so she stared at the items that she and Bilal had collected from yesterday's shopping trip. Bilal had already emptied the truck of their new bounty and it was all sitting in the living room waiting for her to put into their proper places. She decided to feed Raj once again before she tackled the pile of

# Adaptation

provisions. She sat on the chaise and slipped her breast from her bra and offered it to her son. He had been fussy earlier in the day when she had tried giving him a late breakfast and it took him a while to accept her breast.

This time he accepted it readily enough as he concentrated on his tentacle. She kissed his curls and smiled at her beautiful baby boy. And then he chomped down on her nipple and she yowed.

"Whoa Raj!" She pulled her tender breast from his mouth while he looked at her in alarm. His little face screwed up as if he would cry but she kissed his forehead and then placed her forefinger into his mouth and felt his gums.

*Oh my God. He's teething! Three month olds did not teeth ...*

The door swung open suddenly and Bilal was standing there flanked by three wolves. His eyes latched onto hers and only then did he appear to relax.

"Why did you yell?"

Big wolf and Li'l wolf followed him into the house while Girl stayed stationed on the porch stairs as if she was trained to make sure no one would breach the entrance.

"You heard that?" Of course he'd heard it. She slipped her breast back into her shirt. "Bilal we need to talk about Raj. He just bit me — with teeth."

Bilal slipped off heavy duty gloves and his new parka and tossed them onto the end of the chaise. He gave her a confused look while his son strained forward to be picked up by him. He scooped him up and Raj gripped a small fistful of his hair and immediately put it into his mouth.

Carmella couldn't help but to pause at how beautiful they looked together; Bilal wearing jeans, boots and a thermal t-shirt holding his curly haired son who looked enough like both of them that it was spooky.

She stood up and grew serious again. "Bilal he's two months old. Look how big he is."

Raj spared her a curious look before he continued with his exploration of his father's hair, quickly covering his little fist in baby drool.

235

# Adaptation

Bilal's brow rose in confusion. "I know very little about human babies. Human's rarely allowed Centaurians access to their off-spring." There was plenty of data concerning every imaginable topic of human existence but it was uploaded to the Mothership and he had never been particularly interested in the topic.

Until now.

How stupid of him not to have learned every aspect of the developmental phases of a child before impregnating Carmella with a hybrid life form? His rapid development had nearly killed her when she carried him. Why would he think that it would just stop after birth?

He frowned and hefted his son into his arms and looked into his eyes, examining him visually.

"Raj, do you want to play a game?" Bilal asked simply. Raj turned his attention to his father. "What is my name?"

Raj grinned. "Dada! Blaaablaa!"

Carmella felt her heartbeat quicken.

Bilal gestured to her. "Who is that?"

"Mommy." He said clearly. Carmella's eyes widened but she also felt a proud smile tugging at her mouth.

"What's your name?" Bilal continued.

"Rajie."

Carmella beamed with pure love and pride for her baby boy.

Bilal looked at Carmella but he seemed far from happy. Her smile slipped away. "What's wrong?"

"I have to stop this progression. It's too fast. He's developing like a Centaurian ... but he doesn't have a Centaurian's lifespan."

"What?" She whispered, a chill traveling down her spine.

"When he's five years old it will be as if he's fifteen years old. Do you understand? This rapid growth is taking years from Raj's life."

**THE END**

# Adaptation Book 2 available in 2017! Read the exciting preview now.

**Carmella's heart** felt as if it was caving to her very feet. Her breath was knocked from her body and she sank to the couch — had it not been there she would have landed on the floor. She kept thinking, my son is going to grow old and die right before my eyes...

"Mommy!" Raj wailed, his lip quivering. Feeling as if she was in a daze, Carmella pulled herself back to her feet and took her child in her arms. She held him tightly smothering him with kisses, and he held onto her equally as tight. He somehow knew that she was distressed and it distressed him.

Bilal's skin was slowly taking on a black undertone. He pushed back his long hair as he concentrated on his son. He reached out a hand and stroked his curls. Love for his child nearly overwhelmed him. Carmella watched, looking to him for the answer but he had none.

He met her eyes. "Carmella, I have to take Raj to The Mothership."

She opened her mouth to protest but then clamped it shut. "He doesn't go without me."

Bilal nodded once.

**It was** decided that they would discuss it further that night after dinner, when Raj was asleep. Bilal donned his parka and gloves and returned to his chores while Carmella went about the motions of making dinner, lentils with onions and one of the winter carrots that Bilal had scrounged up. She couldn't bring herself to put Raj down as she moved about the kitchen. She even sat him on the counter as she quickly chopped the vegetables. He watched her quietly finding this new attention to his liking.

Bilal returned to his outdoor chores deep in his own thoughts. He swung his axe at the split of wood and watched the blade cut through it with little effort. It was good that it was winter and they needed wood because he needed to cut the wood; the exertion helped to dissipate the anxiety that was building in him.

His mind raced ahead as he thought about his return to the ship with his family. If that happened then Raj would no longer be a secret. What if...what if his parents took Raj from him—in the greater good? It could happen, his parents saw him as a self-indulgent child. In many ways they had been right. He had done things without thinking of the consequences. And once the Centaurian population knew of the hybrid child they would want him. He was the only one and the Centaurians did not consider one individual's wants and needs above the greater good.

He had only to look at the stir it had caused when his first mother had broken away from the family unit to create her own residence on Earth 2. Centaurians still frowned on it, not understanding how it could be constructive to split the family. His joining her caused even more discontent. His mother had not felt the need to explain herself and he really didn't know the reason for her split from the family other then the fact that she was much older and had already birthed two children.

Despite the fact that his parents' sat high on the council, they were still only cogs in the wheel... No, he just couldn't risk exposing their secret. The safety of his family was based on their anonymity.

He suddenly stopped and slumped...He had to go alone. He couldn't risk anyone outside of his family finding out about his human/Centaurian son. He stared at the house that he had grown to love. This was the life that he had always wanted, the family that he had desired.

His face darkened and he picked up the axe and swung it hard at the piece of wood. It cut through sending the two halves

# Adaptation

flying through the air while the blade buried itself into the cutting block.

Dinner was a quiet affair. The only sound was Raj's babbling as he played with his sensors and gnawed on a wooden spoon. Carmella had to keep his coveralls unbuttoned on one side to give his tentacles room to move. Also, Raj seemed to find it uncomfortable to now have his right side confined by clothing.

Carmella watched him and suddenly had an idea. She took a spoonful of the stewed lentils and offered it to her son. One of his sensors went into it first and then he opened his mouth for it. By that time most of it was on his clothes but what remained was spooned into his mouth.

Bilal watched with interest when Raj realized that he rather enjoyed eating. His tentacle took the spoon from his mother — it seemed to have much more coordination than his pudgy fingers did. He plunged the spoon into the lentils and Raj opened his mouth as the spoon barely missed his eye and landed in his mouth. There were more lentils on the table and him than in the spoon but his next spoonful was much better.

She grinned at Bilal. "Wow, that was much easier than..." the smiled slid from her face as she thought of Micah, "than I thought it would be."

Bilal tilted his head at her, not missing the pause in her words. "I wonder when he will be able to change his own diaper."

The spoon clattered to the floor when Raj realized that his fingers were able to shovel more food into his mouth more quickly than his sensor. But the grey, snakelike appendage continued to explore the food and Carmella sighed in acceptance of the mess that she would need to clean up. A baby with two hands could be quite destructive but a baby with that and two tentacles was turning out to be a force she would have to reckon with. With another wave of sadness she realized that it was time to move Raj from her lap and into his own high chair.

After dinner Bilal gave him his nightly bath and then took him upstairs to bed while Carmella went outside to process one of the chickens for tomorrow's dinner. She didn't know how long they would be away from the farm and she wanted to have at least another good earth meal before they left. She picked a small cabbage to sauté and there were still plenty of potatoes and onions in the root cellar. During winter she didn't need to waste the tanks of propane to keep her small refrigerator running when the root cellar kept everything nearly as cold. Along with a stove that only needed wood to operate Carmella had managed very well without electricity.

She had everything prepped and the dishes washed but Bilal still hadn't returned so she went upstairs to investigate. He was in Raj's room, standing over his crib. He had removed his shirt and Carmella took a moment to admire the strong muscles that lined his back. He was beautiful. He had pulled back his hair into a knot that fell down his back between his shoulder blades.

She came closer and saw that his tentacles were buried in their son's chest. She gave him a curious look but his eyes were nearly closed in concentration. Raj was sound asleep on his back wearing just his diaper. His own tentacles had retreated back into his side where the only evidence of their existence was a darkened and bumpy patch of skin.

She stood by the crib and watched for about half an hour before she had to use the slop bucket. When she returned Bilal was finished with whatever he had been doing. He was covering their son with his blanket and he met her eyes but she couldn't tell anything from his expression. He was closed—which was unlike him.

"What were you doing?" She asked.

He closed the baby's bedroom door.

"Carmella…" he sighed. How could he explain this to a human? They didn't understand that Centaurians experienced everything through the use of their sensors. He couldn't explain the language they spoke or the understanding that came from just communicating through colors and vibrations and emotions…

He felt her touch his arm and his attention returned to her. She was afraid. "Is it bad?"

# Adaptation

"I don't *know* what it is." He couldn't bring himself to meet her eyes; he couldn't bear the pain and fear that he saw there. "This is a language that I don't understand."

"A language? What do you mean?"

He gestured that they go downstairs and she followed him while he tried to gather his thoughts. He finally took her hands. "Raj is healthy...his white blood cells have fought off the onset of...a cold? That's what you call it...a cold. He is a perfect mixture of Centaurian and Human. Our physical development is much more rapid than a human's. For instance, I was nearly full size by the time that I was ten earth years old.

"Raj has acquired many Centaurian traits while still appearing human—which was my intent. I wanted him to look human. I wanted him to have sensors."

Carmella gave him a look of surprise. She remembered that Bilal had pointed out the location of their son's appendages when he was first born, but she hadn't realized that Bilal had actually designed him this way.

"They would serve him well in his life," He explained. "But in my ignorance I didn't realize that his human condition was also at odds. Being carried to full term by a human mother, for instance..."

He ran his hands through the loose strands of his hair. Carmella knew that he was blaming himself but she needed him to get to the point. What was it that he saw when he examined their son?

"Bilal—"

He took a deep breath. "I can't calculate his maturation rate! I can't read it! It's not something that I understand because it is too intertwined. My hypothesis is that he has thirty years."

She grew cold, her limbs went numb. Bilal gripped her arms. "Or...he could stop his human growth once his body matures and live as long as a Centaurian can." Bilal's face fell. "But that is doubtful—the human body can't withstand the wear and tear."

"But he can repair his damage. You even said that he's healthy."

"Indeed, he is."

Carmella saw that he didn't believe that even a Centaurian enhanced human could prolong his own life. And suddenly the meal that she had recently eaten threatened to come up. She covered her mouth and then quickly placed her hands on her knees and tried to catch her breath.

Bilal lifted her silently, cradling her in his arms. For one horrible moment Carmella stiffened before she finally melted against him and buried her face against his neck. He felt her hot tears against his skin and it hurt him as much as daggers.

After a short time, Carmella finally looked at him. His face held not a look of sadness but determination. Something shifted in her. She knew two things as sure as she knew anything else; if Raj died she would take her own life, and that if there was an answer to save their son then Bilal would move heaven and hell to find it. She wiped her eyes and moved to stand. He stood as well and held her close.

"When do we do this?" She asked bravely.

"*We* do not. I must to go alone."

"But-"

"No one knows about this. My parents' shielded me as I changed and they secured the information deep within the Mothership where no one but the five us will ever be able to find it."

He shared his fear of exposing their existence to the other Centaurians and Carmella's fear grew.

"Bilal...are you saying that you truly only have five years here with us?" Because she heard him clearly say that this was just a test. A test was just until a conclusion could be made.

His hands tightened on her arms. "I'm never leaving you. Do you understand that?" She remembered his promise just last night and she nodded, relaxing. He bent and kissed her lips. "I'll never leave you," he whispered. Then he released her and turned. "Now I must go."

"What? Uh..."

# Adaptation

He smirked. He was making a joke. Something lightened in her. She smiled. He was becoming more and more human. No...not human. He was just becoming more and more the Bilal that he always wanted to be. And oddly she had a memory that came out of nowhere. She couldn't remember the face of her mother, or the smell of a banana but she remembered a simple Dr. Suess rhyme.

*Today you are You, that is truer than true. There is no one alive who is Youer than You.*

**The next day** Bilal left the house without his parka or his gloves, but he barely felt the cold. A fine layer of snow covered the ground but he began a fast run, never slipping. Li'l Wolf followed and for a moment he considered making him stay behind. Instead he set a fast pace that the young wolf easily matched. Together they sprinted to the nearest sensor post, which was a few miles from the farm located in the middle of an empty field.

Humans had long ago figured out that the posts were for the Centaurians to communicate with each other as well as with their Mothership. But it was also used to summon his transport pod.

Just one day ago, he would have been forced to use the sensors in his tongue to call the ship. Now he gratefully lifted his thermal shirt and the tentacles in his chest emerged, his sensors stretching forward and connecting to the post.

Li'l Wolf sniffed the post and then urinated on it before exploring the area attempting to decipher the strange smells. He could smell the remnants of the ship, something not quite mechanical but a living organism. He understood this better than a human who thought of technology in terms of lifeless mechanics.

The pod emerged from the sky with a quiet speed that caught the young wolf by surprise. He leaped into the air at the sudden appearance of the large oblong shaped object.

# Adaptation

Li'l wolf gave his pack master a searching look but saw nothing but fearlessness. It gave him strength to fight down his own fear and to stand alongside the man that was not a human.

Once the pod landed gently on the snow-covered grass, Bilal reached out his hand to touch it. It was grey and hard, smooth and reminiscent of metal and yet it was warm—alive. A vibration met his fingertips as the pod reacted to his touch and then an opening formed, just large enough for him to step inside.

Li'l wolf whined, not wanting to be swallowed by the object. Bilal met his eyes. "No," he said plainly, not believing that the wolf would understand his words but he would understand his intent.

Li'l wolf edged towards the pod.

"No!" Bilal said sharply and the young wolf skittered away with his tail tucked between his legs. "You stay," he said softly. The opening in the pod closed and two seconds later it disappeared into the sky.

The wolf whined and then darted into the nearby woods where he hid and watched the post suspiciously.

**As soon as the** opening to the pod closed, Bilal was enclosed in the womb-like interior of the ship. The familiar hum comforted him as he joined with it. He was the ship now. He was speeding through the sky and then further—among the stars. For an uncomfortable few moments his lungs stopped working when there was no more oxygen. It was fine; the ship knew that he could 'breathe' with or without it. It was his lungs that had grown use to it and protested before his body took over and he relaxed.

If he had Carmella and Raj the ship would breathe for them. It was like the Mothership in that way. He didn't want to think about how the Mothership had changed all of the humans so that they could survive on Earth 2. There were thousands of humans that lived on the Mothership because they refused to go to Earth 2. He didn't blame them…once a human went there they could never leave.

# Adaptation

"Mother-Mina," he said. He was too far away still and she couldn't 'hear' him. He relaxed and watched the earth recede, growing smaller as his pod moved further from it. Soon he began to feel the Centaurians. He called his mother again.

"Where are you, Bilal?"

He was surprised that she asked. If he was close enough to communicate with her through his sensors then she normally knew his whereabouts. Curious.

"I'm on my way to the Mothership. Please meet me there. I need your help."

"Have you communicated with your other parents'?"

"No. Just you. Please don't say anything to them."

"Bilal, I can't keep a secret like this from them-"

"Secrets? No, just me making an unplanned visit to my First Mother."

There was a pause. "Are you hurt?"

"I'm fine."

Another pause. "Fine. I'll find you a private dock and then we will meet in our rooms." He was relieved that it appeared that she would keep his secret for now. He carried samples of his son's DNA, chromosomes, cells, spinal fluid in his own body. With his First Mother's help, he would feed it into the ship. The only one he trusted to give him a fair shot was Mina. The others meant well— except for Mother-Baba. But they would want to monitor his son more than ever if they knew that there was something wrong.

He frowned. And because there was something wrong Baba would just want to destroy it.

To be continued…

# Adaptation

# PEPPER PACE BOOKS

STRANDED!
Juicy
Love Intertwined Vol. 1
Love Intertwined Vol. 2
Urban Vampire; The Turning
Urban Vampire; Creature of the Night
Urban Vampire; The Return of Alexis
Wheels of Steel Book 1
Wheels of Steel Book 2
Wheels of Steel Book 3
Wheels of Steel Book 4
Angel Over My Shoulder
CRASH
Miscegenist Sabishii
They Say Love Is Blind
Beast
A Seal Upon Your Heart
Everything is Everything Book 1
Everything is Everything Book 2
Adaptation
About Coco's Room
The Witch's Demon book 1

### SHORT STORIES
~~***~~

Someone to Love
The Way Home
MILF
Blair and the Emoboy
Emoboy the Submissive Dom

**Adaptation**

1-900-BrownSugar
Someone To Love
My Special Friend
Baby Girl and the Mean Boss
A Wrong Turn Towards Love
True's Love
The Delicate Sadness
The Shadow People
The Love Unexpected
The Vinyl Man

COLLABORATIONS
~~***~~
Sexy Southern Hometown Heroes
Seduction: An Interracial Romance Anthology Vol. 1
Scandalous Heroes Box set

Written under Beth Jo Andersen
~~***~~
Snatched by Bigfoot!
Bigfoot's Sidepiece
Mated to the Bigfoot!

Written Under Kim Chambers
~~***~~
The Purple World book 1

Sign-up to the Pepper Pace Newsletter!
http://eepurl.com/bGV4tb

# About the Author

Pepper Pace creates a unique brand of Interracial/multicultural erotic romance. While her stories span the gamut from humorous to heartfelt, the common theme is crossing racial boundaries.

The author is comfortable in dealing with situations that are, at times, considered taboo. Readers find themselves questioning their own sense of right and wrong, attraction and desire. The author believes that an erotic romance should first begin with romance and only then does she offers a look behind the closed doors to the passion.

Pepper Pace lives in Cincinnati, Ohio where many of her stories take place. She writes in the genres of science fiction, youth, horror, urban lit and poetry. She is a member of several online role-playing groups and hosts several blogs. In addition to writing, the author is also an artist, an introverted recluse, a self proclaimed empath and a foodie. Pepper Pace can be contacted at her blog, Writing Feedback:

http://pepperpacefeedback.blogspot.com/
PepperPace.tumblr.com
pepperpace.author@yahoo.com

# Awards

Pepper Pace is a best selling author on Amazon and AllRomance e-books as well as Literotica.com. She is the winner of the 11th Annual Literotica Awards for 2009 for Best Reluctance story, as well as best Novels/Novella. She is also recipient of Literotica's August 2009 People's Choice Award, and was awarded second place in the January 2010 People's Choice Award. In the 12th Annual Literotica Awards for 2010, Pepper Pace won number one writer in the category of Novels/Novella as well as best interracial story. Pepper has also made notable accomplishments at Amazon. In 2013 she twice made the list of top 100 Erotic Authors and has reached the top 10 best sellers in multiple genres as well as placing in the semi-finals in the 2013 Amazon Breakthrough Author's contest.

# Adaptation

Adaptation

Made in the USA
Columbia, SC
21 August 2017